T0356725

ELIZA, FROM SCRATCH

Eliza, from Scratch

SOPHIA LEE

Quill Tree Books
An Imprint of HarperCollinsPublishers

Quill Tree Books is an imprint of HarperCollins Publishers.

ISBN 978-0-06-337263-4

Typography by Jessie Gang
25 26 27 28 29 LBC 5 4 3 2 1

First Edition

For 엄마 and 아빠
for giving me the most interesting parts of myself

Eliza Park's Recipe for Senior Year

INGREDIENTS:
- 1 try-hard salutatorian
- 1 annoying and (annoyingly) cute boy
- A handful of Korean recipes (measure with your heart)
- The spice of competition, to taste

Mix until well combined. If mixture becomes too tough and you think you're doing something wrong, you probably are. Keep going and hope for the best! You'll know things turned out right when final product is sweet, spicy, and tastes like home.

Chapter 1

I wake up to the smell of miyeokguk.

The direct translation is *seaweed soup*, which is technically accurate, but contextually bereft. Seawood soup prompts the image of slimy kelp floating around in a bowl, like you dipped a dish into murky seawater and set it on a place mat. Bon appétit.

Miyeokguk is a soup of tradition, a symbol of celebration, and although today marks the first day of my senior year, that's not the type of celebration that warrants my mom making miyeokguk this morning. Especially lately. She hasn't been doing much of anything since June.

But when I roll out of bed, I forget to wonder what the celebration today might be. I'm too focused on letting my nose lead me down the stairs and into the kitchen. The unmistakable aroma of savory broth and tangy mussels wakes up my stomach. My mom has always been the best cook I know—something I'm reminded of when my stomach cramps with craving, a Pavlovian response to hearing my mother clink around downstairs.

It's been a long time since she's really cooked for us. She must spend some amount of time in the kitchen because she keeps the banchan, or side dishes, in our fridge stocked, but the kitchen has essentially spent a season without her.

That's why the image of my mom standing behind the stove, gently stirring the miyeokguk with a slim wooden spoon, is almost startling now. Her hair is cropped at her chin and pulled back with a thin headband, highlighting the gray hairs at her temple. I used to pluck them out for her, but now they battle the black for majority. Ever since I started high school, she would say she doesn't know what makes her older: her gray hair or the fact that she can't sleep past six a.m. anymore. Meanwhile, my dad, who mainly teaches long seminar classes in the evening, rolls out of bed once the sun has already made its way halfway across the sky.

"Smells good," I say. The sleep in my mouth makes the words come out sticky.

She glances up at me. Or in my direction, more accurately. I can't remember the last time my mother looked directly at me. That's something I never thought I'd take note of. "You have drool on your chin, Yeji-yah," she says in Korean.

My defense comes in English. "It's toothpaste," I reply, raising the back of my hand to wipe off the crust that is very clearly drool. This is the unspoken agreement between us—she speaks to me in her native tongue, I speak to her in mine. I know from years of her demanding my enrollment in Korean school on Saturdays, she thinks that in an ideal world, I would speak only Korean at home. But there's a feeling of suffocation that comes with needing to simplify my thoughts into the limited vocabulary I know, a dull pang of shame when I can't arrive at the correct formal conjugation. So I continue to use English and she'll continue to ask me not to.

My mom shakes her head, her hair brushing along her jaw. For a moment, I think there's a flicker of something written across her brow, but her expression instantly returns to indifference.

"Is . . ." I clear my throat before trying again. "Is something wrong?" It's unnerving to ask a parent this, like a marked subversion of human nature, and it makes me feel suddenly much more awake. Part of me wonders whether it's a question even worth asking. Have I had a conversation with my mom that lasted more than a few minutes? Certainly not since June. We used to spend entire afternoons together, getting reflexology massages, then buying the week's groceries at H Mart, then debating whether to take a hot bath or a nap. It's not like that anymore.

This is why I'm surprised when, after a moment's hesitation, she says, "You know it's tradition to make miyeokguk on someone's birthday?"

I do know this. "It's someone's birthday?" I comb over dates in my head. My dad's birthday is in February, mine is in April, and my mom's is in December. Who am I forgetting?

"Did I ever tell you why miyeokguk is eaten on birthdays?"

Something faint pulses in my memory. "It's good for pregnant women, right? Lots of calcium or something in the miyeok." Miyeok is the seaweed that serves as the entire identity of the soup. My mom swears that the quality of the seaweed and where you buy it from makes all the difference, which is maybe what she says to justify shipping hers all the way from Korea.

"Yes, but more importantly, after pregnancy, the mom has just gone through something very difficult and lost lots of her nutrients. Eating miyeokguk on birthdays is not really about whose birthday it is. It actually comes from taking care of the mother." This last part is almost pushed out, and that's something new about her, too. The way she sometimes ends her sentences like an additional word would cause her to collapse.

And that's what it takes for me to finally understand. "It's Halmeoni's birthday?"

My mother meets my eyes. They're misty, and my instinct is to look away, like I'm not supposed to see her like this. We both pretend that it's from the steam of the soup. My mom murmurs, "She would be eighty-three."

My grandmother on my mom's side passed away earlier this year, in the middle of June, which coincided exactly with when my mother takes her annual trip to South Korea. It all happened suddenly, like reading a book and skipping pages at a time. A nasty blood clot that traveled to Halmeoni's lungs. The pure luck that my mom was there for Halmeoni's hospitalization. My father and I flying out to meet her for the funeral. Next chapter. After only a couple of days, I returned by myself so I could take my SAT. My father had insisted it wasn't worth rescheduling. Shortly after, my dad returned, too, for work, and then eventually, weeks later, my mom returned on her own. Although it's deep into August now, and although my mother doesn't lock herself in the master bedroom after dinner anymore, I know she's always one memory away from unraveling again.

I don't know what to say to my mother's mistiness. What is there to say to your own parent about something like that? *Sorry for your loss? Do you want to talk about it?* In no world can I imagine opening that type of conversation with her. I'm her daughter, not a licensed counselor, and we hardly even speak the same language sometimes. The whole thing would feel feigned anyway. It wouldn't help to tell her that the woman she's grieving is someone I felt like I barely knew. I would see my halmeoni once every few years, and our time spent together was usually limited by my broken Korean and her insistence that I need to lose more weight. Nonetheless, I try to think of something comforting to say before too much time has passed.

It's like my mom can sense my awkwardness. She gives herself a small shrug, a tight roll of her shoulders, and asks why I'm up so early.

I check the time on the microwave clock. It's almost seven thirty a.m. If anything, I should already be getting ready. "I have school today," I say.

She looks up at me with wide eyes. "Today?"

"First day of senior year," I remind her.

"Eomeo," she says, which is essentially the Korean version of *oh my God*. In this instance, the real translation is, *I totally forgot school was starting again.* I'm sure in her head, it's still June. Time stopped in a Korean hospital. "I didn't pack your lunch."

"I packed one last night." The truth is that I knew this would be a possibility. It's not like the hints of the upcoming school year weren't there. We bought the few school supplies I needed at an H-E-B trip a couple of weekends back. I also asked for a pair of new white sneakers to wear to school and even went to the Korean salon to get my annual haircut. My mom was there for all those things, but only literally.

Once upon a time, my mother would have had a lunch packed with a handwritten good luck note stuck onto a Tupperware of thoughtfully sliced fruit. She would have asked me yesterday what I was planning on wearing for my last first day of school, so she could give her nod of approval. She would have reminded me to set my alarm especially early for this morning so I wouldn't miss picking up my schedule before the school day starts. But those are all remnants of a lifetime ago, a version of my mom lost to me now.

"Oh, Yeji-yah," my mom says, stirring the miyeokguk, "mianhae." *I'm sorry.* Her voice sounds brittle.

I give her a lighthearted shrug. "I'm going to get ready."

After a crawling summer of SAT studying and tutoring middle schoolers, senior year has taken its sweet time to finally arrive. On the first day of the semester, all the students come to school early to pick up our printed schedule cards from our designated school counselor. If you ask me, I would've transitioned to an online model years ago and allowed everyone to get that extra thirty minutes of sleep, but the sleep schedule of Eliza Park does not seem to be on Highland Hills' priority list. The in-person schedule pickup is sort of a tradition at Highland Hills anyway, and I'm pretty sure it's only so that our counselors see our faces for a quick check-in before the school year starts.

I understand the intention. Highland Hills is undoubtedly one of the wealthier schools in Austin, and the parents in the zoning district expect the administration to use that money to properly care for their children. I'm pretty sure this school is the whole reason my dad decided to buy a house in our neighborhood, even though it's considerably the smallest place on the block. Just to clarify, I'm not too dense to recognize that I'm lucky to go to such a good school, especially one that brought me to Kareena and Meredith. But to wait in line for however long just to have a two-minute-long chat and grab cardstock printed with my class schedule? Seems a little exhausting.

Admittedly, my annoyance this year is compounded by the fact that I haven't seen my guidance counselor, Mrs. Porter, since I informed her that my halmeoni died. After months of ignoring her well-meaning, but overly frequent emails checking in on me, I don't exactly feel thrilled to slide back into her office. It'd be easier to ghost someone if you weren't assigned to meet with them throughout the school year.

I'm kicking myself for not realizing that ahead of time as I wait in line for last names *N* through *R*. When I hear my name called, it still feels too soon.

Mrs. Porter smiles at me. Her coral lipstick is pristine. "Elizabeth Park!"

"Eliza," I correct, taking a seat across from her. As usual, her desk is threateningly neat, like if I moved one sticky note out of place, she'd smack away my hand out of instinct before apologizing.

"Right, I know that!" she trills. "It always throws me off to see 'Elizabeth' on all the paperwork. But yes, Eliza, how are you?"

"Fine. How are you?" I just want to grab my schedule and be out the door, but I force myself to engage politely.

I don't want to give the wrong impression of Mrs. Porter. I genuinely used to enjoy my chats with her. She's always been a supportive and enthusiastic school counselor. But she was also the faculty adviser for the school's summer tutoring program, where Highland Hills students tutor kids from the local middle schools. I had to request a leave to go to South Korea for the funeral, and I couldn't get approved for it without letting Mrs. Porter know what was going on. I still remember her reaction when I told her. The gaping mouth and the hint of tears welling in her lined eyes. The hot stab of shame, seeing how my guidance counselor had a bigger reaction to my grandmother's death than I did. I couldn't look at her without feeling guilty about my own nonchalance, so I successfully avoided interacting with her the rest of the summer. Until now, of course.

Mrs. Porter tucks her hair behind her ear, or more so does the motion of it but doesn't seem to realize that it was already neatly tucked. "Listen, Eliza. I want to . . . I'm really worried about you."

"Oh, please don't be. I'm doing great," I say, with what I hope is convincing enthusiasm.

"Well, you didn't respond to my emails from the summer after you left for your grandmother's funeral. Maybe you didn't receive them," she says generously. I morph my face to suggest that this is totally a possibility. "I wasn't sure if you were okay."

"I still made all my tutoring sessions," I say, trying to erase the defensiveness I fear is already there. I actually took on more sessions than any of the other tutors in the last half of the summer, but I don't need to mention it, because if there's one person who would know that, it would be Mrs. Porter. I did more than my share of work, and I did it well. What can she fault me for?

"Right, and I'm proud of you for doing that. You had some of the best reviews from the students I've seen in a while. But I also want you to know that I'm here for you. All of us at Highland Hills are here for you, okay?" Mrs. Porter looks at me with pleading eyes, like she's desperately waiting for me to crack open into a vulnerable display of emotion I don't feel.

When it's clear that I'm not close to crying anytime soon, Mrs. Porter sighs quietly. "You know, if this affects your academics or your extracurriculars, just let us know and—"

"It won't," I interrupt.

"Of course. We know you're such a good student, Eliza. Still hanging in there as our projected salutatorian, it looks like. Which is why I especially want to check in with you. You've worked very hard and when events like this happen in the family, sometimes students do better when they take school a little easier. Also, as your counselor, I am all too familiar with the fact that some students have a very hard time reaching out for help when they're going through difficult times. Especially our high achievers."

I find myself gritting my teeth. I release my jaw and say, "Thank you, Mrs. Porter. May I have my schedule?"

Mrs. Porter pinches the card, and I notice the beginnings of a frown as she slowly hands it over to me. "Now, I do want to bring to your attention—"

"Culinary Arts?" I say in disbelief, looking at the square cardstock in my hands. Whoever printed these made a huge mistake because, there, in the last slot of my schedule, is a class I certainly did not rank, nor is it something I even knew Highland Hills offered. Whose idea was it to turn a hobby into an academic course? "This is a mistake. I signed up for AP Physics."

"Right. But unfortunately, there's only one section of AP Physics and it conflicts with you taking AP Calculus BC, which is also only offered fourth period. When you ranked your classes last semester, you put calculus above physics, so this is how things worked out." Mrs. Porter's expression is guarded, like she knows I'd react this way.

"But Culinary Arts isn't weighted." I say it softly, just to subvert her expectations.

"Right."

"And AP Physics is."

"Right."

"So my GPA is going to drop."

Mrs. Porter purses her lips. "That's not true. It won't *drop*, unless you do poorly in the class. If you get an A—which, given your record, I'm sure you will—then your GPA will stay the same. It just won't get that extra weighted boost."

"But other people are going to be taking all weighted classes,"

I say. "I won't be salutatorian."

She stares at the schedule in my hands like she wishes she could take it back. "Now, Elizabeth, let's not—"

"Eliza. What are the other eighth-period options?"

"Band and orchestra are the other electives. AP Chemistry is also offered, but it looks like you took that junior year."

I slump back in my seat. "So there's nothing I can do?"

"I think you'll enjoy Culinary Arts a lot, actually. Mr. Treviño is probably one of the most beloved faculty we have, and a lot of students want to make this elective work into their schedule, but can't! So really, it's a little bit lucky, Eliza."

"I feel really lucky," I mutter. Then I squeeze my eyes shut. "Sorry, Mrs. Porter. I don't mean to be . . . well, you know." I don't know how to finish the sentence, so I don't.

Mrs. Porter gives me a gracious nod. "If you don't mind, I think I'll change the subject. Something else we're asked to discuss with our seniors is plans for college. It's time to start thinking about your personal statement, who to ask for letters of recommendation, and which schools you might want to apply to. Have you thought about these things?"

I nod. "I'd really love to go to MIT. Study computer science. My dad's an engineer."

"Great!" Mrs. Porter says. "Well, I'd love to see a draft of your personal statement pretty soon, okay? No rush, but it should be something to be working on in the background. And I'd also love to see a list of schools you're planning on applying to, just so I can make sure there's a good balance of competitiveness. MIT can be the goal, but we have to round out the list, too."

I nod again. I am half listening, because mainly I'm still hung up on the fact that my GPA might drop and I won't graduate salutatorian and what have I even worked for these past three years if I can't finish strong? The difference between rank two and rank three feels insurmountable. One has a title, and the other doesn't. One gives a speech, and the other doesn't.

Mrs. Porter reads my expression, and something there makes her give a small sigh. "I know senior year can be stressful, even without family matters."

Ah. She's mistaken my silence for grief. Maybe a reasonable assumption for anyone other than me. "I'll be fine. I promise," I say.

I can't explain to this woman that my grandmother's death affected me like a stranger's, that the only time I cried during the funeral was when I saw my mother fall into her brother's arms like a dropped doll. Saying these things out loud would make me sound like a villain, and I desperately want to believe I'm not one.

"Listen, Eliza. We really want you to succeed. So don't be afraid to take it easy."

Now is not the time to take things easy, I want to say. I can take things easy when I have a college acceptance in hand and have given my salutatorian speech at graduation to a room of weepy eyes and all the work I've invested throughout the last three years has finally turned into something real. But of course, I don't say these things. Instead, I give her a wide, warm smile and sling my backpack over my shoulder as I get up. "Thanks, Mrs. Porter. Have a good day."

I leave her office before she can tell me once more that she's always here for me.

Chapter 2

At least my homeroom selection went according to plan and I get to reunite with Kareena and Meredith. The two of them are already sitting in the front row, comparing their schedule cards. I guess they weren't delayed by awkward dead grandmother talk with their counselors. They look up when I join them.

"Hey," I say dejectedly.

Kareena already has her hand out for my schedule. I surrender it without a fight.

"Culinary Arts?" she says with possibly even more disbelief than I had. "What the hell?"

Meredith and Kareena's schedules are identical. They have been for the past three years. I look at their eighth-period slot: AP Chemistry.

"I asked for AP Physics," I say. "But apparently that's only offered fourth period, which is when we have calc."

"So they put you in *Culinary Arts?*" Meredith says. Her blond hair has remnants of the electric blue dye she used over the summer from when she worked at some young senators camp. Unnatural hair colors are technically against Highland Hills' dress code, but I doubt the administrators would do anything to Meredith, who easily is in the top ten of our class and takes the school's mock trial team to state every year.

"Can you cook?" Kareena asks.

Meredith rolls her eyes. "Come on, Kareena, be serious. When has Eliza ever brought something she cooked to the picnic?"

Every year, starting from middle school, Kareena, Meredith, and I would have a picnic in Zilker Park after the first week of classes. It started when we were too young to have our licenses and we had to get our parents to drop us off. We used to bring whatever we had at home—lone packets of Gushers, reheated samosas, Nutella sandwiches. It didn't really matter what we brought to eat. It was just a way to squeeze in some last-minute relaxation before the work of the school year consumed us.

"Oh, so you two will be making something gourmet for this weekend, then?" I say with a raised brow.

Kareena shrugs. "I feel like I could if I tried, is the difference."

"I'm not completely inept. Like, I know Bagel Bites taste far superior in the oven than in the microwave."

"Okay." Meredith draws the word out into an impressive number of syllables. "So you'll be learning."

I sigh. "This is unfair."

"Worried about salutatorian?" Meredith asks.

"Don't tease me."

Kareena puts her hand on mine. She is the projected valedictorian, as she has been since our freshman year, and it's obvious why. She's the kind of student who is effortlessly smart and seems to have been born knowing everything about everything. Not to say she doesn't have excellent work ethic, because she has that, too. Ever since the start of high school, we've planned on giving our graduation speeches together, and I know that we're both thinking about that right now.

To any other two nerds, of which Highland Hills has plenty, giving a speech at graduation probably isn't that much of an incentive to grind for valedictorian or salutatorian. But for Kareena and me specifically, it's been a small dream of ours, with more details added each passing year—us standing in front of a podium, thanking our immigrant parents in a way that is both public and embarrassingly sentimental. An undeniable confirmation that their sacrifices have amounted to something, that in this white and wealthy school district, the children of parents who left their home countries with very little still came out on top. If it sounds too dramatic, it's probably because it is, but when you've let a dream grow for three years and counting, it feels bigger than yourself. We both want this so badly, have pictured it for years, and I refuse to let my chance go at the eleventh hour.

Kareena squeezes my hand and says, "It'll be okay. One class isn't going to tip things too much."

I try not to huff, because even I know I'm being obnoxious. It's probably true that one unweighted class isn't going to kill the dream Kareena and I have, but does it have to be a class I have absolutely no interest in taking? They could've chosen any science or foreign language and I would've happily made do. But despite my mother being one of the best cooks I know, I have never really spent much time in the kitchen. It's also occurring to me that I've never tried to remedy that.

Meredith grins. "You know, it's actually a blessing in disguise. You see, young one, cooking is an essential life skill. As women, we need to learn how to cook so that we can keep our future husbands' bellies full every night. Pretty sure I'm quoting this straight from the *Code of Hammurabi*."

Kareena gags.

Meredith, who would rather have her toes cut off than marry

a man, raises her eyebrows in mock innocence. "You should enroll in midwifery next. Cooking and childbirth—what else are women good for, right?"

"I promise you are not as funny as you think you are," I say.

"Honestly, this is punishment for you not taking AP Biology with us last year and choosing chem instead," Kareena says. "If you'd just stuck with us, your schedule would be fine!"

Meredith nods in agreement.

"If I wanted to be lectured on my poor decisions, I would just let my internal psyche be a little louder, okay?" I say. At the time, the decision made sense. The AP Chemistry teacher, Mrs. Pearson, is also the faculty adviser for Science Bowl, which I've been a part of since freshman year. I wanted to make sure I had an actual class with her before I asked her for a letter of recommendation this semester. But now, with my cursed schedule in hand, all the logic of last year has dissolved into simmering frustration.

"Maybe Culinary Arts will give you a great anecdote to write about for your personal statement," Kareena suggests. She started writing hers at the end of summer and already has three separate drafts, none of which she's let me read yet under the excuse that they're in too poor a state for any respectable eyes. Her words, obviously. Based on what little she's said about it, I get the sense that volunteering at the hospital over the summer was her writing muse. Not entirely surprising considering Kareena has had her sights set on medical school since sophomore year.

"This is like *High School Musical*," Meredith says suddenly, like she's been grappling with this thesis in her head and things have finally clicked together. "People think you're just a go-getter nerd archetype, but then you're going to whip out some crème brûlée by the end of the semester, and the nonsense of you being a *multi-dimensional person* with *several hobbies* is going to make the rest of us spontaneously burst into song and dance."

Kareena and I blink at her.

Then, Kareena says, "Eliza's right. You're not as funny as you think you are."

"Am I Zeke or Gabriella in this situation?" I ask.

"Both, obviously," Meredith says. "Like I said. *Multidimensional.*"

The rest of the day goes smoothly, especially with Kareena and Meredith in all my classes. There's a different energy this year, with all of us being seniors and college applications being right around the corner. It's like we're letting ourselves go on autopilot, finally doing things by muscle memory.

That is, of course, until eighth period rolls around.

The location on my schedule card simply says Culinary Kitchen. There's not even a room number to go off, and I'm left clueless, like I haven't been going to this school for the past three years. I speedwalk to the cafeteria because my first instinct is that maybe kitchens are next to other kitchens. But the cafeteria is empty with the exception of one lunch lady who is wiping down a table.

"Hi, do you know where the student culinary kitchen is?" I ask her.

She looks at the schedule in my hand. "I think that's in one building over."

"There's a separate building?"

She nods. She tells me to walk across the courtyard and look for a small green building. I thank her and leave, just as the tardy bell rings. I sigh. Making a bad impression on a new teacher by walking in late on the first day is something I once had a nightmare about, I'm pretty sure.

I finally manage to find the promised green building. A tiny tin placard on the side of the door reads Culinary Kitchen. Who knew this place even existed? Helpful lunch ladies excluded, I mean. I open the door, interrupting the teacher, who has already started his spiel. He's a Latino man with a little bit of a belly and curly salt-and-pepper hair.

The entire class stares at me when I walk in. Okay, so apparently, everyone else knew this place existed. There aren't too many students, maybe a dozen or so, and I realize the class size is probably restricted due to cooking equipment. But even so, having a dozen pairs of eyes on me as I walk in late is not my ideal way to start the semester. All the students have already found a place to sit around the large aluminum countertop that takes up the center of the room. Along the perimeter of the kitchen are what look like individual workstations with stovetops and ovens and sinks. There's only one empty seat left at the center table and I awkwardly shuffle toward it.

The teacher looks at his attendance sheet. "Elizabeth Park?" he asks.

"Eliza. I'm so sorry, I had trouble finding this place."

"No worries, that's what the first day is for. Glad you found us." He claps his hands together and resumes, "As I was saying, I'm Mr. Treviño and this is an introductory class to culinary arts. In this class, we'll not only learn to prepare and cook food, but I'll also be testing you all on topics like equipment, nutrition, and sanitation.

But I want to assure you, this class will be more *Great British Bake Off* than *Hell's Kitchen*."

The class laughs. I smile, even though I'm not sure what the joke is.

"Now, how many of you would say you have cooking experience?" Mr. Treviño asks.

My stomach drops as the entirety of the class raises their hands. My hands feel like lead in my lap, but for a second, I wonder if I should put one up, too, just so I don't call attention to myself.

The boy sitting to the left of me turns to stare. "Not any?" His dark eyes are wide in surprise. I wonder where the surprise is rooted. The fact that I'm in this small class with other people who are clearly interested and experienced in the subject? Or that I'm a girl and naturally should have made a casserole or two at least once in my life?

"Wesley, we're not here to call anyone out," Mr. Treviño chimes with a jovial chastising tone. "I promise this class is for all skill levels."

I give Mr. Treviño a half-hearted smile. I'm trying to convince myself that I'll easily be able to find my footing. Isn't cooking like science anyway? I've always been pretty good at science. I'm even serving as the cocaptain of the Science Bowl team this year, which reminds me that I need to notify them that we're starting practice this Wednesday.

Mr. Treviño passes out a quiz to all of us. "Don't panic. It's just a diagnostic, to see where you're at. No grades today."

The boy next to me, Wesley, hands me the stack after he takes a quiz. He gives me a smile that can only be accurately described as a smirk. Why does this guy think he can smirk at me like that? "Good luck, salutatorian."

I take a quiz and pass the others to the next person before it occurs to me that he knows my rank. That must mean he's a senior, too, but I don't think I've ever seen him before. At the very least, I've never had a class with him. I put this thought on pause as I take a look at the quiz and feel my body go cold.

Not to sound too obnoxious, but never have I ever been this lost looking at a school assessment. I know Mr. Treviño said it wouldn't count for anything, but still, the concept of filling out a quiz and not acing it feels illegal. The quiz itself is technically straight-forward. There are equipment-identification questions. I guess on them. There are technique questions. I guess on those, too. The only question I know for a fact I get right is the boiling temperature of water and that's only because it's a chemistry essential.

When Mr. Treviño calls time, I put my pencil down and see Wesley steal a glance at my paper. If he's looking to score a few points, he really chose the wrong class to sit next to me. But to my surprise, he cracks a grin. Smirk adjacent, but not quite there.

"Number five is a mandoline."

I look down at what I've written. *Grater.* Like what he's doing to my nerves. I narrow my eyes at him. "A mandolin is an instrument. Like a musical one, not a kitchen one."

He laughs like I'm making a joke. His round eyes crinkle when he does, making him look so youthful. Then his smile drops as he realizes I'm serious and I watch as disbelief visibly replaces his mirth.

Mr. Treviño makes us self-grade our quizzes. He goes over each question and asks the class for the answer. I go down my paper, marking question after question as incorrect. Mr. Treviño announces that the equipment pictured for question number five is indeed a mandoline and my cheeks burn. I don't have to look up to know that (a) Wesley is smirking smugly in my direction and (b) I'm doing the worst on this quiz out of the entire class.

I hate feeling incompetent, so I let the hate spill over to the boy next to me. I can't believe he thinks he's so much smarter than me. The only person who I'd allow to act this haughty is Kareena, and she fundamentally would never. So what if his quiz is barely marked up? Not that I'm looking. Really, I was just trying to confirm his name and my eyes snagged on how long it looked all written out. Wesley Ruengsomboon.

After what feels like far too long, the bell rings to signal the end of the school day. I immediately stand up and make a beeline for the exit, glad to be done with the class. I could honestly switch into band or orchestra and have the same entry-level skill. It would even be more useful, I think, to pick up a new instrument. Maybe the cello could be fun. Maybe the mandolin.

A shoulder brushes mine and I immediately jump.

I turn and—of course. "Wesley, right?"

His hair is short on the sides, but the top lifts up like it's been intentionally tousled. He walks alongside me as if I've invited him to. "I was just curious. How does one get to be salutatorian of a school full of try-hards without knowing a single thing about an everyday subject?"

"So you know what a mandoline is. Your Nobel is coming any day now."

He laughs, unfazed. "Eliza, I watched you grade your quiz. Let's not pretend that's the only thing you didn't know."

I refuse to let shame flood my cheeks. "Stop looking at my paper, creep."

"All the red caught my eye."

I halt to face him, straightening my back to make myself feel taller, but he's still got a head over me. "So it's just coincidence that you know my rank and were looking at my paper?" I ask.

He shakes his head and I watch his hair bounce. I want to tell him that we're not in a shampoo commercial, but then it would expose me for paying too much attention to him in the first place. "Does everything revolve around rank to you?" There's a marked shift in his tone, like it's been drained of humor and replaced by wariness. It's clear that he is not thinking about my role in a shampoo commercial.

"That's not what—"

"No, I get it. You're one of those kids where school is, like, your entire life. But you know what they say about being at the top."

Without my consent, I hear myself saying, "What?"

"Only way left to go is down," he says, and I don't even need to see Wesley's face to know his mouth is curled into the smirk I'm already coming to despise. "I hope you're as good of a student as you think you are. Winning the cook-off won't be fun without any real competition." Then he easily rushes past me, sauntering off into the emptying hallway. In no time at all, he's out of sight, and I realize he'd been slowing his pace to walk by my side. Cursed tall boys with their cursed long legs and equally cursed long stride.

"Get over yourself," I say, but he's too far away to hear me.

Chapter 3

By the time I get home, my mom has a student over for a lesson. She doesn't normally have one at this time, but I can tell it's a student because the notes of a staggered minuet reach me from the garage.

My mother teaches private piano lessons to a dozen kids in my city. She didn't always want to be a piano teacher. Her undergraduate degree in South Korea was for journalism. But then she and my dad moved to the United States, where her degree didn't seem to matter and what used to be her best strength—her wield on language—became her largest hindrance. So she ended up settling on a more universal language: music. There were still some translations to be done, but the biggest victory was that private piano tutoring required no extra degrees or licenses.

The student stumbles through the piece as I walk into the house. I heat up the pot of miyeokguk and check the rice cooker to see if there's anything left in there. I'm blessed—it's full. I scoop a heaping mound of sticky rice into a bowl and let my eyes scan the kitchen as I wait for the miyeokguk to warm. On the ledge of the countertop, a pile of papers is strewn around, like my mother didn't have time to put them away before her lesson. I can't help but inch closer to investigate.

The papers are soft and yellow tinged, with the occasional tear in the corners. Faint stains and powdered fingerprints stamp across handwritten Korean in black ink. I can't decide if the papers are old or have just been amply loved. Although my Korean reading comprehension stays generously at a third-grade level, I can easily tell that these are recipes. I pass them through my fingers as I look at one after another. Kimchi jjigae, dakdoritang, japchae . . . I recognize each dish as things my mom has made for me growing up. The handwriting prevents me from making out all the instructions. Reading Korean is difficult for me when it's perfectly printed by a machine, let alone when it's handwritten, but I think I can decipher the gist. I'm so absorbed in studying the different recipes that I don't notice the piano stop and the front door close.

My mom walks into the kitchen, saying, "The miyeokguk is boiling. You need to take the lid off." She turns the heat off and tilts the lid so that steam escapes. "Did you stir it at all? It smells like the miyeok might be burning." Then she looks at me, and I know the exact moment she understands what I've been doing because she wilts, nearly imperceptibly if I weren't watching her so closely. She walks over to me with her mouth pursed, like she's holding her breath or biting her tongue, or maybe both.

I start to feel like I'm trespassing. I stack the papers together, being careful not to crinkle the edges further.

My mother's voice interrupts me. "I was looking at them today because I missed her."

My hands still. "Halmeoni wrote these recipes?"

"She wrote them for me when I told her I was moving to America. She said she would never forgive me if I forgot how to make the dishes she made me growing up. When I first moved here, I made these recipes so often, I knew them by heart within the first two months."

For some reason, I feel choked. A sudden guilt prickles at my skin like a wool coat when I realize that I have never shown interest in my mother's cooking before. I never questioned where she learned her recipes, or whether I would ever learn them, too. And I never made the connection that what she made for me, in turn, might have been made for her when she was younger.

"In fact," my mom continues, "your dad got sick of me making the same dozen dishes all the time. He would say, 'We're in America. Let's experience American food! There's McDonald's on every corner and it's so cheap!' If he wanted to eat somewhere nice, we would go to Olive Garden." She smiles as she says this, and I can't help wondering what exactly she is remembering. "We gained a lot of weight," she laughs. "Halmeoni hardly recognized me the first time she came to visit us here."

"That's the real American experience," I say.

My mom nods in agreement. "These recipes are a great baseline, but even now, my taste has become Americanized. I'll find myself adding more salt or more sugar than what your halmeoni wrote down."

I nod, mainly because, once again, I feel like I have nothing to contribute. In another life, maybe I'd have grown up learning these recipes from Halmeoni herself, in some kitchen in South Korea, wearing a public school uniform with Park Yeji stitched across the right chest, speaking Korean with a fluid tongue instead of a tied one. But in this life, these recipes are just markings on a page, remnants of a mother-daughter relationship I did not see and a grandmother-granddaughter relationship that did not exist.

I want to hear my mom continue to talk because this is the loosest I've heard her in months, but I feel frozen. Ever since June, there's been this unspoken but undeniable wall between us. Anytime it seems to be in the process of being deconstructed, one of us builds it back up again. I worry that maybe it's me this time.

She suppresses a sigh and it's like she senses my thoughts, knows that I feel like I've forgotten how to have a conversation with her. She takes the stack of recipes and places them in a clear folder, sliding it behind jars of flour and potato starch. "I have to get back for my next lesson. Your rice is probably cold." Then she exits the kitchen to make her way back to the lesson room.

I realize belatedly that the miyeokguk does smell a bit burned The frustration burns inside my chest like an open flame. I can't even heat up a premade soup without messing something up. Am I *that* pathetic?

I'm eating alone at the dining table when my dad gets home. He comes in with his suit jacket tucked underneath his arm. He's a professor at the local university where he teaches classes in electrical engineering, mainly to graduate students. Most of the courses are in the evening, so I don't see him for dinner that often. My dad is one of those people who are steeped deeply in the minutiae of academia. It takes a special kind of person to spend years in school and decide, oh yeah, they would like to spend the rest of their careers in school, too. I mean, I like school as much as the next nerd, but choosing academia for the rest of my life sounds like too much for even me.

"Hi, Appa," I say with a mouthful of soupy rice.

"Hey, Yeji-yah. How was school?" he asks. He speaks to me in English most of the time. Part of me thinks it's because he's always in professor mode.

"Fine," I say. I'm about to tell him about my shitty day in Culinary Arts, but I stop myself. If there's anyone who would be more upset than me about not being in AP Physics, it would be my dad.

The relationship between Appa and me is simple math. He loves school. I am good at school. By the transitive property of immigrant familial dynamics, we get along great. This has been the foundation of our kinship since elementary school, when my first-grade teacher read aloud my book report to the class as an example of what to do. When he found out I was ranked second in my class at Highland Hills, a school known to send dozens of kids to top-twenty schools every year, he insisted on calling me *salutorian* the whole day. He has trouble saying the word *salutatorian*, and in his defense, the word probably does have too many syllables.

This is all to say that, although my father and I are close—maybe even closer now that my mother is barely a part of our family— I can't find it in myself to volunteer information that he most certainly will interpret as my rank being in jeopardy. Instead, I let my eyes fall to the table as I ask, "How was school for you?"

"Great," he says, walking into the kitchen and scooping himself miyeokguk as well. He spoons rice and pulls out different banchan dishes from the fridge, stacking the Tupperwares like Jenga pieces. Kimchi, bean sprouts, spinach—a tower of things my mom somehow still makes for us despite never being seen in the kitchen anymore. I consider my dad to be a smart and capable man, but I wonder what he would do for himself if my mom truly dropped all her chores on us.

My dad sits at the dining table with me. "Where's your eomma?"

"Piano room. I think she has a lesson soon," I answer.

"How is she?" he asks as he begins eating his dinner. As he chews, the corners of his mouth turn down. "Did she burn the miyeokguk?"

If I've been scared to talk to my mom since Halmeoni's death, then my dad has been absolutely terrified. He's hardly interacted with her since she came back from Korea, letting her have her alone time, tiptoeing around conversations, and never asking her a direct question. I mean, not that I've been much better, but isn't there a different responsibility when it's your spouse? I can't imagine my dad feels as awkward around my mom as I do. I think he believes space can reset everything, but in the meantime, he asks me to connect the bridge between them. I obviously have not been doing a very good job at it.

"She's definitely not herself today," I say. "It would've been Halmeoni's birthday. But she's trying her best." I don't know what compels me to skip over the recipes I found. Given that my mother made them frequently enough that my dad would ask for McDonald's instead, I'm sure he would recognize what I'm talking about. But remembering the ease of my mom's speech when she was reminiscing in the kitchen, the relaxation in her shoulders . . . part of me wants to hold on to that just for myself.

My dad nods, tossing cubes of kkakdugi, or radish kimchi, into his mouth. "She always does. And so do you. That's why I'm proud of you. That's why you're salutorian."

"Thanks, Appa," I say, getting up from the dining table and going to wash my dishes.

When I go upstairs to my bedroom, I consider reading the Culinary Arts syllabus to prepare myself for tomorrow. But the idea is so exhausting that I end up falling asleep without even unpacking my backpack.

Chapter 4

Culinary Arts the next day is an absolute shit show. Even reading the syllabus would not have helped my ineptitude.

I come to class, actually on time, but people have made a pattern of the first day and sit exactly where they sat yesterday, giving me no choice but to take my seat next to Wesley Ruengsomboon again. We both sit in silence, staring straight ahead and very pointedly not looking at each other.

Mr. Treviño takes his place at the front of the classroom when the tardy bell rings and flashes us all an impish grin. "I forgot to mention this yesterday in class, but one of your classmates—who is already keeping me on my toes—asked me about it today after seeing it on the online syllabus. We do something a little bit different for the end of the semester here in Culinary Arts. No paper exams from this guy," he says with a hearty laugh. There is something weirdly joyous about him, like he genuinely wants to be here with us. "What we like to do instead is block off an evening where everyone is free, which shouldn't be hard with this small a class size, and have a cook-off! Throughout the semester, everyone is expected to come up with three original recipes for an appetizer, an entrée, and a dessert, and then cook this three-course meal during the cook-off." Then Mr. Treviño drops his voice conspiratorially and wags his bushy eyebrows. "The winner even gets a special prize!"

"What's the prize?" someone asks.

"Why is that always the first question?" Mr. Treviño replies with joking exasperation. "Can't you all just be excited to win for the sake of winning?"

I snort. Wesley glances at me from his periphery.

"To answer the question," Mr. Treviño says, "the prize is a brand-new cookware set. A trusted source, namely the guy who's been teaching this class for the past five years, says that he thinks there's a nice Le Creuset Dutch oven in the mix, but you didn't hear it from me."

Some students perk up in their seats. I guess it makes sense that people who actually cook would be interested in cookware. I feel even more like a farce in this class, as I'm pretty sure my classmates' idea of a Dutch oven does not involve bedcovers and noxious gas.

Mr. Treviño holds his hands up dramatically and booms, "But wait! There's more!" He is clearly having too much fun with this. "In addition to a sparkling new cookware set, the winner also gets something priceless . . . a GPA boost! Whoever wins the cook-off will get an additional 0.5 added to their final grade, which means you can earn higher than a 4.0 if you try!"

My heart falters in my chest, like my own atria are gasping. Then it thunders like a bulldozer. No one else seems to be as astounded by this news as I am. Am I the only one who understands what this means? The additional 0.5 is the equivalent to a *weighted* course. My mind races. If I somehow got an A in this class *and* won the cook-off, it would be the same as taking AP Physics. No anxiety about dropping in rank necessary, no need to ever mention this class to my dad, and my beautiful, poignant, will-leave-not-a-single-dry-eye-in-the-auditorium graduation speech secured! I try to reel myself in. That's a lot of ifs and I already seem to be the furthest behind in the class.

I try to give up on the thought almost as soon as it pops into my head, but my chest continues its palpitations. Let me think about this logically. Even I can admit that it's already a stretch to think I'll get an A in this class, so it would be nearly impossible to beat the other students in the cook-off. But an admittedly annoying and arrogant part of me can't help but think that if I just believe in my ability to work hard, the reward will come naturally. It's probably an American Dream–like fallacy, but maybe I'm exactly like my dad and foolish enough to believe in it. It's not like I've been proven wrong yet. And now it's like I've followed my logic down an ouroboros that has led to exactly what I wanted to avoid in the first place: the alluring glimmer of hope. My leg has begun to bounce up and down to reflect my anxiety, but I don't notice until I accidentally bump Wesley's leg.

"Sorry," I murmur out of instinct.

"Peeing yourself over the chance for extra credit?" he taunts. My expression must be pretty transparent and I wonder what he sees there. Some distortion of rank-obsessed fervor, probably, to confirm that I'm exactly what he thinks of me—a grade-hungry monster.

"Just imagining your reaction when I win," I say.

I'm talking nonsense, and I know it. But what a perfect solution it would be. I could maintain my *salutorian* title, I'd learn an invaluable new skill, and I would prove to Wesley that sometimes the people at the top are there for a reason.

Mr. Treviño's voice cuts through my thoughts. "Today's another diagnostic day," he says while rolling out a cart stacked with grocery items. "Here I have a random assortment of ingredients. Some baking basics, like flour, salt, sugar. Some pantry items: pasta, chickpeas, canned tomatoes. Lots of fun goodies up here. Throughout the class period, I want you to make something. It can be literally anything, as long as it's finished by the end of class. The final product doesn't really matter to me, although ideally, I'd like it to be edible! I just want to watch you all in your processes, see where your skill levels are in action."

He lets us roam free, pointing out where certain equipment is if someone asks. One student asks for an immersion blender, which sounds like a blender you would use underwater. People have to be trying to flex, right? There's no way these students have just casually spent their ten thousand hours in the kitchen. Mr. Treviño walks around as people grab ingredients and find counter space at one of the workstations on the periphery. Mr. Treviño comes up to me, and that's when it hits me that I've been standing and staring at other people moving while doing nothing myself.

"Looking around for inspiration?" he says.

"Something like that."

"Well, you've got to start somewhere."

I nod. We both stand there. He waits for me to move. I don't.

"I meant today, Eliza," Mr. Treviño grins.

"Actually, Mr. Treviño," I say, "I really shouldn't even be in this class. I didn't sign up for it. I know other people genuinely want to be here, and I think that's great for them, but I was only placed here because it fit with my schedule. If I tried to cook, I might burn this place down, which I'm sure would be pretty upsetting. And who knows what the school's insurance policy looks like?"

Mr. Treviño laughs. I like that he laughs with his full body like a cartoon character. "I was serious about this class being for all skill levels. There's no room here for fear of failure. Grab some ingredients. Can you boil pasta?"

I give him an unconvincing nod, which makes him laugh more.

"Try your best," he says. "Like I said, no grades today."

I wonder what part of me exudes anxiety about grades so greatly that he feels the need to drill this point in. Maybe my reaction to the GPA boost was embarrassingly evident to more than just Wesley. Inspired by Mr. Treviño's quasi–pep talk, I grab a box of spaghetti and the can of diced tomatoes. I have no idea how to make pasta sauce if it isn't already wrapped up in a Prego label, but considering no one's going to be tasting this, I figure I'm not endangering anyone's gag reflex by just using the can of tomatoes.

I find a stovetop and a pot. The pot is too small for the spaghetti so half the strands cook before they're soft enough for me to push the upper halves in. When I pull a strand out to test it, one half has a soft crunch. That should be fine, right? People like al dente, and half of each strand is just extra al dente. It's textural variety. I drain the water and visit three other students' stations before I finally find a can opener. I pour the diced tomatoes over the pasta and stir it around to mix it up. It looks pretty okay, if you excuse the lumps of tomato and maybe stare at it long enough until your vision starts to blur, but I am in no rush to taste test. Mr. Treviño said it was about the process anyway. Hopefully, he watched my process. From afar, ideally, where my mistakes could possibly be concealed.

I must have spent too much of the period standing around doing nothing in the beginning, because by the time my dish is ready (I know I'm using both *dish* and *ready* generously), class is almost done and Mr. Treviño is walking around to inspect people's finished products. I only notice because from my station, I hear him say, "Wow! Now that's impressive."

Of course, when I look up, he's standing in front of Wesley

Ruengsomboon, who is proudly holding up some sort of chickpea curry dish. It looks magnificent. Even from where I'm standing, I can see he took the effort to plate it properly and added a sprig of something green as a garnish. Since when are high schoolers Iron Chefs?

"Where'd you learn to make this, Wesley?" Mr. Treviño asks. "I don't do any taste tests on diagnostic days, but your dish is trying to tempt me otherwise."

Wesley grins. I inspect him, desperate to find flaws, and am annoyed to note that his smile practically gleams. "I found a chana masala recipe online when I was a kid and tweaked it over the years. It was a little tough to make it here because I didn't realize there wouldn't be garam masala. Had to improvise with the cumin and coriander."

"This reminds me of something I once had at Grain and Garlic," Mr. Treviño says thoughtfully.

"Oh, come on," I mutter to myself.

Known as one of the most successful restaurants in Austin, Grain and Garlic is the kind of place where you have to set an alarm for when reservation spots drop. I've never dined there because my parents don't splurge for food and the tasting menu at Grain and Garlic is upward of a hundred dollars, but everyone in the Highland Hills zip codes knows the general reputation. I'm fairly confident it was started by some guy who made it onto one of those network cooking competitions.

I intentionally tune the rest of the conversation out, refusing to let myself feel nervous about my diced-tomato-sauce pasta. Of course, I thought that some of the students might have been cooking for years, but the confirmation of it aloud—by Wesley especially—makes me feel uneasy. The naive hope of winning the cook-off and keeping my rank seems increasingly silly. And how absurd is it to compare this random high school kid's food to a chef who was on TV?

When Mr. Treviño comes around to my station, he looks at my spaghetti and gives me a warm smile. "Look at you, Eliza! That's something."

"Something inedible," I agree.

"Leave that part to me," he says. "A semester is a long time to learn something new. Did you save your pasta water?"

"Did I what?"

Someone in the room literally gasps, like I've committed an unforgivable sin.

"It's okay," Mr. Treviño says. "We'll learn about emulsification later."

My Science Bowl brain tells me I know exactly what emulsification is. My Culinary Arts brain is the equivalent of a blinking cursor in an empty Word document.

Once Mr. Treviño has come by your station, you're free to clean up and dismissed from class. He moves on from me and I'm about to scrape my food into the trash bin when someone says, "You don't want to take that home?"

I look up to see Wesley holding a Tupperware container of his chickpea curry, his backpack already strapped onto his back.

I glance down at my pasta. "I thought you would say something more along the lines of 'I'm glad you found where that belongs.'"

"You don't need me to lecture you on food waste, do you? So your tomato sauce looks like salsa. That doesn't mean it's not salvageable."

I return the pasta back to my station. "I think it's impossible to waste *waste*? It's definitionally . . . waste." I've said the word *waste* too much.

"Here," he says, handing over his chickpea curry. "Let's trade."

"What?"

He walks over to a cabinet to grab another Tupperware container and brings it back. He starts transferring my salsa-pasta into the tub before I can protest. "I'll take this home. You can take mine."

"Who says I want yours?" I say. It's hard to sound indignant when he's seen my cooking failure up close, but I'm doing a fairly good job.

"I promise you won't hate it," Wesley says. There is unmistakable confidence in his tone and it makes me want to wipe the grin off his face. But I know I have no leverage here so I let him continue.

"What are you going to do with mine?" I ask. Resigned, I take my dishes to one of the sinks to wash them.

He follows me. "Not sure yet," he says, "but it doesn't look too hard to improve."

I flash him a withering glare. "Why won't you just let me throw mine away?"

"One student's trash is an even better student's treasure, or whatever it is they say." He gives me a shrug and looks away. "Enjoy the curry, Eliza. Eat it with some rice—any kind will work." The way he offers unsolicited advice, dripping with condescension, grates on my nerves. What annoys me even more is that I don't even know what *kinds* of rice there are besides white and brown, but I feel like that's not what he means. He finally heads out, leaving me with sudsy dishes and a Tupperware container full of obnoxiously immaculate food.

Chapter 5

When I get home, my stomach growls and I realize I've been ignoring it on purpose. I open the fridge door but find nothing suitable in its contents and end up having a staring contest with Wesley's Tupperware. Part of me is undeniably curious to see if it tastes as good as it looked in class, all plated up so perfectly. Was Mr. Treviño's reaction—or even worse, Wesley's confidence—warranted? The other part of me wants to throw the curry away out of spite. I only have his food because he was watching me try to throw mine away. He wouldn't be able to see if I did the same to his.

My stomach then releases a noise that convincingly sounds like a kitchen sink's garbage disposal, so I swallow my pride and make the decision.

I wash some white rice and set it to cook in the Cuckoo rice cooker, which is perhaps the best I can do in the kitchen without assistance. Why is spaghetti so long anyway? Rice always fits in the pot.

As I wait for the rice to cook, I pull out some homework. There's not much to do, since it's only the second day, but my mom's current student provides a pleasant enough soundtrack. The rice finishes cooking and I heat up Wesley's dish in the microwave. When I pull it out, it smells so intoxicating, my stomach cramps a little bit.

My first thought when I take a bite is that I despise Wesley Ruengsomboon. I despise him for creating something so delicious, fully knowing his own talent, and giving it to me in exchange for my sad salsa-pasta. The chickpea curry has just the right sting of spice and it's impossible to isolate the individual flavors because it melds so perfectly together. I never considered myself partial to chickpeas before, but this dish could easily make anyone a convert. By the time my mother finishes her lesson, my bowl is spotless.

"What is that smell?" she asks when she walks in and sees me.

"Chickpea curry."

"From where?"

I hesitate, unsure how to phrase it. I haven't told either of my parents about Culinary Arts yet, which sounds ridiculous because a class schedule doesn't seem to warrant secrecy. Still, I can't risk telling my mother and having her mention it to my dad. "A friend gave it to me." *Not technically a friend*, I think to myself, but I won't tell my mother that I accepted food from a stranger. Or worse, an enemy.

Just the situation of it all gives me pause for a moment. Why did Wesley give me his dish in the first place? Despite the fact that he knows my rank, we don't actually know each other, and there are plenty of students in the class who I'm sure made edible, even tasty, things. Was he trying to intimidate me, to let me know that I shouldn't bother trying to beat him at the end of the semester? A Trojan horse of sorts: *Here's some delicious food and a reminder that you'll never be able to catch up to me!*

An idea comes to me then.

What better way to hone my skills—and more importantly, beat out Wesley Ruengsomboon—than to take lessons from my mother, who just so happens to have written recipes for her most signature Korean dishes? I don't know a better cook than my own mom. No matter how amazing Wesley can make chickpeas taste, I just know my mom could do better. She could teach me, and the prize, the rank, the bragging rights—they would all fall right into my lap. I need to chill out before I start twirling my mustache.

But it all sounds temptingly perfect. Even more perfect than Wesley's curry.

"Eomma," I say. "You know those recipes from Halmeoni?"

"Mm," she says in agreement.

"I was thinking maybe you could teach them to me?" The uncertainty in my voice makes it come out like a question. I guess it is a question. I'm never sure anymore how much I can push my mom in a conversation before she vanishes again, so every statement feels like it requires permission.

Her voice is cautious, too. "Why?"

Because I want to beat Wesley Ruengsomboon.

Because I want to keep my rank.

Because I want you to see me onstage at graduation.

"You miss Halmeoni so much" is what I actually say. "Maybe it would help me miss her, too, to learn her recipes." I'm startled by my own words. Do I mean it? It's either something I subconsciously believe or Highland Hills taught me to be such an excellent bullshitter that I can't even tell the difference for myself.

If I let myself be candid, I don't think I've ever been interested in learning more about my halmeoni before. And I certainly have never wanted to spend time in the kitchen voluntarily.

But still, even if my actions are only reactionary to the whole schedule mishap, maybe that doesn't have to be the only reason. Or at the very least, maybe my mom can believe it's not.

She looks to me then, and her eyes are bright. Alive, even. When was the last time I saw her like this?

I find myself thinking of the day before my seventeenth birthday.

I don't remember when the tradition first started, but it's one of those things that feels like it's always been there, a cornerstone of my relationship with my mom. The thought stings, a reminder that the current version of my mother is not who she once was.

Every year, my birthday arrives in late April, just when the lingering Austin winter finally surrenders to the sudden heat of a Texas spring. Texas weather is unpredictable, but this is a pattern I can expect without fail. I always know my birthday is coming up because the temperature jumps up like it's trying to celebrate with me.

The day before April 27, my mother will say to me, "You know what this weather makes me crave?"

We could be sitting on the couch, watching one of the Korean dramas she claims she doesn't care about but watches almost daily. Or driving home from a duo trip to HomeGoods where we bought a total of zero items, but still managed to spend half the afternoon investigating bottles of avocado oil and manuka honey. Regardless of where we are or what we're doing, when she asks this question, there's only one correct response.

"Gaja." *Let's go.*

The bingsu place we like best is nestled between a Japanese stationery store and an overrated Korean barbecue restaurant. Bingsu is a heaping mountain of shaved frozen milk topped with a variety of fruits, rice cakes, or syrups. I always ask to get the strawberry, but my mom prefers the old-school one, which includes sweet red-bean paste, known as pat, and injeolmi, rice cakes coated in a fine golden powder made from ground dried beans.

When the bingsu is ready, she'll bring the tray over and sing

"Happy Birthday" in Korean, very quietly so only we can hear.

"It's not my birthday," I said the first time she did it.

"Well, I can't take away your actual birthday from you spending it with your friends. That would be selfish of me. But the day before can be for us."

We always act like this bingsu is better than the one we got last time, finishing the whole bowl and licking our spoons like greedy cats. We say things like, "They must have changed their chef!" or, "The ice is really in season!" knowing full well that how much we enjoy it is proportional to how heavy-handed the pouring of condensed milk is. It was my idea to alternate between strawberry and injeolmi each year, but usually, we can't actually remember what we got the time before and my mom insists that we must have gotten injeolmi, so let's get strawberry this time.

April was an easier version of my mother, and it's in this moment that I can clearly see what a shell she is now. She didn't have this constant sadness weighing her down, and her daughter didn't know she was running out of time to know her grandmother. I wonder if I would've acted differently had things been less sudden. Would I have tried a little harder to make conversation with Halmeoni during my trips to Korea? Would I have asked her for stories about my mom when she was little?

An ugly prick of shame starts in my stomach. I don't know if it would've made a difference at all. My nonchalance has been so ingrained for years, it's hard to imagine myself without it.

But now, with her eyes just the slightest bit brighter than they were before, I see the faintest glimmer of my April mother as she shuffles through the stack of Halmeoni's handwritten recipes. "It would be fun to teach you how to cook. When I was your age, I'd already learned how to make food for me and your samchon." She uses the word to mean my uncle, her younger brother.

I wonder what was missing from her generation to mine that I've gotten this far without knowing what to do in the kitchen. My parents were only a few years older than I am now when they decided to uproot themselves from South Korea and immigrate to America without knowing the language or a single neighbor. It's humbling to think that they made the most life-altering decision of all time at the age where I can't even write a personal statement. I get the sense that my parents grew up so much faster than I did. Then I remember how disturbingly good Wesley is in the kitchen despite being the same age as me, and I think maybe I'm using generational differences as an excuse when it's really something missing inside me.

My mom checks the clock on the microwave. "I can't do it today, I have my next lesson." She pulls out her phone and checks her calendar app. My heart pangs just a little. She was supposed to put the first day of my senior year in weeks ago, but all I see are the highlighted blocks that represent each of her scheduled piano lessons. She swipes to next week. "I can do Tuesdays before my seven thirty p.m. lesson. Does that work?"

I don't need to check anything. I know I'll make myself free.

Chapter 6

During lunch break, Kareena, Meredith, and I like to eat in the classroom of our Spanish teacher. Señora Molina leaves the classroom open for us so we have the space to ourselves. Meanwhile, she spends her lunch break across the hall with Madame Granger, who teaches French.

The routine is simple. Meredith pulls up a playlist on Señora Molina's computer. We catch up on homework. We eat our lunch. It's been a faultless formula since freshman year.

"What time for the picnic on Saturday?" I ask.

"How about noon?" Kareena says. "I checked the weather and it shouldn't be too hot until, like, three p.m."

"Works for me," Meredith says. "The boba shop will miss us."

We typically spend at least one weekend afternoon at our favorite boba shop. We even have a signature table in the corner of the store—the one with the greatest amount of natural lighting and copious outlets—that we usually claim while we do the week's homework together.

"They'll be fine without our business for one weekend," I say.

At that moment, someone knocks on the open door of the classroom.

We all look up to see Jess Archibald hovering in the doorway. She's dressed, as usual, in an outfit that looks like it was lifted directly from a storefront mannequin, and she has a folder tucked against her chest.

There are three important things to know about Jess Archibald. The first is that although everyone who lives in the district for Highland Hills has a decent amount of money, the Archibalds have *money*. Jess had a Disney Channel pop star perform at her sweet sixteen and she'd invited everyone in her classes. Kareena, Meredith, and I went just to see the spectacle of it all, and the Archibalds certainly did not disappoint.

The second thing to know about Jess, more important than the first, is that Jess is the person most likely to take my salutatorian title if I lose a weighted class. Technically, Highland Hills tells only you of your rank so that it's private information, but people talk and rumors spread, especially in a school as competitive as this one. My friends and I don't really interact with Jess, so I can't confirm it directly, but I am more than aware that people say Jess Archibald holds rank number three.

The third thing is that Jess Archibald is a liar and a cheater, but that's a separate story.

"Hey," Jess says from the doorway, not fully entering the classroom. She must correctly get the sense that the Spanish classroom is our specific territory. I'm also fairly certain that Jess takes French, so I'm even more confused as to why she's here. I turn back to my friends to see if they're just as perplexed as I am.

Kareena doesn't meet my eyes. Instead, she looks at Jess and smiles. "Hey, Jess."

What the hell?

"I was wondering if now's a good time to go over our chem homework?" Jess asks.

Kareena gets up and grabs her chemistry folder from her backpack. "Yeah, let's sit out in the hallway." She leaves the room with

Jess following. She never meets my eyes.

I look at Meredith with confusion and a thrum of annoyance. "Since when does Kareena talk to Jess?"

Meredith shrugs. "She sat next to us in chem on the first day and they talk every so often, I guess. I think they volunteered at the same hospital over the summer?"

"Of course she sat next to y'all." I put down my granola bar, suddenly uninterested in eating it.

"I know what you're worried about," Meredith says, rolling her eyes. "Jess isn't going to beat you out."

The image of Jess giving the salutatorian speech infiltrates my head. Her onstage wearing a designer sundress and thanking her parents, who have enough money to rename the school if they wanted to. "She might," I say, careful to keep my tone neutral. "Especially if she's checking answers with Kareena. Kareena's answers are never wrong."

That's the day that Culinary Arts somehow gets even worse.

At the start of eighth period, Mr. Treviño makes an announcement that genuinely makes me consider dropping the class and picking up orchestra after all. The cello is suddenly calling my name.

"All right, so I know I said that yesterday was diagnostic only and that it didn't count for anything. That wasn't necessarily true."

I feel myself about to have a heart attack.

Mr. Treviño meets my eyes and gives a reassuring smile. "Although yesterday didn't count for a grade, it did help me understand where everyone's comfort levels are in the kitchen. Cooking and food are a gorgeous way of connecting with and learning from other people. It's also part of my teaching philosophy that y'all should learn as much from one another as you do from me."

His words sound suspiciously like the introduction to a group project, which means my blood begins to curdle.

Mr. Treviño continues, "As part of the class, I've assigned you into pairs. If you look online on our course page, you'll see I posted a new bulletin with a list of dishes. I want each pair to work through the dishes over the course of the semester, as a way to make sure you're getting extra practice outside of class. Some of the selections are complex, and some will demand difficult technique. But don't worry, the grade will not be about how well the dishes come out! Instead, I want you to take a selfie with your dishes and submit them online in the folder I've set up for this class. That will be our method of accountability, a way to see what you've made, and that both partners were present and involved. The actual grade will not come from the dishes—not their taste, not their appearance—but from what you personally have learned. Each of you will complete a reflection essay about how you've grown as a chef by learning new culinary techniques with a colleague. The deadline for the essay usually falls around Halloween, but feel free to submit it earlier if you're ready."

Here's the thing about loving school and being a bona fide nerd: group projects are the absolute worst. You're always the one pulling all the weight and everyone gets to enjoy the blanket score that you've single-handedly earned. At least, that's how it typically works for me. I'm suddenly nervous that I'll be the one pulling my partner down, a concern I have never once before had in my life. The reality of this class is that I don't know that there's a single person he could pair me with that wouldn't be markedly better than me.

Mr. Treviño adds, "I've intentionally tried to make it so that each pair has a balance of skill level. It's about teaching to, and learning from, each other. There's not a lot of that if both people know the same things, right?"

Oh God. Oh no. I freeze in my seat and my mouth tastes like acid.

"The Culinary Arts kitchen will be open after school until six p.m. during the school week for pairs who need a common space. Plus, if you'd like to get any extra cooking practice, if you'd like to use it as a study space, if you'd like to make yourself a little afternoon snack—it's all free real estate. The janitor will come kick you out by six p.m., though, so make sure you're done and have cleaned up by then. Let's not make it harder on him, all right? Now, as for the pairs . . ."

I know without Mr. Treviño announcing the names exactly who I'll be working with for the next couple of months.

When he says my name followed by Wesley Ruengsomboon's, we briefly make eye contact and both look away. His expression is as sour as mine. The acid surges back up in my throat.

Then, Mr. Treviño has the audacity to launch into what I would consider to be more "textbook" curriculum, as if he didn't just doom us to the most torturous semester of all time. All the goodwill he's earned from me in this first week has instantly dissipated.

I force myself to take diligent notes, trying to revel in this sense of normalcy and taking advantage of the fact that it gives me something to do other than work with my paired partner. There are new terms, new structures to learn, and although some of my classmates look bored, I am chasing the slightest feeling of relief. This is the stuff I can learn on my own if I make the effort. I can read a textbook chapter, make flash cards, hold information in my head long enough to get questions right on a quiz. Doing things hands-on, having things come out badly despite good effort, is where I get lost.

When the bell rings, Wesley makes no move to gather up his things. The other students in the class hustle out of the room, but he still remains seated.

"I'm guessing you want to talk about the group project," I mumble, pulling out the empty and washed Tupperware container from my backpack. I walk over to the cabinets and put it back in its place. "Look, I'm not stoked about working with you either."

He rolls his eyes. "The sooner we get through his recipes, the sooner we can be rid of each other. What days are you free?"

"What do you mean?"

"Aren't you president of every club this school has? I'm sure you'll have to squeeze it into your schedule if we want to work in the kitchen after class."

"I do have to go to Science Bowl right now," I say, checking the time on my phone. "I'm cocaptain this year."

He does me the favor of saying nothing, but I can practically hear him rolling his eyes again.

"Fridays," I say, zipping up my backpack and slinging it over my shoulder. "I'm free on Fridays after school. I gotta go."

"Are you not going to comment organically on my curry or are you going to make me ask?" Wesley says.

I snort. I should be walking to the door, but something holds me there. "When people fish for compliments, it's usually less transparent than this."

"If you fished for anything regarding your dish, I don't trust what would come up," he says.

I narrow my eyes. "You'll have to wait for Friday."

Then I leave, making him the only person in the Culinary Arts kitchen. I walk to Science Bowl practice and I should be thinking of strategies to get to state this year. But really, I'm thinking about how I've essentially promised away my Friday afternoons to someone who gets under my skin worse than Jess Archibald.

When Friday comes, I can barely take notes during Mr. Treviño's introductory lecture about foodborne illnesses because I'm so nervous about cooking with Wesley after school. He hasn't spoken to me since Wednesday, despite the fact that we sit approximately six inches apart during class. He hasn't given me any indication as to which dish we're tackling first.

I looked at the list last night. I had the document open for all of two seconds before I wanted to close it. Most of the words on there weren't even English—at least, not really. Words like roux, béchamel, au gratin—and that was all under one dish! The only thing that sounded straightforward was tomato sauce, but the memory of my salsa-pasta made my cheeks burn. Why do I feel like Mr. Treviño added it to the list just because of me?

Each dish had culinary techniques written in parentheses that he wanted us to practice. Tomato sauce had *mince, dice, sauté*—all of which I actually knew the definition of, even if I wasn't confident I could carry them out. But the other things on the list were a mystery. Even something as simple as chocolate chip cookies had *browning butter* in parentheses. How do you suck the joy out of making cookies by putting in nonsense like that?

To Mr. Treviño's credit, the list is pretty short. It only has five dishes, so if Wesley and I meet every week, we can be done with plenty of time to spare before the Halloween deadline.

The final bell rings and within minutes, there's only Wesley and me left in the Culinary Arts kitchen.

"This is the first time there hasn't been anyone else here," he says. "Guess everybody wants their Fridays to be free."

"Oh," I say. "I'm sorry. I didn't even ask if you—it was just that Fridays are the only days I don't have something."

"It's fine."

"Do Fridays work okay for you?" It's a bit of a useless question at this point, since Mondays are Student Council, Tuesdays are Honor Society, Wednesdays are Science Bowl, and Thursdays are Key Club. I guess technically, I could miss the Honor Society meetings if I needed to, since I'm not an officer. Kareena is Honor Society president, so I'm sure she'd understand. Suddenly, a thought occurs to me and I'm forced to backtrack. "Wait, you've been staying after school every day?"

He shrugs and avoids meeting my eyes. He looks almost bashful.

"You're really trying to get ahead, aren't you?" I say.

He turns to fully face me and his eyes go cold. "Some people think cooking is more than just a way to get another A. I know that's hard for you to understand."

I straighten my spine, pulling my shoulders back. "No one said they're mutually exclusive. But anyway, if you want your weekends back, I can maybe do Tuesdays—"

"Fridays are fine," he says. He's brusque.

"You don't want to start your weekend?"

"No."

There are other questions that fill the space between us, but I am not brave enough to ask, and I'm sure he wouldn't want to answer.

"Okay, so which recipe should we start with?" I say. I try my best to keep a neutral tone of diplomacy that I hope can defuse whatever tension has been building.

It works in part. His expression is a palimpsest of earlier smirks. "I think it's about time you knew how to make a tomato sauce."

"I was wondering, do you think he added that in because of me?"

He raises his eyebrows. "Do you want me to answer that honestly?"

I sigh. "Forget it. Not everyone can whip up an amazing curry on day one."

The corners of his mouth quirk up even more fully. "Amazing, huh?"

"Don't make me say it again."

"So she can't cook, but she does have taste," he says, nodding to himself. He flashes me a smirk, and although it's annoying, I think I do prefer it to his scowl. "All right, salutatorian. Let's see how you chop an onion."

"Sure." I grab an onion from the supply pantry and bring it over to my cooking station. I won't say aloud, of course, that I've never chopped an onion in my life. I also don't voice that I didn't know we needed onions to make tomato sauce. The name is tomato sauce, after all, not tomato-and-onion sauce.

"So do I take off its jacket first?" I ask, running my finger along the brown skin. It's paper thin, so I could easily just slice through it.

"You're not asking me if you need to peel an onion. . . ."

"That's not an answer."

"Eliza. Tell me you're not being serious."

I roughly peel the skin off, accidentally tearing off a layer of what I think is likely the actual onion, before starting to chop. But as I cut farther into the onion, the layers start to separate, the upper layers sliding out over the ones underneath, and my fingers turn sticky with what I can only presume is onion sweat.

"Keep them together," Wesley demands.

"I'm trying," I snap.

But the layers continue to slide, and my knife doesn't cut as straight as it should in my head. My diced onions range in shape from a pencil eraser to a domino. A rough chop, one might say.

"My God, how are you this hopeless?" Wesley's words are meaner than his tone.

"I'm *not*—you're just—oh," I say. My voice drops to a whisper. "Oh no."

Burning. My eyes are burning.

It happens all of a sudden, my eyes filling with tears I absolutely did not consent to. It's like my corneas are fighting off the world's most noxious bug spray. I blink and blink, but the sting keeps mercilessly returning.

"Oh shit," Wesley says. "I'm so sorry. I didn't mean to hurt your feelings like that."

"It's the *onion*, you—you *oaf*!"

"*Oaf?*" he repeats, but he's laughing.

Admittedly, I don't spend much time insulting people out loud. I had nothing at the ready.

Still, I spit, "Like I'd ever cry over you!" The heat of the words is sabotaged by the way I cannot stop leaking onion tears. For a second, I take a mental note to look up what exactly in onions irritates the lacrimal glands so much, because it would make for a pretty good Science Bowl question. But for the time being, all I can do is blink and sob.

"Eliza, why are you even in this class?"

I look up at him through foggy vision, unable to decipher whether he looks bemused or frustrated. "What do you mean?"

"This isn't AP. You're obviously not interested in cooking, nor do you have the slightest chance of winning the cook-off. Why even take Culinary Arts?"

At last, my eyes start to calm down and the tears clear. "Wesley, I don't know what it is about me that makes you think you know me so well, but—"

"Come on, you're a walking stereotype," Wesley says, and I'm surprised to hear such venom in his tone. "I don't even have to talk to you to know exactly what your priorities are. Getting an A? Winning the cook-off to pad your already perfect GPA? Thirsting after early admission to Harvard?"

MIT, actually, I almost say. But I can only stay quiet.

"Cooking isn't something you can just study for and be good at," he continues. "It's a bit of intuition and a hell of a lot of practice." The condescension is sickening. I can't believe this random guy who likely has never taken an honors class in his life is lecturing *me*.

But hating my group-project partner does not bode well for my grade. So I swallow my pride. It goes down like knives. "Well, it's good that I'm paired with you, then," I say evenly.

He looks at me, and although I'm still learning to read him, it looks like he's surprised I'm not fighting back. I'll take that as a victory in the battle I'm aware might only be happening in my own head. Wesley lets out a laugh that is mainly breath.

"Listen," I say. "If there's one thing I'm good at, it's taking a group project seriously. So I'll see you here every Friday. Every Friday, we'll work on one of Mr. Treviño's recipes, and if Fridays aren't enough, I'll take your Saturdays, too. Your Sundays, even. Then I'll write the most incredible reflection essay about what you've taught me, even if I have to lie, and Mr. Treviño will weep when he reads it. And then, at the end of the semester, I'll present my three marvelous dishes, win the cook-off, and you'll feel humiliated that you ever doubted me. Sound like a plan?"

This time, when Wesley laughs, it's much more than an exhale. It fills the empty kitchen and bounces off the stainless steel appliances. He pretends to wipe away a tear, and I wonder if that's a callback to my onion fiasco. Finally, his laughter dissolves and he looks straight into my eyes to say, "Oh God. I'd love to see you try."

Chapter 7

Exactly ten minutes before noon, Kareena arrives in her navy-blue Volkswagen. Meredith is already in the passenger seat, so I crawl into the back with my tote bag filled with paper plates, plastic cutlery, and a Tupperware.

When we get to Zilker Park, there are already dozens of picnic blankets laid out. You've never seen so many golden retrievers in your life until you go to a green space in Austin. From her tote, Kareena pulls out the same pale gold blanket we've used since our middle school picnics and spreads it across the green grass. Her family bought it in India before Kareena was even born, so the colors are worn with age and there's a big hole in the upper left corner, which is the only reason Kareena's mother lets us use it outdoors.

"All right, girls, get excited," I say, pulling out my Tupperware. I take off the lid and reveal rows of perfect little Bagel Bites. "Looks great, huh?"

"Eliza, a little effort would've been nice," Meredith says and pulls out a bag of tortilla chips and a container of queso with the Torchy's logo emblazoned on the circumference. Although we all agree that you can find better tacos than Torchy's on practically any street of Austin, they do nail a perfect Tex-Mex queso.

"Are y'all kidding?" Kareena cries. "Am I the only one that made something?"

Kareena reveals three slices of what I think is supposed to be a cheesecake, but it's bright orange and the surface is dimpled.

There's a dollop of whipped cream at the edge of each slice.

"Didn't think I'd ever live to see the day where Eliza brought the best picnic food," Meredith murmurs. "Kareena, is that pumpkin pie? In August?"

"The whipped cream looks like it might be melting," I say helpfully.

Kareena rolls her eyes and pushes her thick, black hair behind her shoulders. "It's a mango cheesecake! I tried to be creative and neither of you even tried to match my energy. And yes, maybe it didn't set or bake properly or whatever, and yes, maybe I didn't whip the cream for long enough, but it still tastes good!"

"Cooking's hard, isn't it?" I say smugly, snapping a cheesy tortilla chip into my mouth.

"Girl, I can cut an onion," Kareena says.

Obviously, I keep the girls up-to-date on every detail and every interaction in my life in our group text that inevitably changes names every week or so. Right now, it's called "vaxxed against senioritis," but only because I changed it from Meredith's "two nerds and a crybaby" after I sent them my onion story.

Maybe it goes without saying, but Wesley and I did not finish making our tomato sauce on Friday. He condescendingly showed me how he cuts an onion and demanded that I mimic his steps until we had cut through three full onions and an entire bulb of garlic. It was both so demoralizing and patronizing, I seriously considered throwing a handful of onions in his eyes just to get him off my back. By the time Wesley said that the janitor would be coming soon, the collar of my shirt was visibly wet from my constant stream of onion-induced tears. I woke up this morning with my fingers still reeking of garlic. How many weeks will it take before I can make tomato sauce—a question I ask myself and also what Kareena renamed the chat before Meredith's crybaby contribution.

Kareena continues, "Half of cooking is sautéing onion and garlic anyway."

Well, actually, it's a bit of intuition and a hell of a lot of practice, I want to say, but stop myself when I remember who I'd heard it from. I'm not used to making callbacks to people who aren't Kareena and Meredith. The feeling is unsettling.

"I can't believe you have to keep working with that guy," Meredith says. "Sounds like a group project from hell."

I sigh. "I can't believe my senior year is being ruined by some regular kid whose only definition of AP is all-purpose flour."

Meredith stifles a cackle with a tortilla chip.

"The way you know different types of flour," Kareena preens. "Our little girl is *learning*."

"He talks to me like he's smarter than me. It's so infuriating." I hold a Bagel Bite so tight in my hand, I almost squash it. "Like, go back to learning your times tables or whatever it is you do in your other classes and stop breathing down my neck!"

Kareena laughs. "My God, Eliza. I don't know if I've ever seen you like this. He really riles you up, huh?"

Meredith waggles her eyebrows. "You're not in chemistry class with us, and yet, could this be . . . *chemistry*?"

"I would rather drink bleach," I say witheringly. "Also, speaking of chemistry, I think I've waited long enough before respectfully bringing up this topic." I shift myself to face Kareena and try to keep the grimace of judgment from overtaking my features, because the last thing I want is our picnic to turn into an awkward argument. "I must be missing something, because since when are we friends with Jess Archibald?" I purposefully use *we* to remind her of her loyalties.

Kareena instantly looks down, letting her gaze land on the Bagel Bites. Jesus, it's worse than I thought. She looks so guilty. How can so much have happened in the first week alone?

"Kareena?" I say.

Meredith nudges my knee with hers. "Give her a minute! Damn. It's a picnic, not a cross-examination."

"Taking time to respond gives the impression that you're trying to make up a story," I say. "If you're friends with Jess, you're friends with Jess. I just want to know why. And why now? She could easily take my speech by the end of this semester. The timing is just . . ."

Kareena sighs. "I truly mean this with so much love, but not everything is about you, okay?"

"I know. I'm sorry," I say. "I'm just anxious. I think Culinary Arts is going to be the lowest grade of my lifetime, and Mrs. Porter asked me about my personal statement earlier this week, and it just feels like I'm not where I should be in any of this."

Kareena takes a Bagel Bite and weighs it in her hand. "My dad's taking me to Philly in a few weeks to tour Penn. My cousin there said I could sit in on one of her lectures. Maybe you could scope out MIT and inspiration will strike?"

"Wait, maybe I should tour Brown," Meredith says, shifting into the encyclopedic image of piqued interest. "There's this class on decolonization that went kind of viral and I'd love to investigate." As viral as something can be in the tiny corner of the internet that pays attention to Brown undergraduate courses, she means.

Each of us has had our sights set on a dream school since freshman year. It's been convenient that none of them have overlapped, but it does make me worry about being lonely in college. Our academic drive is what bound the three of us together originally, but I don't know what I would do in a school where that's already the shared common ground. At least at Highland Hills, there are people who don't take AP classes, like Wesley. I'm sure everyone in college will have been the maxed-out versions of all three of us, so where do I go from there?

"You don't have any ideas on what to write about?" Meredith asks, bringing me out of my thoughts. I've already read and edited a draft of Meredith's personal statement she wrote over the summer. It's a heartwarming story about coming out to her parents and finding power in public policy. It's excellent. It's quintessentially Meredith.

I just don't know what it means to be quintessentially Eliza. Writing about wanting to be a girl in computer science feels overdone. And it's MIT—I'm sure every woman applicant is saying some variation of the same thing.

Kareena offers, "You could write about Science Bowl?"

Meredith nods along. "Or Key Club and how you organized the women's hygiene drive for the domestic violence shelter?"

"Yeah, maybe," I concede.

"You got this," Kareena says. "You're so smart."

"And if your Bagel Bites come out this good," Meredith adds, tossing one in her mouth, "then it sounds like the cook-off is yours to win."

"The way you talk with your mouth full is very charming," Kareena says.

Meredith adds a tortilla chip into the bagel mush and exaggerates her mouth movements when she says, "Thank you, Kareena.

I'm equally as charmed by your disfigured cheesecake." Meredith dodges quickly before the tortilla chip Kareena throws at her face can hit its mark.

The next Tuesday, my mom walks into the kitchen looking lost. I wonder if even she feels the absence she's left in this house. Does she recognize the same things I do, and like me, keep them to herself?

For our first lesson, we are making doenjang jjigae, or fermented-soybean-paste stew. It's a Korean staple, something that every Korean parent knows how to make and a dish that's even blossomed in Western popularity by being a common addition to a Korean barbecue meal. It's one of my mom's favorite dishes, something she will always order during the rare times we go out to a Korean restaurant, because it's the epitome of a comfort meal. She chooses the recipe easily from the stack, neatly replacing the rest in their folder with an excruciating level of care. "Every Korean should know how to make doenjang jjigae," she says.

The lesson starts out quietly. She asks me to read out the list of ingredients as she pulls them, one by one, from the fridge.

I bring out a pair of cutting boards and knives. I select an onion and give it a rough chop, taking care to make the cuts even. I feel the familiar sting of tears prick my eyes, but I manage to make it through. By the time I've cut a single onion, my mom's cutting board boasts piles of zucchini, potato, and tofu already uniformly prepped. Her remarkable efficiency is not dissimilar from watching Wesley's last Friday, but I ignore the thought.

"When did Halmeoni teach you how to make this?" I ask, trying to prompt her into opening up.

She ponders the question while she minces the garlic. I note the way she curls her fingers so they don't get injured and try to mimic it with my own hand as I slide it across the countertop. "You know what's funny? I taught it to myself."

"Really?"

"Halmeoni was feeling sick one day when I was in sixth grade and Harabeoji had already gone to work. So I tried to make doenjang jjigae for her to eat and feel better." She begins to work on making the soup base from dried anchovies in our coal-colored earthenware pot called ttukbaegi. She fills it with water and sets it to boil.

"How did it turn out?"

"Oh, not so good. But Halmeoni ate it. And she felt better! And then she told me that if she's sick, she would like to be made dakjuk instead." She smiles to herself at the memory. To my grandmother's point, chicken porridge does seem more like a sick-person meal than a spicy stew.

"So she wasn't grateful?"

"She was. But that was her way. She never really said things explicitly, but you could tell what she really meant."

Maybe that was part of the problem with Halmeoni and me. There were too many things missed in between the lines, further lost in translation by my bad Korean and her lack of English.

I help my mom transfer the chopped veggies into the pot. So far, the recipe seems simple enough. "That was very sweet of you to do," I tell her. "I'm sorry I never made doenjang jjigae for you when you were sick."

"It's not the child's job to take care of her parents. Not yet," she says.

I shrug. "I think it could still be a little more equitable." Then, because I don't know that she would know the word *equitable* in English, I clarify, "More even."

How many moments over the past few months did I see an opportunity to help care for my mother, and then proceed to ignore it? The guilt that comes afterward is nauseating, battling the good smells in the kitchen.

"Doenjang jjigae always reminds me of home," my mother says abruptly. "It's like childhood." She goes someplace else then, her face clouded over with lost focus and reminiscence.

Let me in, part of me wants to say. *Tell me where you go when you disappear like this.*

Stop leaving me, the other part of me coldly demands. *Focus on the family that you have left.*

But neither part says anything until it's time to stir in the doenjang paste. By then, the dish is almost ready and my mom goes back to the piano room to prepare for her next lesson.

It shouldn't irritate me as much as it does that Wesley Ruengsomboon stays in the Culinary Arts kitchen after school every day. After class, he's never in a rush to leave. Sometimes, he doesn't even bother to pack his backpack up. He leaves everything splayed out and open, like he's made a home out of this space. On Wednesday, the last bell rings and he stays seated on his stool. I do, too.

"Do you ever have anything to do after school?" I say.

"Like what? Sports?"

"Sure, maybe. Or clubs. Extracurriculars. You know, the things you put on your résumé."

His annoyance is written across his brow. "You trying to play guidance counselor?"

I narrow my eyes at the diversion. There's no way I can ever catch up to him with my once-a-week lessons with my mom, especially if he's putting in kitchen hours literally every weekday. "Just curious as to why a high school senior would want to spend all his afternoons at school."

"Some people have passions, Eliza. We're not all just regurgitations of others' expectations."

My sharp inhale is embarrassingly audible. "What is *wrong* with you?" He talks to me like he's already cracked me open and found something rotten inside.

Wesley doesn't give me the decency of turning in my direction. "Aren't you late for Science Bowl practice?"

Unwittingly, I glance at the time on my phone. He's right.

I hold my tongue, mainly for the sake of our grades, but in this moment I feel very tired of playing peacemaker. I don't know how I can get through a semester of this kind of tension when we can barely talk to each other without throwing insults like weapons.

But you don't succeed by rocking the boat. So I leave him in the kitchen. Neither of us says goodbye.

Chapter 8

When class ends on Friday, as soon as people leave the kitchen, Wesley slides out a DVD case and ambles over to Mr. Treviño's computer. He fiddles with the controls that connect the computer to the projector.

"Are we working today or not?" I ask.

"We are," he says.

Eventually, he gets the projector to mirror the computer screen and the DVD he brought starts to play. From the intro, it seems to be a Disney film, but I can't exactly tell which one.

"I must be missing something," I say, "and I don't miss much."

He hits pause on the film before it can really begin playing and walks over to sit directly next to me. I don't remember the last time, if ever, Wesley has turned his entire body toward me like this. Our knees are practically overlapping. Something about it feels nerve-racking, although I don't know what about this could possibly scare me.

He meets my eyes and I have to stop myself from immediately looking away. Can't he say what he has to say without boring into me like that? "I'm sorry, Eliza, for what I said to you the other day," he says. The sincerity in his voice is undisguised, if not a little baffling.

Despite my surprise, I don't let myself miss a beat. "Thank you."

"I thought we could watch a movie to set the tone," he says, clearly finished with the topic of his apology.

"What movie?" And what tone?

Instead of answering my question, Wesley gets up and returns to Mr. Treviño's computer. He clicks the play button.

The narrator's voice comes from the projector speakers. "Although each of the world's countries would like to dispute this fact, we French know the truth: the best food in the world is made in France."

My laugh comes so suddenly, I almost choke on it. "Oh my God. Is this *Ratatouille*?"

"Clever, right?" he says. He begins moving around the kitchen, collecting ingredients and equipment. I wonder if I should be following him around. "Great film, but that first line is a huge pile of bullshit. No one who's ever grown up in a non-white household would ever think France has the best cuisine."

"I haven't seen this," I say.

He almost drops a pan. "*What?* Never?"

The intensity of his disbelief makes me reconsider. "Maybe I've seen it once a long time ago? I don't really remember, honestly."

"Well, I normally like to think my cooking is the star of the show, but in this case, the movie might actually upstage me."

"Is that what you're going to teach me to make? Ratatouille?" I ask. "I didn't see that on the syllabus."

He scoffs. "Shocking, right?"

I furrow my brow. "I don't know what you mean."

He shakes his head and I catch myself watching how his hair moves. "I mean, I love Mr. Treviño, but the syllabus was pretty . . . Eurocentric."

"Oh," I say. "You mean, it was just white-people food."

His eyes flicker up to mine in surprise. Something in Wesley's expression is softer than I've ever seen it, like he's seeing me for the first time this semester. "Right."

"Definitely a lot of French words."

"*Ratatouille* makes even more sense, doesn't it?" He looks pleased with himself.

"So are we not remaking the tomato sauce? Which, by the way, I think the Italians claim," I say, peering at his collection of ingredients. There's an onion, some garlic, and a can of tomatoes like last time. But I notice a bell pepper, nearly half a dozen eggs, and a collection of spices he's pulled from the cabinet, all of which I'm pretty sure we did not use last week.

"We are. Kind of," Wesley says. I hear the smile in his voice without even looking at him.

"Again, I don't know what you mean. I can't read your mind, Wesley."

"We're going to make shakshuka."

I blink at him. "Am I supposed to know what that is?"

He sighs. Whatever softness he had earlier is completely erased. "I forget that you're—"

"Just skip to the part where you explain what it is."

"It's a North African dish. Basically like eggs in a tomato-based sauce."

"I don't remember seeing that in Mr. Treviño's bulletin." I wish I didn't sound so much like a teacher's pet, but I can't fight against the fabric of who I am.

Wesley waves his hand dismissively. "What's Mr. Treviño's goal in making us make tomato sauce from scratch? The techniques. The dicing, the mincing, the sautéing, cooking out the flavors without burning them or pushing them too far until they're bitter." The words flow so fast out of him that he forces himself to take a breath. "I figured we could still do all those elements that he wants us to practice, but make something more interesting. You don't think it's kind of ridiculous that practically the entire list is French?"

I shrug. "I didn't really think about it. It would be kind of silly to have us make miyeokguk. Seaweed soup, I mean. Right?"

He meets my eyes. There's a brightness there that disarms me. "Why would that be silly?"

I think I'm generally good at answering questions. It's part of my identity. But for some reason, with Wesley's eyes shining in the fluorescence and something similar to eagerness on his face, I feel like I'm at a loss for words. "I don't know. Because no one else in the class would eat it? It's just something my mom makes sometimes."

"I would." He says it without hesitation.

"Really?"

"Of course. Miyeokguk sounds awesome. And honestly, how many times are you personally cooking tomato sauce at home? Because for me, it's never."

He's right. I don't know why I'm resisting saying it out loud. The image of my mom making tomato sauce from scratch instead of buying a jar at the grocery store is nearly outlandish. "Don't you think it's important to follow our teacher's instructions rather than writing your own? Plus, he's going to be checking our photos. He'll see we strayed from the syllabus."

"I don't think he'll care," he argues. "Like I said, we're learning all the right culinary things, and technically, shakshuka is a tomato-based sauce anyway. Plus, the photos aren't even graded! So what are you worried about?"

"I don't like breaking rules."

Wesley looks away, and for a split second, I register a trace of what looks like disappointment. I hate how that makes me feel, like I had the wrong answer. Or more like I've closed him back up.

I let out a noisy breath, making a show of huffing. "Fine. We'll go with your revised syllabus."

"Seriously?" I can't tell if his disbelief should be offensive.

I roll my eyes. "As long as you make sure we're hitting the points he wants us to hit. I'm not showing up to class and everyone else has mastered the techniques and I haven't."

"Oh, Eliza . . . I'm not a miracle worker."

"Shut up. I'll chop the onion."

We work in silence as the movie plays in the background. Wesley lets me command the onion and garlic, while he seeds the bell pepper and dices it.

He arches a brow as he watches me work. "Better than last week."

"Thank you."

"Though it was maybe impossible to get worse."

I scowl at him. "This knife is sharp, you know."

He is completely unfazed by the threat in my voice. "If only you knew how to use it." His smirk is so aggravating, I look away to ensure that the only thing I cut is a vegetable.

The shakshuka comes together surprisingly easily. The sauce simmers with crushed tomatoes and the enticing smells of paprika and cumin. Wesley makes small wells in the sauce and cracks an egg into each space before covering the skillet with a lid.

He glances up at the projector screen. "Looks like it'll be ready just in time for my favorite scene."

To be completely honest, I haven't been paying that close atten-tion to the movie. Just making sure the onions didn't burn when we cooked them to what Wesley said was "translucent" was enough to take up my entire reserve of brain power. But now that all we have to do is wait for the eggs to cook, I let myself actually watch.

I have to admit, *Ratatouille* is absorbing. Enchanting, even. It takes little effort to find myself invested in Remy and Linguini's success. When Colette returns to help them, Wesley waltzes over to join me on our normal stools at the main table. He places one plate in front of each of our seats and hands me a spoon. The tomato sauce still bubbles from the heat and the yolks of the eggs shine like gold. It smells so good, I'm tempted to stick my nose into it, but I remember the cayenne Wesley threw in and restrain myself.

"Wow, Wesley. This looks incredible," I say. My mouth waters and I have to swallow audibly.

Wesley stops to take a photo of us with the plates before he sits down to eat. "It does. Not even you can mess it up. That ought to inspire you."

I glare at him, but the second I lift my spoon to my mouth, I'm overwhelmed. I didn't know what's essentially just tomato and egg could feel so comforting, like a warm hug. And I didn't know I could help make something like this just by chopping up some vegetables.

Wesley, who has been watching my expression, grins. "Better than tomato sauce?"

"Not even a comparison," I say. "How did you know how to make this?"

He shrugs, breaking one of his eggs with the back of his spoon. "I didn't really grow up around anything special. Not like you and miyeokguk. Nothing feels like it belongs to me, so I just try out every kind of cuisine I can figure out."

A question I've had in the back of my mind, but never asked aloud, comes out unchecked. "Aren't you Thai?"

"Did the hundred-syllable last name give it away?" He looks like he's about to say something else, too, but then his eyes catch on the film again and he shushes me.

"I wasn't even talk—"

"Shh," he says, even more aggressively. "It's about to be the best part."

I turn my attention to the screen. The long-faced, overplucked-eyebrowed food critic is about to taste Remy's dish. The first bite transports him back to childhood, moves him so markedly that he swallows the idea that a rat cooked his food.

"That's my favorite scene," Wesley says, still whispering. "It makes me cry." Sure enough, when I look at him from my peripheral vision, his eyes seem just a little glassy.

My first instinct is to make a joke. I want to wound him, poke fun at his vulnerability, and take the chance to restore the power balance. Then I chastise myself for the thought. We've been civil for about a minute, which is maybe a new record for us, and it's best that I don't ruin it. When I look back at the screen, something strikes me.

"It reminds me of my mom." I say it low enough that part of me hopes Wesley hasn't heard.

He turns to me with surprise. There's that brightness again, like he is seeing me with a different lens. "Your mom's a villain?"

"No—what? I mean, the part where he gets reminded of childhood. My mom's been trying to teach me some of her mother's old recipes. I think she's so excited about it because she gets to remember being a kid again," I say. Why am I saying so much? I haven't talked about my mom's cooking sessions with even Kareena or Meredith, but now, the words slip out so easily. I didn't know I had these thoughts until they're already out in the open.

"That's sweet," Wesley says. After a moment, he adds, "My mom's probably the villain in my story. If it's not actually me, that is." His voice has a trained nonchalance, like he's playing it off as a joke and hoping it's convincing enough. His gaze returns to the screen and seems to lock itself there.

I pause. "Is that why you stay here after school all the time?"

He eats a spoonful of shakshuka. "I could add some more cumin. Needs to be a bit punchier. And I forgot to garnish with cilantro. Or maybe parsley?"

"What's your mom like?"

"You ask a lot of questions."

"Do I?" I say instinctively, then laugh. "Maybe you could try answering some of them."

"Do being nosy and a ceaseless overachiever go hand in hand?" he says with faux curiosity.

"Kind of a wild thing to bring up without elaborating, in my opinion." I glance at him sideways. He's still staring ahead. "But I won't pry."

"Great."

We eat the rest of our shakshuka in silence. The movie finishes and the credits begin to roll.

"That was an excellent movie," I say. And it really was. I can't believe I hadn't seen it before.

"Obviously," Wesley says. "I also thought you might like one of the film's mantras."

"Which one is that?"

"Anyone can cook." He flashes me a grin and it's so quick, so unexpected, that it catches me off guard. He's back to looking at me now? "Even you, Miss Salsa-Pasta."

To my chagrin, I have no witty response at the ready.

"We should start cleaning up. It's almost six."

I nod slowly. "Yeah, that's kinda late."

"It's when the janitor comes to lock up the kitchen," he explains.

"Oh. Right."

He says it with the ease of someone who has clearly internalized this schedule. It occurs to me that I should be considering the length of his stays in addition to their frequency. For the first time, I sense that he doesn't use his kitchen time just to get ahead, but maybe also to stay away. I want to know more. Dozens of questions tumble around in my head, but the memory of his chastisement is still fresh. If he won't answer, I will dampen the curiosity.

I wash our dishes while Wesley straightens up the kitchen and retrieves his DVD. When we're done, we grab our things and leave the kitchen, just as the janitor comes in our direction.

"Like clockwork," Wesley says. "Good to see you, Mr. Wilby."

Mr. Wilby chuckles and gives Wesley a friendly wave. "Hey, kiddo. Have a good weekend, all right?"

"You too."

Wesley and I walk to the parking lot together. It's silent between us and I wonder if I should make up an excuse to go in a different direction.

"Thank you," I manage to say. "For the culture. I mean both the film and the food, of course."

"Of course," he says. "You can write about it in the reflection essay. How I introduced you to culture."

Finally, we reach my car and I realize we haven't diverged yet. "You didn't have to walk me," I say. "Where are you parked?"

"Over back." He gestures to a far corner of the parking lot. There are only a few cars left. I wonder which is his. "See you Monday."

I nod. "Yeah. Thanks again."

As I pull away from the school, I catch a glimpse of Wesley in the rearview mirror. But he isn't in the parking lot, or in a car. He's on the sidewalk, walking home.

Chapter 9

My mother has started accepting lessons on the weekends, so the sound of the piano scatters throughout Saturday. The occasional melody is the only reminder that it's not just me and my dad in the house.

My dad calls me down into the living room on Saturday morning. "I was thinking we could look over your physics textbook together. I want to see what they're teaching you at school."

"You called me down on a Saturday morning to talk about school?"

"Oh, come on, Yeji-yah. When you were a kid, you asked if there could be school on the weekends, too. Do you remember that?"

"You have to be making that up."

"It's true! Also, it's physics! That's not even work. It's beauty." I wish I could say that my dad was saying this in a joking manner, but he is not. He genuinely thinks physics is the most elegant subject of all time. Sometimes I think that if I were to ask him if he loves my mom or physics more, he would have a difficult time answering.

"Appa," I say, sitting down on the couch. I don't want to come clean, but I know it's better now than down the line. It's good to prepare him for bad news—rank drops, no speech at graduation. "I'm not in physics."

He blinks at me through his black, wire-rimmed glasses. "What?"

"They couldn't get me into physics. There was a conflict with the scheduling." The excuse sounds weak to my own ears, but I have no other defense.

"So what are you taking? Another science?"

I shake my head. "No, it's more like . . . an art class."

"Huh?" he says, his voice raised. "Like AP Art? I think Mrs. Oh's daughter did that, too. She still went to UCLA."

I shake my head again. "No . . . it's called Culinary Arts."

"Culinary Arts?" he repeats. His disbelief echoes Kareena's from the first day in homeroom, and mine from my meeting with Mrs. Porter. "That's like cooking?"

"Yeah."

"I didn't know they had AP classes like that."

"It's not . . . AP. . . ." I feel my face twisting into a visible cringe as I say the words.

His expression looks unfazed. "Is it honors, then?"

"No."

"No?" I can tell he's trying to compute things and they're not adding up. "So it's . . . regular?" He says *regular* like it's derogatory. I can't blame him, because I know with sudden clarity that it's a habit he got solely from me. There's no way that's something he's picked up on his own from his years in America.

"Yes," I confirm.

"You are about to apply to college and they put you in a regular class?"

"Yes."

His mouth gapes open and his eyebrows reach his hairline. "I need to call the office."

"Appa, it's Saturday."

"There's no way they can get away with this! You ranked physics!

I signed your form!" His eyes burn wild with outrage.

"Appa, I know. There's nothing we can do. I already asked. My best chance at keeping my rank is getting an A in this cooking class." I make the conscious decision not to tell him about the cook-off. It's not that I think he would pressure me into winning, but I know it would just be another way to disappoint him if I didn't.

"Ah, Yeji-yah . . . but you don't know how to cook."

"Wow, thank you for the support!"

He shakes his head. "Oh, this is not good."

Even though I agree with him, I find myself wishing that he could express a little more optimism. "I'm going to try really hard. Eomma is going to help me."

"Good. She said she can help you get an A?"

I bite my lip. "Well, she thinks I'm asking for her help to get to know Halmeoni's recipes better. She doesn't know that it's for class."

"That's a great idea, Yeji-yah!" he exclaims. He doesn't spend a second thinking about the deceptive angle I just admitted to, which makes me wonder if I'm overthinking that in my head. Or whether he even heard me. "Halmeoni was one of the best cooks in her whole region."

I nod. "I also think it's helping Eomma be . . . less depressed. She seems happier when she's remembering Halmeoni."

But my dad ignores this and says, "That was smart to ask Eomma for help. My salutorian."

"Salutatorian."

"Right." He leans back in his leather armchair and rests his hands on his slim belly. "Yeji-yah, I've watched you these past three years. Staying up late to finish work. Going away on weekends for competitions or service trips. You've worked really hard, and now that it's finally time to apply to college, it's your opportunity to show off what you've done."

"I'm still working hard, Appa. I promise."

"Of course you are. I already told my golf friends that they could come watch your graduation speech."

"Appa!"

"What? I'm so proud of you. I want everyone to come see my daughter."

I'm happy to hear him say it, I really am. It's just that this is the first time it feels a little bit like suffocation.

On Tuesday, my mom pulls a recipe from the stack and says, "This is the simplest one, so I thought we should learn it early."

I look over her shoulder to see which one she's selected. There are barely any instructions or ingredients written on the page. I read the title tentatively, "Kimchi bokkeumbap?" Kimchi fried rice is one of my favorite things my mom makes when she's short on time. I'm convinced that there must be some science behind the indisputable fact that anything with a blazing red color immediately tastes worlds better. The idea that we eat with our eyes has some merit.

"It's a very easy recipe," she says. "You really only need a few basics. The most important part, of course, is the kimchi." She walks over to the fridge and pulls out a tub of the red cabbage. "I was fifteen when your halmeoni taught me how to make my own kimchi. It's an important skill."

"Really?" I ask. "It seems like so much work." It has never once crossed my mind that I would ever make my own kimchi as an adult, let alone as a fifteen-year-old.

Growing up, it was easy to tell when it was a kimchi-making day in our family. The pungent smell of the ingredients seeped into every corner of the house and notified you, regardless of if you wanted it to or not. I would come downstairs to see my mother sitting on the tiled floor of our kitchen with plastic gloves on her hands and colossal stainless steel bowls in between her legs. Large heads of napa cabbages would roll around in the bowls as she slathered each leaf with spicy red paste. I would choke on the smell as I walked closer to her, and my mother would react by teasingly sticking her nose deep into the bowl and inhaling. Each time, she would make enough kimchi to last months, so the process didn't happen often, but it always looked laborious. I don't eat nearly enough kimchi to make the process seem remotely worthwhile.

"It's a lot of work," my mother confirms, placing the tub of kimchi on the countertop and moving expertly to the different cabinets to gather ingredients. "But it's worth it. You should always be able to make your own kimchi."

"It seems much easier to buy it," I say.

"And a lot of people do," my mother agrees. "I think most store-bought kimchi is too sweet. That's the worst. But when you make it yourself, you can cater to your tastes and make it however you want. I think my kimchi tastes the best." She allows herself a small grin at her own self-indulgence. "Maybe Halmeoni's kimchi is the best, and mine is a close second."

The image of my fifteen-year-old mother sitting on the floor of Halmeoni's kitchen in South Korea forms in my head. Two heads of black hair hovering over bowls of cabbage and paste, laughing and smiling and feeding each other the small leaves that fall off. It makes me long for a memory that's not my own.

"Your halmeoni would usually host a kimjang at our house for all the ladies in the neighborhood. We had so many cabbages and bowls, I could never see the floor," my mom says. My vision corrects itself. Instead of just my mother and my halmeoni, I now imagine dozens of women with overlapping limbs, coming together for their kimjang, which my mom once explained to me as the event of preparing kimchi. Suddenly, my memories of my mom alone on our tiled kitchen floor here in Austin feel much colder. Something that used to be a symbol of community turned into solitude. Why did I never join her? Why didn't my dad?

"Read out the ingredients," my mother instructs.

I do as she says. There aren't many surprises. Kimchi and rice, obviously. Gochujang, which is spicy pepper paste, for seasoning. Sesame oil for the unmistakable aroma. Cut strips of gim, or toasted seaweed, for garnish. My mom was right about the simplicity. It seems hard for even me to really mess this up.

We go through the recipe line by line. My mom tells stories in between each one if it sparks a memory. There's an ease in the way she talks about her mother, like the stories are always waiting there just below the surface, willing to be dipped into if you just break through the surface tension. She tells me of a time when she offered to help Halmeoni cut up the kimchi, which is the first step to making kimchi bokkeumbap. She was young, young enough that my uncle was still a baby, and didn't have much knife experience. She ended up slicing her middle finger. The blood ran and mixed with the kimchi juice on the cutting board, and the kimchi had to be thrown away. My mother cried, but my halmeoni only laughed at her tears and bandaged her finger. "I'll make it this time," my halmeoni told her. "Once your finger is healed, you make it next time."

I can't count the number of times my mom spread a dab of Fucidin cream over my cut and wrapped it with a SpongeBob or Hello Kitty bandage. I try to imagine my mom being the one with the cut, looking up at Halmeoni with tear-sodden lashes and a chin dimpled with distress. It's weird to know that my mom was once a child, too.

"I was always in a rush to learn as a kid," my mom says.

"Not anymore?" I ask.

"Not so much anymore."

"Why?"

She shrugs. "I came to America with a degree and college journalism awards, but it didn't really matter for me. I realized you can be in a rush to learn everything, get to a new place, and have everybody believe you know nothing. Like only a certain sort of knowledge is valuable." Her words sound serious, but her expression remains completely serene. She made peace with this reality long ago. Once again, I'm struck by how much she's sharing after being so quiet for the past months. There's something about cooking that seems to soothe her and lower her guard.

She opens the fridge and takes out a large bowl of white rice that's been covered with plastic wrap. I can see the tiny drops of condensation that say it was originally wrapped when the rice was still a little warm. "You can make kimchi bokkeumbap with any kind of rice, but white rice tastes the best, especially if it's a day or two old." She fries the diced kimchi in a wok before adding the rice and heaping spoonfuls of gochujang. "Your halmeoni didn't put it in the recipe, but I love adding a fried egg on top with the yolk still runny. Do you want to fry the eggs?"

"Sure," I say. I grab two eggs and heat a small skillet next to my mother. I oil the bottom and crack the eggs. They stay transparent.

"You want to wait for the skillet to heat up properly before you crack the eggs in," my mother says.

"Oh, sorry." Gradually, the bottom of the eggs begin to turn opaque, but the yolks remain raw. I try and press one down with my spatula in an effort to apply more heat, but the yolk pops open and runs a connecting river to the second egg. By the time I've success-fully divvied them up with the edge of my spatula and flipped them over, the bottom sides have burned into a brown crisp. I hate the way my mind instantly goes to the way Wesley expertly cracked and cooked the eggs in our shakshuka. He made it look so effortless, it didn't even occur to me to pay attention to how he did it.

Meanwhile, my mother adds sesame oil to the rice and turns off the heat. The smell of sesame oil does something indescribable to my body's physiology, like it single-handedly activates my hunger. "I like to add the sesame oil as late as possible. The more it cooks, the more you risk ruining the flavor. And now," she says, giving the fried rice one last toss in the wok, "it's time to plate! Easy, right?"

"Right," I say, unconvincingly.

She divides the kimchi bokkeumbap into two bowls. "Are the eggs done?"

"Maybe?" I say.

My mom slides one egg into each bowl. She garnishes each dish with a sprinkle of crumpled gim. "It's so easy, but it looks nice, right?"

It really does. The red of the gochujang, the white of the eggs (if you ignore the parts I burned), the dark green of the gim. It looks a little bit like art. My mom takes the bowls into the dining room and I bring two wooden spoons. We dive in.

There are few things that taste better than warm kimchi, in my opinion. The heat opens up the tang and spice, turning it into something so much more complex. It makes me think of kimchi pajeon, a pan-fried pancake, another perfect vehicle for sharp spice and heat. If I ignore the parts of the egg that are too black and too crispy, this is a perfect comfort meal.

"Did you salt the eggs?" my mom asks.

My spoon pauses on its way to my mouth. "I forgot." Did Wesley salt the eggs? Why can't I remember?

She grins. "That's okay. You'll remember next time." She continues to eat, unbothered by my burnt, unsalted eggs. She doesn't seem to care that the only responsibility I had in cooking this dish, I messed up.

But I care. I think about the final cook-off, I think about Wesley's curry, I think about how possible it is to learn enough in a semester to beat people who have years of practice. I eat my fried rice, and with every bite of burnt egg, the idea that I can catch up to anybody else gets harder and harder to swallow.

Chapter 10

The next Friday, after Culinary Arts ends, the whole class evacuates the kitchen within minutes, leaving Wesley and me alone, just like last week. I wonder how many times we'll have to go through this without it feeling so awkward. It'd be easier if we were friends, or maybe if I didn't have the single goal of beating him in the cook-off at the end of the semester. It'd also be easier if he didn't think I was a walking stereotype, and if I could convince myself that I'm not one either.

"I'm ready to learn," I say cheerily, trying to break the silence. "I was thinking we could get matching aprons or those tall chef hats with our names embroidered on them. Wouldn't that be cute?"

"A toque."

"Huh?"

Wesley rolls his eyes at me. "The chef hat you're talking about. It's called a toque. And no offense, but I don't think you're qualified to wear one of those yet."

"Oh, please. You meant that with full offense."

That earns me one of his smirks. "So I did."

"What's on the agenda for today, Chef?" I ask. "Which of Mr. Treviño's selections are we tackling?" He looks at me with such amusement that I can't help but sound defensive when I say, "What?"

"Just wondering if it's killing you to have to learn from another student. And worst of all, a *regular* student." He imbues *regular* with mock disgust, a caricature of me and others like me.

"Oh, it absolutely is," I say. "But as you know, I'll do anything for a good grade. Even play nice with the *regulars*."

He barks a laugh. "So she does has some self-awareness."

"And he randomly speaks in third person. We're learning so much about each other."

"So chummy. Might as well make an order for those matching aprons now."

"You joke, but if it makes Mr. Treviño more likely to give us a good grade, then it will be done."

"My God, you really are such a greasy little grade-grubber."

"I was kidding," I say.

He shakes his head and meets my eyes with a challenge. "Only partially."

I let my smile turn saccharine. "Only partially."

"I was thinking we could tackle potatoes au gratin today."

"That's how you pronounce that? Why does it kind of sound like 'oh rotten'? I feel like they could have workshopped the name a little more," I muse.

He shrugs, like he can't be bothered to indulge me.

"And 'roux' is pronounced like 'rue'? And 'béchamel' looks like it should be 'belch camel,' but it's not."

"Am I witnessing you discovering the French language?" Wesley says, his mouth pursed in annoyance.

"Weren't you the one complaining in the first place that the recipe list was too white?"

Wesley sighs. "If we don't start soon, we're not going to finish in time. And I think we both would like to spend as few Fridays together as possible. So are you done?"

I cross my arms. "Fine."

Wesley walks over to one of the equipment cabinets and brings out the cursed utensil that I know now to be a mandoline. I've already decided that it's my least favorite thing in the kitchen.

He sets it on the countertop of our workstation. "This recipe calls for your favorite stringed instrument."

I stand corrected. Wesley is number one, and the mandoline is number two.

"This is one of those things in the kitchen that are equally helpful and dangerous," he says with gravity.

"We have to slice a bunch of potatoes on it. I got it. Let's get into it."

Wesley looks like he's going to argue, but only sighs.

We make quick work peeling the potatoes. I decide to take initiative with the mandoline. Wesley watches me sharply. He looks like he's trying his hardest to bite his tongue while I fiddle with the device. I think I figure it out in a respectable time frame. There's a knob that seems to determine how high the knife edge is from the base. It all seems simple enough.

So I get to slicing. I run the first potato back and forth, back and forth, and watch as paper-thin slices collect on the cutting board underneath. The uniformity of the slices is something close to beautiful. Maybe I judged this damn not-a-grater, not-a-musical-instrument too fast. "Wait, this is kind of easy," I say with a grin. Is this actually fun? The thought almost makes me laugh.

"Slow down," Wesley warns.

"Why? You're the one who said we're short on time." I'm almost down to the nub anyway and we have two more potatoes to get through. Not to mention we haven't started the béchamel. I keep going, letting my hand get lost in the motion of sliding against the blade. I'm about to tell Wesley that he can stop hovering when almost instantly, faster than a blink, I see a drop of red that turns into a small rivulet. The sting comes after.

"Eliza!" His voice sounds thunderous, and I realize it's because he's instantly moved to my side. "I told you to be careful!" Wesley snatches my hand away, keeping me from contaminating the heap of potato slices. He runs my bloody finger under the sink faucet. "Are you okay?" The words are a begrudging grumble.

"I'm fine," I say, still in minor shock. "I don't know how that happened."

"People slice themselves on mandolines all the time. That's why they sometimes come with gloves." Wesley leaves me at the sink to fumble through one of Mr. Treviño's desk drawers, but that does not keep him from continuing his didactics. "When you're at the end of the vegetable, it's better to stop and use a knife. You don't have the proprioception to know how close you are to the last slice. You don't know if there's a half inch or a quarter inch until it's the pad of your finger running against the blade."

He comes back with a tube of Neosporin and a box of bandages.

"Wesley, you don't have to—"

"Don't go so fast. I know it kills you to listen to someone you think is so terribly unintelligent, but sometimes I know what I'm talking about." Despite his barbed words, he is gentle when he takes my hand and dries it with a paper towel. He smears a dab of ointment across the slash of scarlet, then carefully wraps a bandage around my finger, taking care to make sure the two edges line up perfectly.

"Thank you," I say. I'm embarrassed that the words are barely louder than a whisper. Is it my pride or the surprise at his tenderness that's blocking my windpipe?

"I'm going to wash the mandoline and then we can finish the potatoes."

I don't argue. I feel too chastised.

When Wesley sets up the newly cleaned mandoline, he glances at me. "How's your finger?"

"Fine," I say.

"Good. Come here. We're going to try again." He cleaves each potato and says, "It's safer to have a flat edge. More stability that way."

I primly grab one of the pieces and align the flat side with the slant of the mandoline. I slowly slide the potato along the blade, but I go so slowly that the slice comes out uneven.

Wesley has been watching over my shoulder and grabs my wrist to pause me. "Not like that. Here." Seamlessly, he guides his hand over mine and together, we glide the vegetable along the incline. He pushes my hand to apply even pressure and tucks my fingers into his so that our knuckles are curled. "You always want to protect your fingers. Just like when you're using a chef's knife." His words are soft and I can't tell if I'm imagining the flutter of breath that tickles my ear. It occurs to me that he must take cooking so seriously if he didn't even hesitate to wrap his arm around mine. Or maybe he thinks of me as so far from an actual girl that our proximity doesn't even register to him.

I tell myself to ignore the strength of his grip around my hand and the warmth that burns at the nape of my neck. I ignore the way that for the first time, I notice what he smells like. Some cousin of vanilla, but warmer. Spicier. I turn all my brain off, because my thoughts are too scrambled to be coherent. I watch with glassy eyes as dozens of even, pale discs fall from the blade. The action feels safer when his hand is pushing mine through the correct motions.

My mouth did not get the memo to shut down. I hear myself say, "You could've just said that you wanted to hold my hand."

Wesley snorts, but he immediately lets go. I try to continue the inertia of what he was showing me. It works to an extent. He lets me finish the rest of the potatoes. He even directs me on how to use the chef's knife to slice the last nubs, but does so verbally, not once coming closer than six inches from my hands again. Maybe he thinks it's unsafe considering my skill level.

"Let's start making the béchamel," Wesley says, weighing out flour and butter on the kitchen scale. "Technically, to make a béchamel, we start with—"

"A roux," I supply.

He can't conceal his shock, or he's not trying to. "How do you know that?"

"I'm a nerd. I did my reading before class."

Wesley arches an eyebrow. "Tell me what you learned."

I clear my throat dramatically and recite what I read online last night. "A roux is when you mix an equal amount of flour and fat. When you add milk, it turns into a béchamel. And a béchamel is a white sauce that's one of the French mother sauces. Like tomato sauce, which we've already made."

"For the first time, I kind of get why you're salutatorian. You memorized all that?"

I nod.

"I didn't know about the mother sauces," Wesley admits. He

doesn't look embarrassed to say it. In fact, it's almost like he's happy to store the information somewhere under his fluffy hair. Does Wesley *like to learn*? Do we actually have something in common?

"You bring the street smarts, I bring the book smarts," I say with a wide grin.

Wesley lets me take the lead on making the roux, but by that, he means that he stations himself at my shoulder to watch scrupulously while dispensing unsolicited tips. "You don't want the flour or the butter to burn, so keep the heat low," and, "Don't stop stirring! You'll get a lumpy sauce," and, "Okay, stop, *stop*. We're making a béchamel, not a gumbo." It is both irritating and helpful, which somehow just exacerbates the irritating part.

Eventually, the sliced potatoes are resting in the oven under a bubbling cheesy béchamel sauce. I'm surprised at how relatively painless the whole process was. Minus my cut finger, of course. I've been ignoring that part because remembering the way Wesley wrapped the bandage around my finger so gently makes me feel like I might disintegrate.

The potatoes au gratin come out beautifully. Wesley taps the crisp golden crust with a serving spoon and plates the steaming dish into two shallow bowls. He uses a paper towel to wipe the dribbles of béchamel around the edge of the bowls for a pristine presentation, and I want to be annoyed by how much effort he puts into something that's only for the two of us, but there is a part of me that's impressed. His care when cooking isn't for show, but for himself. That's something I can respect.

And then we taste.

"Wesley, talk your shit about French food all you want, but this is . . . perfect." It's salty, cheesy, creamy, and buttery—all my favorite things. I want to kiss the blade of the mandoline for producing potatoes like this.

"You can't go wrong with potatoes and cheese," he says. "It's predictable."

"It's perfect," I repeat. I scoop steaming heaps of creamy potatoes into my mouth and let out a muffled cry as the roof of my mouth gets scalded. "Hot!"

Wesley sighs. "How many injuries are you going to sustain in a single afternoon? I'm not going to rub Neosporin into your mouth."

I scowl at him, but I'm not sure how effective it is when I'm simultaneously blowing out air through my potato-packed mouth.

"Oh, that reminds me," Wesley says. "Picture time." Before I can say anything, he whips out his phone and quickly takes a selfie of us with our plates, my face glowering and my cheeks bulging with literal hot potato.

"Delete that," I say.

"Not a chance. It's our accountability, remember?"

I try to shove his chair away by kicking its legs, but it barely even causes a bump. Wesley snorts at my feeble attempt.

When we're finished eating, Wesley volunteers to do the dishes. He says it would be a waste to get my bandage wet so soon, but I suspect his peculiar brand of chivalry comes naturally. It just battles against his equally natural asshole tendencies, I guess, which is very, very tough competition. Regardless, I sit at the table and get my things together.

I swear I don't mean to be nosy. It's just that the corner of a quiz peeks out from his unzipped backpack. Really, it's not my fault he keeps all his things so splayed out. From what I can see of the rest of the page, it looks like a math quiz. Maybe precalculus? Much more obvious is the red C minus circled at the top of the sheet. Just the sight of a score in that range makes my blood run cold. I'm shocked Wesley has been acting so nonchalantly throughout this entire session. How is he holding up so well?

I turn to look at Wesley, who instantly recognizes what I've seen. Almost immediately, he's beside me at the table and shoving everything into his backpack. It's obvious he's prioritizing speed over order, because he crinkles the quiz I was peering at with a forceful punch. The red grade gets swallowed from sight.

"Hey, are you okay?" I try to sound gentle.

"Mind your business, Eliza," he says through gritted teeth.

"It's just one quiz," I say. "I mean, yes, even one bad grade can feel absolutely devastating, but I'm sure—"

"I said, mind your business." The glare he gives me feels like it could qualify as first-degree murder. He rushes out the door without saying goodbye.

I stand there for a second, wondering what I could have said to have made him react better. Did he think I was judging him for his grades? It was just one quiz. That's hardly enough to make some kind of character judgment. Should I have tried harder to comfort him? It seemed like my abbreviated attempt was already enough to revolt him.

Eventually, I gather my things and leave, too, so that I'm not found here alone when Mr. Wilby comes by.

Apparently, I'm arrogant enough to assume that my limited time with Wesley would turn me into a master chef, because when my mother teaches me to make gimbap on the following Tuesday, I expect to impress her.

In my defense, gimbap looks deceptively simple. Every ingredient in the roll needs to be prepared beforehand, even the rice. It's often mistaken as sushi by people who don't know any better or think unique Asian cuisines are interchangeable. I remember my mom used to pack me a roll of gimbap for lunch in elementary school and kids would recoil. *You're eating* seaweed? they'd say, their hands holding strings of cheese and craggy chicken nuggets. I'd asked my mom to stop packing me gimbap for lunch. She didn't ask why, but I have a suspicion she knew anyway.

Asking my mom to stop packing me gimbap for school seemed like the obvious choice at the time. But now, I wonder how my mother felt when I asked. I can't imagine giving part of your culture and childhood to your child and having them come back ashamed, full of rejection, and petulantly annoyed by what you've given them. I'm reminded of all the times I left my mother alone on the kitchen floor on kimjang days, plugging my nose and complaining about the smell instead of sitting down to help her. There's a newfound guilt, an uncomfortable prickly feeling. When my mom suggests gimbap as the recipe for today, I enthusiastically agree, as if this can assuage the shame that's been building recently.

"Gimbap is really customizable," my mom says to me as she watches me wash the short-grain rice. That's one thing I didn't have to be taught—the obligation to wash rice before you cook it. "When I was little, I was a picky eater. I didn't like danmuji. So your halmeoni would make one roll without danmuji for me, and one roll with extra danmuji for your harabeoji."

The process of making gimbap takes a surprising amount of time. The first thing we do is set the rice to cook. Once we've set the rice cooker, we move on to our ingredients. "Your halmeoni uses bulgogi, but I trade that in for imitation crabmeat and fish cake."

"Why?" I ask. I expect a childhood memory or some special association with the ingredients she prefers.

But my mom simply explains, "You have to make your own bulgogi. Crab and fish cake come prepackaged."

I smile. No story, just laziness.

I quickly understand the desire to cut down the steps, because there are a lot of them. The spinach, eggs, and carrots need to be cooked and seasoned. The rice needs to be mixed with sesame oil and salt and then set to cool. The danmuji, or pickled radish, and fish cake are cut into strips. It seems like preparation is the bulk of cooking. I remember how long it took to slice all the potatoes for the au gratin.

"Now is the fun part," she says. "The rolling." She pulls out a bamboo rolling mat and lays it flat against the cutting board. "And this is the part where you can customize. Add more of your favorite ingredients. Less of another. Rolling looks easy but takes practice."

She places a sheet of gim on the bamboo mat and spreads a layer of rice. Then she begins to assemble, placing each ingredient in a line near the bottom edge. She shows me how to roll the bamboo mat so that the mat doesn't get stuck inside the gimbap. She tells me when to give the roll the occasional squeeze to make sure it's secure enough. When she's done, a sleek black roll emerges. It looks so perfect, I can't imagine how it's possible to mess this part up.

Then it's my turn. My rice layer is lumpy, with the occasional patch of green gim peeking through areas of sparse grain. I pile in the other ingredients and make an effort to keep things from bleeding too far into the center of the rice. My mom seems to have some kind of instinctive gauge on how much to put of each ingredient without things toppling over. When I begin rolling, the filling starts to spill forward, so I stuff the ingredients back in and try again.

"Curl your fingers to keep it in," my mom advises. But the help comes too late. The shape is coming out all wrong. When I'm done, my gimbap roll looks saggy, like a flat tire.

I slam the bamboo mat down. "What did I do wrong?" The gimbap somehow deflates even more as I watch it, like there was no point in wrapping it at all.

My mom laughs at my final product, and the sound makes me start.

When was the last time I heard that?

She continues, "I told you rolling was hard! You were a little too loose. But if you're too tight, it tastes bad." As she slices up her gimbap roll, I'm still reeling from what could be a revelation. All this time, was unlocking her old self as easy as trying to cook with her?

My mom plates the cut gimbap. As expected, hers look gorgeous. The colors of the green spinach, orange carrot, and yellow danmuji are like a springtime garden. When she slices up mine, the gim doesn't quite stick together and the ingredients start to fall out. I can't believe we spent an hour prepping the filling just so I could botch the final product.

My mom and I continue to roll gimbap until we run out of ingredients. Each one my mom does comes out flawlessly. When I try the next time, it doesn't fall apart, but it's now too tight. She opens her mouth to say something, but I interrupt, "Yeah, I know. Rolling is hard." Just as hard is ironing out the annoyance in my tone. It's like every time I step into the kitchen, I'm forced to confront my new ineptitude all over again. Like a video game that doesn't save the last level you were on.

"Don't be upset," my mom says, using her fingers to manually iron out my wrinkled brow. "You can't expect to be good at everything from the start."

Since when? I want to say, but I shove one of my misshapen gimbap into my mouth. She's right. When it's too tight, it tastes bad.

She checks the clock and pulls off her apron. "It's almost time for my lesson. Good work, Yeji-yah."

When my father comes home, he looks at the towers of sliced gimbap, stacked neatly on our dinner plates. "Eomma made gimbap?" he asks, surprise coloring his voice.

I nod. "She was trying to teach me."

He blinks in surprise. "Really?"

"Well, I asked her to."

"Huh," he muses. He pops one into his mouth. "Not enough danmuji, don't you think?"

I shrug.

"I'm glad you're asking Eomma to teach you things. But you can ask me that stuff, too."

"You can cook?"

My dad waves his hand like he's swatting at the idea. "I mean, I could teach you physics. One of your parents is a professor, after all."

I eye him warily. "And the other is a teacher."

"I'm just saying, one of us can teach you something that'll help you in college." He picks up one of my mother's gimbap, a perfect, colorful circle that took hours to create, and squints at it with one eye. "This is just hobby, not science." Then he eats it and walks out of the kitchen.

Chapter 11

As is routine, the girls and I are spending lunch in Señora Molina's classroom, and I'm once again staring at a blank document, trying to rack my brain for a single thing worth writing a personal statement about. I've written approximately thirteen different first lines, twelve of which were intolerable garbage and the thirteenth was an AOC quote, which felt like cheating. Like clockwork, my document has been reset to its daunting emptiness while I ponder what AOC's personal statement must have been like. This, of course, leads me to the rabbit hole of reading her Wikipedia, where I learn that she graduated from Boston University with Latin honors despite her father passing away her sophomore year. My first thought is, *How do people that impressive exist?* My next is, *Mrs. Porter would've been a great guidance counselor for AOC.*

A knock on the open door pulls me away from my screen. It takes incredible discipline not to let my eyes roll when I see who stands in the doorway.

"Hey, girls," Jess says. She shakes her chemistry folder in her hand like it's enough explanation for her to be infiltrating our space yet again. "Do y'all mind if I borrow Kareena for a second?"

Once Kareena is out in the hallway, I turn to Meredith. "You don't think it's weird that Jess doesn't ask to check answers with you, too?"

Meredith shrugs. "Kareena and I check answers in homeroom, so I guess it's all the same."

I can't tell if Meredith is intentionally missing the point, or if I really am being unreasonably wound up.

"How's the cooking class going, by the way?" Meredith asks with a grin. "Earning Michelin Stars yet? Which, by the way, *is* the tire company. I looked it up."

I slink back in my seat. "It's kind of kicking my ass." It feels embarrassing to say out loud, that this class everyone else sees as a joke is somehow taking the most effort on my part. How I am quite literally getting both physically and emotionally injured by my cooking incompetence.

"You are not letting people who see a marshmallow man as the One True Food God get you down, Eliza Park."

"Marshmallow? The Michelin Man is made of tires. But, like, white tires."

"Like that makes any more sense. The point—there's no way you're not better than every kid in that class. I already know that. In time, everyone else in the class will know it, too." Meredith says it with such casual honesty, like it's impossible to be anything other than scientific fact.

If only that weren't becoming so hard to prove.

Ever since I caught a glimpse of Wesley's quiz, he has been notably icing me out. He doesn't talk to me in class, not that he did too much of that in the first place. But he doesn't even let his eyes move in my direction. When I raise my hand to answer a question Mr. Treviño asks (we're learning about sanitation and safety, and Science Bowl definitely gives me a leg up on foodborne illness), I might as well be invisible.

So when Friday afternoon rolls around, I don't even know if he plans on us still working together today. There are a few dishes we're supposed to work through, and although Halloween is well over a month away, I know that we both would rather get our assignments completed sooner than later.

When the classroom clears out, Wesley silently moves toward the refrigerator to collect ingredients.

"Hey," I call out before following him. "Are you not going to talk to me?"

"Hey," he says curtly.

"Are we working together today or not?"

"Not."

"And you just weren't going to say anything."

"Aren't I making it obvious?"

I roll my eyes. "We are partners, Wesley. It's a *group* project. I think some communication should be the bare minimum."

"Just go home, Eliza. Or don't. I don't care."

I pretend like I'm not wounded. I do want to go home. I want to escape his acerbic tone and his scowling face and his gloomy mood.

But a seed of evil blooms within me. For some reason, I feel certain that the thing that would bother him the most is to stay.

So I walk to the pantry and select an onion. I break off cloves of garlic. I grab a can of crushed tomatoes. I beat Wesley to the supply drawers and take what I know is his favorite chef's knife and one of the wooden cutting boards.

Then I go to work.

As I chop, I try to evaluate myself objectively. The onion still makes me cry. The garlic still sticks to my hands when I try to mince it. But overall, I think my knife skills are getting a little better. Maybe I'm letting myself be slightly delusional. Then I look over at Wesley's station and I see that he has all his ingredients prepped in neat piles, as if they came that way. He wields his knife—notably his second-choice chef's knife—like it's a natural extension of his arm. As if he can feel my stare, he looks up and immediately looks away, reminding himself that he's ignoring me.

When I add the garlic to my sautéed onions, I make the mistake of keeping the heat too high. Just a minute or two of wandering focus—maybe spent looking at the only other person in the room, daring him to look back—and the bottom edges of all my garlic is burned black. I curse and rush to take my pan off the heat, turning down the dial. But the damage is done. The garlic is burned.

"You're really scowling," Wesley comments.

So he hasn't been ignoring me.

"Yeah, maybe your lousy mood was infectious."

He makes a sound that is halfway between a scoff and a laugh.

I look up. "What?" I demand.

"You act like you've never been bad at something before."

"First time for everything," I say.

"Be serious."

"I am." I stir around my burnt garlic and translucent onions. I don't think I can salvage this. "Well, piano, actually. My mom's a piano teacher, so naturally, she tried teaching me when I was younger. I was awful. Quit after two months, and that was in first grade." My mom was understanding. She said I could always pick it back up whenever I wanted. It just never happened.

"So you didn't even give it a shot."

I raise my eyebrow. "Did you not hear the part about two months?"

"As a *first grader*. You don't think you were being unreasonable?"

"Is there a way for a first grader to be reasonable? Plus, Mozart was composing by age five."

"So you've always just given up the second you found out you weren't going to be the next Mozart," Wesley says, shaking his head. "Even more unbelievable that you're in this class. I guess you'll do anything for a GPA boost."

I let my wooden spatula clatter to the countertop. "Don't pretend like you're any different."

"We couldn't be more different," Wesley argues.

"We want the same thing. Why skirt around that?"

"No, I want to win the cook-off because I love cooking. It's something I'm *passionate* about." He draws out the syllables like he's trying to introduce a new word to a toddler. "You don't have things you're passionate about, only things that you're good at."

"What's the difference?"

"You're absurd."

"You know what? Maybe I will go home," I declare, moving toward the sink to wash my hands. I scrub them furiously with soap to wipe off the garlic juice that somehow lasts the entire weekend.

"Giving up because you're not good," Wesley observes. "At least you're consistent."

I know he's trying to egg me on, so I deliberately dry my hands and make my way back to the table, not even bothering to put away my equipment or ingredients. If Wesley cares so much, he'll clean it up. And it's his fault that I'm leaving anyway. He's practically forcing me out.

Once again, Wesley has left all his things haphazardly strewn across the table. I see the same quiz through the gaping zipper. Although last time, the grade was a seventy-two, and this one is a seventy. And last time, the quiz looked like precalculus, and this one looks like biology. I see the words *transcription* and *mRNA* in the question stems. This time, I don't even hide how I gawk. I pull it out to study it further. It's easy stuff, just introductory biology. For the first time all day, I think of Wesley and feel a tug of empathy. Was Wesley sick last week and I didn't notice? Or maybe he was sleep deprived and couldn't focus? Is this the explanation for his sour mood all week?

"Jesus Christ," I hear him say before a hand snatches the quiz from me. "Did I not tell you to mind your business?" Like déjà vu, I watch him as he once again crumples it into his backpack, like the faster he gets it out of my sight, the faster I'll forget what I saw.

"Is something going on?" I ask.

He zips his backpack up with such force, it's a testament to the manufacturer that the zipper doesn't fly right off. "Like what? Having the most invasive group project partner who can't respect people's boundaries?"

I hear Mrs. Porter's words echo in my head: *When events like this happen in the family, sometimes students do better when they take school a little easier.* I look at Wesley with new eyes. Have I ever asked him about anything other than Culinary Arts? Besides the one time he mentioned not getting along with his mother, has he ever spoken about himself? His world outside school could be crumbling apart and I'd have no idea because I never took a second to consider him as anything other than an obstacle in the way of a prize.

"I don't know, and I don't mean to pry either," I begin, "but sometimes when life outside of school gets crazy, it's harder to do well in class." I let the implication waver in the air between us.

He stares at me, scanning my face for—I'm not sure. Sarcasm?

Judgment? "You think I'm getting these grades because something is going on in my life."

I can't read his tone. Is he impressed that I guessed accurately, or embarrassed that I know something deeper about him now? "It occurred to me as a possibility."

Wesley's back straightens and it registers that he is taller than I remember. He literally looks down at me to say, "Maybe it should occur to you that some people just get these grades. Not because anything is happening in life, not due to some personal tragedy, and not because they slack off. In the way that some people get As, some people also get Cs."

I blink at him, trying to process this revelation with the most neutral expression possible, but I feel my face get warm. Is it possible that Wesley, who knows so much about cooking and speaks with such authority about the things he cares about, could be a *bad* student? Or at the very least, poorly ranked? It seems irreconcilable in my mind with the boy standing in front of me. I knew he wasn't in any AP classes, but I figured he would at least be good in his regular ones. "Wesley, what rank are you?"

He looks away, but I notice his fist curl tighter around the zipper of his backpack. "I'm fourth quartile." Based on his tone, he says this like it could not be less relevant, but there's a flicker in his eyes that suggests . . . embarrassment?

"So you need this GPA boost, too," I say.

For a long moment, I wonder if he won't respond. I watch a fiber of muscle in his jaw contract silently. Then he meets my eyes and there's an anger, or a frustration, there that expels his words out. "It's the last semester before college applications. It would be nice to show that I'm good at this thing that I'm actually really good at.

Instead of losing it to some carbon copy honor student whose transcript looks like the keyboard was stuck on the letter *A*. Like, Eliza, if we're going to be serious, can't you admit that there's no way you can prove yourself more than you already have?"

Instantly, my mind is on the defensive. The speech. The title. My family in the crowd at graduation. My father's dozens of Korean friends coming to see me speak. Kareena and me sitting side by side on the graduation stage, holding hands and moving our tassels over. The *speech*. Wesley wouldn't understand. He's right—we're not trying for the same things.

But I know that my best shot at winning the cook-off is to do well on this group project and, in the meantime, learn as much as I can from Wesley's natural talent. He might be a colossal pain, but he makes me a better cook. I'm smart enough to know that I won't get far without him.

"I can tutor you," I say suddenly.

"What?"

"Like I said last time: you bring the street smarts, I bring the book smarts. It's about time this partnership is a little more equal, don't you think? I can teach you how to do better in precalculus, or biology, or whatever it is you think you need help in."

"That sounds—"

"And it would only have to be for this semester, you know," I interrupt. "Like you said, it's the last time that colleges will see our grades. So might as well do it while it still counts, right? Plus, I've tutored middle schoolers before and I was pretty good at it."

"You're comparing tutoring me to tutoring—let me get this right—a middle schooler."

"I'm saying," I clarify, "that I kind of know what I'm doing."

Then, because he doesn't look entirely convinced, I add, "Like you in the kitchen." I don't exactly know why I am pushing this so much. If he doesn't do well in his other classes, who cares? Certainly not me. But maybe tutoring him will open him up, make this group project that much more bearable, and maybe—just maybe—I'll learn enough from him that I can beat him at his own game.

Wesley taps his fingers along his backpack strap, his eyebrows furrowed. He holds my gaze and I watch as his chestnut eyes lose their frostiness and regain some warmth. The longer we stare, the more he seems almost vulnerable, a word I never thought I would associate with him. But it feels like confirmation when he finally says, "Are you going to make me feel pathetic if I ask you for help?"

"Like how you make me feel because I can't chop an onion?"

"Do I really make you feel that way?" There's a softness now, the slightest hint of woundedness written across his brow.

I look away, breaking the eye contact. It feels like I'm forfeiting something that I don't recognize yet. "No, you don't. And I won't either."

Chapter 12

My group chat with Kareena and Meredith—now named "death by ED pending"—decides to make Saturday our boba day for the weekend, which happens to be the beginning of October. Kareena and Meredith have taken the turn of the month to mean that a fire is now lit under their asses for the early decision deadline. For the record, the group chat name does not apply to me. The girls are both applying to schools that do early decision, so their application deadline is the start of November. Luckily, MIT doesn't do ED, so I can at least delay my application until the regular-decision deadline of January.

We meet at the table we've designated to be ours. At this point, I feel like we've funneled enough money into this boba shop that we deserve a plaque on our table with our names engraved. We've spent so many collective hours studying here that the benches should have imprints of our butts. Instead, our table outwardly looks like every other table in the shop, so it's only ours if we get here early enough. Luckily, Kareena has already staked out the table, so I order a jasmine green milk tea—25 percent sweet, with boba—before joining the girls.

Meredith and Kareena are both working on filling out the Common App. The conversation is a lot of:

"What's a better way to say 'I did'?"

"Managed—"

"Executed—"

"Performed—"

"Accomplished—"

"Achieved!"

"Title option for Kareena's memoir?"

And:

"Does this sound okay: 'a unique opportunity to develop'—ugh, wait, I already used the word 'develop' in the last line—ignore me."

And:

"Why do they need to know so much about us? Just take my money and accept me, goddamnit."

Even with all the lip service, I know that both of them are crafting some of the most stellar applications these admissions officers will ever have the pleasure of seeing. It's easy to feel supportive of my friends when I've watched them excel for years. It's one thing to know your friends are smart, but it's another to consider them so competent that it inspires you to be better.

"Are y'all nervous about going to college without each other?" I ask.

Kareena glances up and the glow of her laptop screen makes her doe eyes even brighter. "Because we'll be apart?"

I've just slurped a string of boba pearls so I only nod.

Kareena shrugs. "I don't know, I feel like with FaceTime, no one loses friendships anymore unless they're really not putting in the effort."

"Yeah, but what if that's what we become? We get caught up in all the new experiences of college and it just becomes harder to put in that effort. Maybe we won't want to," I say.

Meredith leans across the table to push my arm. "Is this your way of telling us you're not going to want to talk to us next year?

Damn, it's barely even October."

I laugh, shrugging her hand off. "I'm serious. I just think . . . what are the odds that I find friends like y'all again in this lifetime?"

Meredith covers her eyes. "You're trying to make me cry because I told you I was trying out this new mascara, and I think that is very evil of you."

"Not true, but I did notice that your lashes were trying to stab through the ceiling, so send me the link," I say.

Kareena shuts her laptop screen. "Of course you won't find friends like us again in this lifetime. You'll find other ones in college, for sure, because you're smart, funny, cool, and incredibly well versed in bagel-sized pizzas. And when you find those other college friends, we'll still be there to remind you that we got here first. They can get in line."

Of course, when she says this is when her phone lights up with a text message. Kareena moves to swipe it immediately, but even the shape of the name confirms who I think it is.

"Where is Jess applying?" I keep my voice light and casual and not at all like I'm judging her for becoming so furtively chummy with my only rival. I'm not confident that I'm succeeding.

A rose blush creeps up Kareena's neck. "She's not sure yet. Maybe Vanderbilt. Or Penn."

I raise my eyebrows. "Penn?"

Even Meredith seems surprised. "She's going to follow you there?"

The blush seeps farther into Kareena's cheeks. She opens her laptop back up, attempting to disguise her sudden need for distraction. "It's not like I own the concept of applying to Penn. I might not even get in."

Alarm bells ring in my hand, because too many incorrect things are happening at once. First, Kareena is doubting herself, which unfortunately is just as strong of a character trait as her actual competence. Second, someone else in our year might apply to her *dream* school and she's acting like that's okay? Encouraged, even? And it's not *just* someone else, but the exact girl who's been nipping at my heels for salutatorian and is obsessed with taking Kareena's homework answers? How is everyone acting like this is within the definition of normal, when it is so clearly anything but? I take a forceful slurp of my drink to tame my frustration, but even my boba tastes less sweet.

"So before y'all say anything," Kareena says, even though I wasn't going to, "of course it's okay for Jess to apply. If any of y'all want to apply to Penn, too, please feel free." Her gold rings glint in the sunlight as she starts to undo her braid. Her fingers belie the nonchalance of her attitude. She's always had the habit of braiding, unbraiding, and rebraiding her thick hair when she's anxious. I watch her pointedly until the weight of my stare causes her fingers to still. "Stop staring at me, Eliza."

"I think your braid needs more braiding, actually," I say. Is there an edge in my tone? I cough to pretend it's something in my throat.

"If we all applied to Penn, we wouldn't need FaceTime," Meredith jokes. "We could even live together in a triple! How cute!"

"Hold on," Kareena says. "I said y'all are welcome to apply. If we want to stay friends, there's no chance that we'd room together."

"She means you, Meredith," I say.

"Oh, come on. I am not that messy," Meredith protests.

"I'm not forgetting the time you bought a new set of underwear because you ran out of clean ones," I say.

Kareena nods in agreement. "And your mom does the laundry. You were literally too lazy to pick them off the bathroom floor and put them into a hamper."

Meredith cocks her head. "You can never have too much underwear, so I'm failing to see the issue here."

"The issue is that I don't want to see y'all's underwear," Kareena declares firmly, in just a loud enough volume that the girls at the adjacent table serve us a scornful sidelong glance.

"Okay, let's get back to work or we're going to have to stop coming here out of embarrassment," I say.

"Oh, let's use that," Meredith says, pulling out her phone. Within a minute, I get a notification that our group chat name has been changed to "death by embarrassment at the boba shop."

I grin. "Wait, what about—" The new group chat name pings as "Death! at the Boba Shop."

Kareena shakes her head but joins us in chaotically tapping on our phones. The name changes to "meredith, wash your panties challenge."

Meredith snorts so loudly that, once again, the girls at the next table over give us a glower.

"Okay, y'all, please get it together," I say. "I want to keep coming here."

"No!" Meredith exclaims. "You can't stop it here! You're saying we need to be stuck on the wash-my-panties challenge?"

This must be the tipping point, because the girls at our neighboring table abruptly stand up and leave the shop. They've barely gone through the door when the three of us burst into laughter so forceful, it's nothing but choked gasps and aching ribs.

* * *

My next lesson with my mom starts by her asking, "Do Americans bring food to friends' houses?" She typically uses the word *Americans* to mean *white people*.

"Like a potluck?" I ask.

She nods her head. "Right. That's the word. Well, this recipe is the perfect potluck dish. Easy to make a lot of, nutritious, and, of course, delicious."

Today, we're making japchae, which is one of my favorite noodle dishes. The noodles, called dangmyeon, are made from sweet-potato starch, giving them a stranger, chewier texture than a rice or flour noodle. Like gimbap, all the veggies and meats are stir-fried and prepared individually, so it's another time-consuming project, but when it's with my mom, I don't mind.

My mom slices the beef into long strips while I work on cutting the vegetables. It's a lot of the same heavy hitters in Korean cuisine, like spinach, onion, mushroom, and carrot. The sauce is mainly soy sauce, sesame oil, and sugar. Although I'm not anywhere near well versed in Korean cooking, I like that I can already see the similarities to what my mom has taught me previously. It's easy to see why she felt so comforted by making these meals over and over when she first moved here.

"Tell me something about Halmeoni," I request, taking my time to carefully julienne the carrots without cutting off my fingers. I try to ignore the fact that in my head, the word *julienne* is said in Wesley's voice. It was the answer to one of Mr. Treviño's questions in class, and it goes without saying who had the correct response.

My mom turns to me with a smile. "What do you want to know?"

I shrug. "Anything. Were there ever times you didn't get along?"

She barks out a laugh. "Of course." Seamlessly, she moves from her completed sliced green onions to my other carrot and begins cutting it into matchsticks at easily twice my rate. "I remember one time in high school, I told Halmeoni I wanted to be a journalist. And she said, 'You get to go to school and get a job and you're choosing something that won't make you any money?' Halmeoni didn't get to go to college, you know."

"Wait, really?" I say. I can't imagine not going to college. If I really allow myself to be obnoxious, I honestly can't even imagine going to a college that has a double-digit acceptance rate.

"Oh, it was a very different time. Girls weren't educated in Korea until Western missionaries came and founded schools. That's actually how Ewha, the first girls-only university, was created. Even when *I* was in college, less than a third of girls went to university." By this time, all our veggies have been chopped, mainly due to my mom's miraculous efficiency. She then guides me in starting to stir-fry them.

"So she wanted you to go to college to get a fancier job than the one you wanted," I say.

She nods. "We had a big fight. I didn't eat dinner at home for maybe two weeks. But of course, the funny thing about getting older is that I can understand her perfectly now. That's what a lot of immigrant parents here think, too, right? Appa talks about that all the time, how important it is to take advantage of education and get a good job. But when I was in high school, I thought that was the meanest thing she could say. Why couldn't she be happy that I had found something I wanted to do?"

The first crack in my heart is the realization that I don't know if I've found that something, that thing I want to do so badly that I'd be willing to fight with my parents over it. As much as I say I want to major in computer science, if my parents told me not to, I could easily convince myself to do something else. Maybe Wesley is right about that one thing—I like the things I'm good at, like math and science, but that's not a substitute for passion.

The second crack comes with recognizing that my mom never got to do what she loved. She went to college with her dreams and her passions and ended up here, in the States, with neither. She found an alternative path of turning a hobby into a semiprofession and never complained about how narrow that path was. I almost wish I were cutting onions so I could have an excuse for how I suddenly feel sniffly.

"But you two made up," I prompt.

"Mothers and daughters fight all the time! Halmeoni had so much wisdom. Sometimes I was just too young to see it. It'll be like that for you, too, I'm sure."

I scoff. "You're just saying that so you can try to disguise chores as wisdom."

"I trust you will do these dishes when we're done," she says. The smile on her face makes her look just a little younger. Almost like she's on her way back to being her April self.

This is the secret I've realized: that it's only when she can lose herself in memories that she paradoxically becomes more like herself. It's like watching the scene of the food critic from *Ratatouille* tasting Remy's dish, except I get to watch it every Tuesday, as long as I can get her to talk about Halmeoni.

In the midst of my wandering thoughts, I forget to set a timer for the dangmyeon when I put them into the boiling pot, so they end up being overcooked. I only remember to drain the noodles when my mom notes that it's been a while since we put them in.

When it's time to mix all our stir-fried vegetables and meat with the dangmyeon, my mom slides me a pair of plastic gloves. I've made the dangmyeon so mushy that some accidentally rip as I mix.

Even with my frustration at my own incompetency—how hard is it to cook a noodle right?—there is something relaxing about mixing by hand. That's something else I've noticed about my lessons with my mom. There's a lot of tactility in Korean cooking, whether it's rolling gimbap or hand-mixing japchae or rubbing paste onto leaves of homemade kimchi. It makes me feel like I'm actually a part of it. And maybe all along, it was this easy to be part of it, if only I had been interested enough to ask.

When my mom goes back to her lessons and I'm dutifully washing the dirty dishes, I am thinking about how much wisdom Halmeoni could have given me if only I had the language to hear it.

Chapter 13

In Culinary Arts, we are a week into our basic food preparation unit, having successfully covered sanitation and safety. At the end of each unit, Mr. Treviño gives a brief quiz, and I knocked the sanitation one out of the park. He gave a bonus question for naming the pathogens that most commonly cause foodborne illness. Even if I can't boil a noodle without messing something up, at least I can wax poetic about contamination.

Mr. Treviño says that as we transition to more hands-on culinary learning, he will move away from paper quizzes and favor what he calls "kitchen lab," where he watches us perform kitchen practicals. It makes sense, and I guess that's why we all have individual workstations along the perimeter of the room, but the thought of having everyone in the class be able to witness my inadequacy in action is moderately distressing.

Wesley and I haven't specified when I would tutor him. Part of it is that I'm already so booked after class most days, but the other part of it is that he hasn't revisited the topic with me. And shockingly, it's not because he refuses to acknowledge me. He's finished with his ignoring-me-in-class-even-though-I-literally-sit-six-inches-away-from-him phase, at least. He looks at me when I speak. He even suggested that we exchange phone numbers, which he admits we should have done when we were first assigned as group project partners. Maybe the Cold War is melting.

On Friday, I say that we should tackle the carbonara from the syllabus. It's the first time that I've suggested the dish we work on, rather than him taking the lead. And I didn't ask if he already had a plan for the day.

But, to my surprise, he simply says, "Sure." Then he juts his chin out in my direction, an unconscious display of curiosity. "Any particular reason?"

I shrug. "I think it's finally time I conquer a noodle."

Wesley laughs. "Oh, Eliza. The noodle is not the hard part of this dish."

"Oh, Wesley. Don't you know that every part is the hard part for me?" I give him a look of mock innocence. I further my ingenue cosplay and flutter my lashes. Wesley rolls his eyes and looks away, but the back of his neck turns a rosy pink.

"I did bring a special ingredient for the dish," I add. "I thought we could use it."

"Guanciale?" he guesses. "That's great, because I was just thinking that Mr. Treviño probably doesn't keep it in stock."

I shake my head. I move toward the refrigerator and pull out the slim container of light brown paste I stored there before first period.

Of course, Wesley's eyes and general ingredient recognition are too good. His eyebrows rise. "You brought miso?"

"I thought we could do miso carbonara," I explain. "You said you were tired of how white the syllabus was, right? I found this recipe online last night and thought it looked so good. Here, let me send it to you." I pull out my phone and send him the link to the recipe. It is a blue bubble in an otherwise very sparse text conversation.

I watch as he scrolls through the recipe. He doesn't look as excited as I thought he would be.

I sigh. "What's wrong? They didn't make their pasta from scratch? They're using a nonstick pan?"

His eyes flicker up to mine. "You think this sounds good?"

I frown. He obviously thinks saying yes would be the wrong answer, but I don't understand why. "You don't?"

He sets his phone down on his workstation countertop. "When people blend Asian food with Western food, it doesn't feel like a fun experiment to me," he says. "It feels like they're trying to make our food more palatable to the Western audience, or, like . . . I don't know, like they're trying to disguise it? Oh, you don't like curry? Think of it as an Asian-inspired stew. Dumplings? Ravioli with an Asian twist."

I blink. "I didn't realize you were an Asian-food purist."

"You're smart enough to know that's not what I mean."

I do understand what he's getting at, even if it's an issue I didn't recognize as an issue until this conversation. Growing up, I would've given anything to have the white kids in class accept my packed Korean lunches. But to Wesley's point, there is the question of intention. What counts as celebrating an ingredient versus disguising it?

"Well," I say. "I already battled the hazardous parking lot of H Mart to buy this blond miso specifically to make this dish, so I'm asking you to give it a try."

Wesley lets out a small chuckle. "I love H Mart, but their parking lots make me want to commit murder."

"I don't think it's fair of you to blame that on their parking lots."

"I do recall one of us threatening the other with her knife, and it wasn't me."

I realize I'm trying not to laugh. Do I think Wesley is funny?

"All right," I say. "Let's get started. We'll have to settle for bacon, because obviously I did not bring guanciale."

The first thing we do is set a pot of water to boil. Wesley pours a handful of salt into the water. "Salt is a flavor enhancer," he says. "You want to salt your pasta water so that the pasta can absorb some of it as it cooks." His tone falls back into that effortless authority he has when he talks about food, like it all comes to him as second nature.

While Wesley works on cooking thinly sliced strips of bacon, I grate Parmesan cheese until my arm feels like it's going to fall off. When I whisk the cheese into the eggs, I have to switch hands. I watch Wesley thin a spoonful of miso with a splash of the boiling water and carefully add it to the egg mixture while I stir the pasta to make sure it doesn't stick together.

"What makes carbonara difficult is the balance of the emulsion," he explains. "I still remember how clueless you looked when Mr. Treviño asked if you had saved your pasta water."

I blanch. "Were you the one who gasped?"

Wesley's laugh is just a breath. "Surprisingly no."

"But you wanted to."

He takes over my burner and picks out a single spaghetti noodle with a pair of tongs before placing it into his mouth. "Oh yeah. That's just about ready. Okay, back to the emulsion."

"I know what an emulsion is. It's like us."

"What?"

"Oil and water. They shouldn't mix, but if you shake it up enough, they will. Or you can add an emulsifier, which is the egg. And then you save the water from the pasta and the fat from the bacon, and egg makes the water-plus-fat happy." I narrow my eyes. "Don't look so surprised! How many times do I have to prove to you that I do my readings? Plus, it's science."

He grins. "Sorry, you're right. It's just surprising how you can know so much up here"—he taps my forehead—"but then you watch these guys lose their minds trying to cut an onion." He gestures to my hands. "The pasta water isn't just about the water, though. The pasta releases starch into the water it's being cooked in, which is another emulsifier and also thickens your sauce. That's why people call pasta water *liquid gold*. So then you get this shiny, silky pasta, where each noodle is perfectly and properly coated without any annoying separation."

For a moment, I'm stunned. It takes me a while to name what I'm feeling.

When Wesley talks about cooking, he sounds so intelligent. He knows so much, can explain things better than the articles I'm reading online to prepare for these Friday sessions, and talks about cooking like it's not just science, but art. He's so *competent*. And I realize, belatedly, horrifically, that I find that competence . . . attractive.

He uses his tongs to transfer the cooked spaghetti and bacon into the bowl with the egg mixture. He then dips a measuring cup into the pasta water and adds it as well, mixing vigorously. He rests the bowl on top of the pot of pasta water, using the steam of the water to gently heat the bowl. "This is also another hard part. Wanting to cook your sauce without scrambling the eggs. Low heat, lots of whisking. I would tell you to do this part because I think it's the most important step, but I saw how much you were struggling with grating the cheese." And there it is, the return of the smirk.

Wesley plates the pasta and scrapes large shavings of Parmesan onto the top. I sprinkle over thinly sliced scallions. Together, we look at our dish with admiration.

Begrudgingly, he says, "Okay. This looks really good." He takes our selfie with our dish before we sit down at our normal seats to eat. For a minute, I can't help but stare at the pasta. The pale yellow of the Parmesan shavings, the bright green of the scallions, the golden twirl of miso-coated pasta. It looks even better than the photo on the recipe website. It also smells absolutely mouthwatering, like salty, earthy, cheesy goodness.

As amazing as it smells, it tastes even better.

"Oh, wow," I say. My lips feel coated with the creamy sauce, but it's so good, I don't even feel embarrassed. I could eat this pasta forever and it still might not be enough.

Wesley groans.

"You don't like it?" I say, shocked.

"I do. This is undoubtedly our best work." But he says it with such a deeply etched frown. If my mom were here, she would use her fingers to iron out the wrinkles, warning him that his face might stay stuck that way.

Laughter bubbles out of me. "You seem so upset to compliment your own cooking."

"White people using miso in their pasta doesn't feel like a big victory."

"Maybe we should be glad that the most flavorful ingredient they use isn't cheese anymore. Also, the recipe I sent you is by an Asian lady."

Wesley twirls his fork and I notice how the sauce clings to each noodle like a creamy hug. Who knew science made food so good? "There are so many noodles out there that aren't pasta. I feel like it's a disservice to not learn about those, you know?"

I nod, scooping bits of bacon into my mouth. "Yeah. My mom taught me how to make japchae the other week. Like, a Korean noodle dish from sweet potato—"

"I know what japchae is."

"You do?"

"Eliza, I like food. I like learning about it, all kinds. Is that not clear yet?"

"I guess you do shop at H Mart." I don't think either Kareena or Meredith have ever been to an H Mart before.

"That's so cool that your mom teaches you how to cook Korean food. I've been trying to learn some stuff on my own, but I bet learning from her is something else entirely. And anytime I'm at H Mart, I never know which brand to go with. I guess I just wish . . ." He trails off, like he's said too much. "Anyway, it's cool that you and your mom do that together."

"Your mom doesn't teach you how to make Thai food?" I already know the answer, but I want to hear him say something, anything, to give context for how he feels about his mother.

Wesley scoffs in response. He stuffs a forkful of pasta into his mouth.

"Would you . . . ?" I clear my throat. *Eliza, what are you doing? Don't say what you're about to say. Eliza, stop—* "Would you want to learn how to make Korean food with me?"

Abort.

Cancel.

Escape.

"What?" Wesley says, chestnut eyes widening.

Okay, Eliza, he's giving you a chance to reroute. Let's take it. "My mom has been teaching me some of my grandmother's recipes on Tuesdays. I've . . . well, I guess now that I'm saying it out loud, I don't think I've managed to make a single one without messing something up. Maybe she'd actually like for a dish to turn out like the original for once. If you would want to learn, of course."

Wesley looks like he's about to choke. "You—you want me to meet your mother?"

A blush creeps up my face. "Well, I . . . for cooking purposes."

The silence is awkward—thick—*excruciating*—as he considers the offer. I am all too aware of what a ridiculous ask this is. Bringing this boy, who does not even qualify as a friend, over to my literal home? Introducing him to my mother, who doesn't even know Wesley exists? *Hey, Wesley, I know we don't really like each other, but come spend intimate quality time with me and my mother! Super casual, I do it with all my nonfriends.* For someone generally smart, I am so outrageously foolish.

Why am I doing this? Because it would make me feel less guilty for having a mom who actually takes the time to teach me, when I'm working with someone who would die to have the same opportunity? Because he bandaged my finger like Halmeoni bandaged my mom's, and maybe my mom will see echoes of memories in him, too? Because I see how contemptibly smart he is about cooking, how much he loves to learn, and how I can't help but want to feed into that further? Because the more I see him talk about what he loves, how he knows what japchae is, how he buys Korean groceries, how he learns about other cultures' food not for school but just for himself, I think that maybe I don't dislike him at all?

No, I decide. I don't dislike him at all.

The words have been hanging in the air for too long. I almost take it back. But Wesley says, "That would actually be incredible," and the sincerity in his tone floors me. It fits right into the image of him I'm starting to understand, like filling in the shadows and seeing what comes into relief.

"Really?"

"Absolutely. I would love to join." I can't decide if the wistfulness I detect is legitimately there or if I'm imagining it. Nevertheless, the excitement in his expression is undeniable. There's a warmth in his eyes that I haven't seen before. They're the color of roasted chestnuts, and when his eyes crinkle at the ends, it seems like maybe he doesn't hate me.

"My mom teaches piano most evenings, but she has a break between lessons on Tuesdays. If you want, you could come over after school and we could spend the time before the cooking lesson to work on some school stuff? Or we don't have to. Just . . . if you needed help." God, how did I get through a summer of teaching middle schoolers, who create some of the most savage roasts on the planet, without being able to have a normal conversation with someone my own age?

Wesley smiles at me. It's a surprising flash of warmth, so sweet that it makes me wonder if the conversation was only that awkward in my head. "Thank you, Eliza. That sounds perfect."

Chapter 14

I'm not usually a procrastinator, I swear. It's essentially antithetical to who I am as a person. The second something is assigned to me, it's like the tag of a sweater that will not stop scraping against the nape of my neck. But for some reason, the idea of asking my mom if Wesley can join for cooking lessons feels impossible.

I had plenty of time to ask on Saturday, especially because Kareena asked Meredith and me if we could postpone boba to Sunday. Pickleball tournament! she texted. Since when did Kareena play pickleball? She is on varsity tennis, so it's not completely out of the question, but still. It seems like something she would have mentioned before.

I had plenty of time to ask on Sunday, especially because Kareena canceled boba altogether. Going to my cousin's place in Round Rock for the day. Sorry, I forgot when I asked if we could move it to today, she texted. Kareena did often get dragged along to see her extended family in the area, but still. She usually didn't forget these things. Her Google Calendar is color coded like mine.

Ok so Kareena is buying everyone's boba next time? Lenient punishment for the capital crime that is flaking, Meredith jokes. I type out a text that says, *Maybe her punishment should be revealing who her pickleball partner is*, but I don't want to sound insecure or like I'm prying, so I delete it and let it go.

The point being, I did have time. And I still did not ask my mom if I could bring Wesley.

On Monday night, I'm in my room, listening carefully to hear when her last student of the day leaves. I asked Eomma to start these cooking sessions because I wanted the best shot at the cook-off. But they're something else now, too. They've become this fragile window where the present and the past meet in a way that somehow doesn't pain her. I hope that doesn't change if someone else is in the room with us.

The other worry, of course, is trying to tell your immigrant mom about bringing a boy home.

Somehow, I manage to find the courage to seek Eomma out after her last lesson of Monday night. I knock on the lesson room door and peer in. My mother is wiping down the keys of our glossy Kawai upright with a cotton ball dampened with hydrogen peroxide. "Hi, Eomma."

"Oh, Yeji. What's wrong?"

"Are we cooking together tomorrow?" I say. Easy questions first. She furrows her brow. "I thought so. Are you busy?"

I shake my head. "No, but . . . would you mind if someone joined us? For the cooking lessons?" *Don't look suspicious. Act cool.*

My mother looks confused. "Who? Kareena?" She throws away the cotton ball and lets the ebony keyboard cover fall back over the shiny ivory. I try to extinguish the flicker of annoyance at the suggestion of Kareena, because it shouldn't be such a ludicrous guess. She's the obvious choice, but with how things have been going, I can't imagine inviting her over to cook with my mom. It would be too personal.

I can't tell if what I say next is just a tactic to delay answering the question, or if I genuinely want to give my mom an out. "It's okay if you want it to be just the two of us," I say. "I know it feels private to remember stories from when you were little."

"I don't mind teaching someone else," she says. Then she taps on the closed keyboard. "I'm a teacher, right?"

I nod. "Well, in that case, I know someone who I think would really enjoy getting to learn Korean recipes. He really likes cooking and . . . we're in a group project together in class, so . . ." None of the words coming out of my mouth are making that much sense to her. Maybe because the request itself doesn't make sense. "I think he would do really well learning from you." Apparently, I don't know a word other than *really*.

Of course, the second I say the word *he*, I watch my mom's eyebrows skyrocket to her hairline. It's the most interested she's been in my life since the summer. I can't deny that although the attention is nice, I wish she could find a way to be interested in just me.

I wish I didn't have to come find her in the lesson room. In an alternate timeline, she would meet me in the living room and ask about my day at school, like she used to do every day. She would know instantly who I meant when I said *he* because Wesley would've been introduced to her mental cast of characters starting from the very first day of school. But we don't talk like that anymore. Only our lessons keep us from being completely disconnected.

She studies my face for so long, it makes me nervous. What is she seeing there that I'm not hiding well enough? "So it's not Kareena or Meredith," she concludes.

My eyes flicker from the piano to the songbooks to the piano bench—anywhere that isn't her inquiring gaze. "It's this new friend from class. His name is Wesley."

"Is he white?" she asks immediately. I don't know why this is often the first question my parents ask when I mention someone they don't know. It's always, *What's their race?* inevitably followed by, *What do their parents do?*

"No. He's Asian."

"Korean? No, you would've said Korean."

"He's Thai."

She nods thoughtfully. "And he wants to come learn how to cook Korean food from me."

"And I think he'd be really good at it." *Really*, again. "Like, much, *much* better than me."

My mom smiles. It almost has wattage. "Yeji-yah, I think anyone could do much, much better than you."

"Eomma!" I exclaim. I throw my hand over my chest, clutching my mock wound.

Traces of a teasing grin play at the edges of my mother's smile. "Bring this friend tomorrow, then. Let's see how good he really is."

I widen my eyes. "You aren't going to test him, are you?"

"Of course not," she says, and the smile quirks up unevenly on one side. "We're just going to make something that gets our hands dirty a little bit."

The next day, after my Honor Society meeting ends, I meet Wesley in the Culinary Arts kitchen. Wesley's back is painfully stiff and he keeps brushing his bangs out of the way, even though they're actually too short to be in his eyes.

"Loosen up," I say. "You look like you're about to pee yourself."

"Your mom really is okay with me coming?" he says. I'm struck by his nervousness. I don't think I've ever seen him so unsettled.

"Yes," I reassure him, for probably the fifth time. "Now come on. I'm driving."

We leave the kitchen and make the trek to the parking lot. I'm trying to brainstorm how to ask Wesley about the last time I saw him here—walking home, after he said that he'd parked *over back*—when I notice three girls walking toward a familiar blue Volkswagen.

Meredith notices me first.

Then Kareena.

Finally, Jess.

For a cold moment, we all just stare at one another. It's awkward, painfully so, and further exacerbated by Wesley's witnessing of this. It's so agonizing, I forget to be embarrassed that my friends are watching me walk to my car with someone I've so far only described as my *obnoxiously arrogant Culinary Arts rival*. I see Meredith and Kareena take him in and note all the things I did not mention: tall, dark hair, relatively handsome if you don't know him personally. Maybe even if you do.

Finally, Meredith gives me a soft smile. "Hey, Eliza."

"Hey," I reply. Good, my voice sounds more normal than I expected.

Then I give Kareena and Jess the barest of nods before walking past them. I internally thank Wesley for walking alongside me, silently following my lead. Finally, we get to my car and slide in.

"Okay, I know *I'm* being weird, but that was weird, right?" Wesley says once I've turned the ignition on.

"I have no idea what you're talking about."

"That confirms it. Weird energy with those girls. Are they your friends?" he asks.

I start to drive out of the parking lot, trying to go quickly so that I don't find myself waiting in front of or behind a blue Volkswagen. I'm hurt to see Meredith with them. Kareena and Jess, sure. They check homework together, sit together in chemistry, text on the weekends, maybe have matching pickleball paddles. But Meredith, too? How long have the three of them been hanging out without me? I feel winded. "Yeah. My best friends, actually. Well, two of them."

"And the third?"

"Haven't really talked to her," I admit.

"But you don't really like her," he guesses.

I let Wesley sit with my silence, because I'm not even sure how to reply.

"Is Jess Archibald one of the best friends or the one you don't like?" he says.

My eyes snap to his. "How do you know Jess Archibald?"

He shrugs. "Doesn't everyone?" He then shimmies in the passenger seat and lifts his hand to the radio dial. "Do you mind?"

I shake my head.

He turns it to the oldies station and leans back.

"You like oldies?" I ask, surprised.

"Not really. I just think it's good background music."

"I feel like only white people like the oldies. It's not like Asian kids grew up with our parents playing this stuff around the house."

"My parents didn't play much of anything," he says. I keep my shoulders relaxed so he doesn't see how curious I get when he shares the smallest detail about his home life. He's still such an enigma, even though, barring the girls, I probably spend the most time with him.

I think of what music my parents would play when I was younger. In my dad's car, it was always NPR. But my mom doesn't listen to a lot of English if she can help it. "Trot for me."

"Trot?"

I tap my fingers against the steering wheel as I try to find the best way to describe it. "It's like Korean folk music? But popular, so it kind of counts as pop music, too. It sounds really distinctive, though. Couldn't forget it even if I tried."

"Not a fan, I'm presuming."

"Not *not* a fan. I just would've liked to hear less of it."

Wesley stays silent, and I look over to gauge his expression. He looks like he wants to say something but is holding himself back.

"What?" I say.

"Nothing."

"Just say it."

"I don't want to beat a dead horse."

"What? You want to talk about those girls in the parking lot?"

He gives me a strange look out of the corner of his eye. "Okay, first, very weird of you to refer to your best friends as 'those girls in the parking lot.' Don't interrupt!" I close my mouth and he continues. "Second, the fact that that's what you think is on my mind kind of indicates that that's what's on *your* mind, so maybe you want to talk about it. And third, I was going to say . . . at least you know what Korean folk music sounds like, even if you know it too well. My parents didn't play anything because they weren't really there. I mean, it's nice that I don't have to listen to weird music I don't like, but I also wouldn't know Thai folk music even if it were playing right now."

I look over at him. I do it for long enough that he roughly tells me to keep my eyes on the road. So I turn my attention back to driving and say, "I like it when you do that."

"Remind you not to get us killed? Me too."

"When you keep me in check. I should be more grateful." I pull onto my street and make my way to the back of the house to park in the garage. "All right, we have some time until my mom is free," I say, glancing at the dashboard clock. "Bring your backpack. We're doing work."

I lead him in through the back of the house and we settle at the dining room table. The piano music from the lesson room is perfectly audible through the house. It sounds like a student is playing Burgmüller's "Arabesque." The quick notes come out uneven, which is understandable considering the breakneck tempo, and the bass notes sound heavy. The music stops abruptly for a quiet moment. Then the playing resumes, but with considerable difference. The left hand is lighter and the right hand sounds crisper. I can picture my mother's nod of approval.

I take out my schoolwork from my backpack and gesture for him to do the same. "All right, what's your least favorite subject?"

"Precalculus," he says immediately. He hands me his math folder and I take a look at the last quiz, the one he'd previously crumpled up into his backpack. If I were more poetic, I would make more significance of the fact that he's willingly showing me something he once forcefully hid. Instead, I just scan through the problems to see where he's going wrong.

"I think you're simplifying terms where you can't actually do that," I say. "It's the idea of 'like terms,' and I think there are terms that our brain wants us to think are alike, but they actually can't be combined." I go through his quiz and make a small dot with my highlighter each time I see the same type of mistake. Then in pencil, I complete the problem in the margin so he can see what the next steps should be.

I have Wesley attempt his homework on his own first, using his corrected quiz as a guide. In the meantime, I pull out my math homework, too.

"How is it that you're unable to spend a moment not working?" Wesley asks.

I think of the tag on the sweater. "If you do your work in any free moment you have, you can actually enjoy the free moments you have later," I say.

He gives me a grin. "Maybe you should take up writing fortune cookies. Or horoscopes."

"Do your work."

"That's not a good fortune."

"Wesley."

"Even worse." But he goes back to his math textbook.

We work in silence, so it's noticeable when the piano music stops. I hear a child's voice saying, "See you next week, Mrs. Park." I hold my breath and listen for my mother's footsteps as she walks closer to us.

I look up when she walks into the dining room. "Hi, Eomma. This is Wesley."

Wesley stands up and gives her a small bow. I raise my eyebrows. He clears his throat and says, "Hi, Mrs. Park. I'm Wesley Ruengsomboon."

My mom gives Wesley a cursory once-over. I can tell she's trying not to study him, even though she wants to. I have to suppress my laughter at the noticeable effort she's putting into being nonchalant. "Hi, Wesley. It's nice to meet you. Eliza tells me you're a good cook." It's weird to hear my mother speak in English, although I know she must do it pretty frequently with her piano students. It's like seeing a hidden version of her.

Wesley looks down, looking shier than I've ever seen him. "I'm okay. I've really been wanting to learn more."

My mom gives him a nod. "Good. Let's go to the kitchen." She leads the way and we follow. She wastes no time moving toward the fridge, and soon the countertop is covered with a package of ground pork, bunches of green onion, bundles of sweet potato noodles, and various other things.

"We're making dumplings," Wesley says. I've never heard him sound effusive before, but he does now. His eyes are practically sparkling.

My mom turns to him and smiles. "Right. We're making mandu. Korean dumplings."

I perk up. "This is a lesson I need to pay attention to."

"You like dumplings?" Wesley asks.

"She loves them," my mom says before I get the chance. "She'll eat them for breakfast, lunch, and dinner. Probably for the whole week."

I can't defend myself because she's not wrong.

"Let's start with the filling," my mom announces. She starts her lesson. It's a lot of moving parts—boiling the dangmyeon, blanching the sprouts, shredding the zucchini. Of course, there's always garlic to be minced. I'm convinced my fingers will never not smell like garlic.

Once everything is prepped, my mom gives each of us plastic gloves and we take turns mixing the filling together by hand. Wesley and I watch as the filling squishes through our gloved fingers. It's not dissimilar to making japchae, but this feels more fun. I don't know that I've ever felt this relaxed in the kitchen. With my mother's guidance and Wesley's competency in cooking, things go smoothly for once, like they balance out my entropy.

"How can you make sure you've seasoned the filling well enough?" I ask. "You can't know until the dumplings are done and cooked."

My mom turns to Wesley. "What do you think?"

He considers for a moment. "Maybe you could cook a small part of it. Taste a sample and adjust?"

I know from my mom's expression that he's right before she says it. "You can put a piece in the microwave and taste if you want to." Her smile transforms into more of a smirk. "I don't taste my filling before I fold the dumplings. I trust myself for it to be good."

We then move back to the dining room. Wesley and I push aside our schoolwork to make enough room for the assembly process. Next to the big bowl of our mixed and presumably well-seasoned filling are packages of store-bought mandu wrappers, and small bowls of an egg-and-water mix.

"This is the most exciting part," my mother says. "The folding."

"Is it hard?" Wesley asks.

"There are some types of folds that are for more experienced cooks," she says in reply. "But we'll just do the easy ones." She demonstrates how much filling to put in the center of the dumpling, how to wet the edge of the dumpling wrapper using the egg wash as a sealant, and how to fold it over into a half-moon shape and evenly pleat the edges. "You need to fold it tight so that the filling doesn't come out when you cook it. Like this." Her pleats look absolutely perfect, like the dumpling was sewn by a machine. "Now your turn."

Wesley and I each take a wrapper and scoop a spoonful of filling in the center. I watch him as he dips his finger into the egg wash and swipes it across the wrapper edge. I do the same. Then he crimps the edge into neat pleats and places his finished dumpling next to my mother's. He gives her a big smile. "That's fun."

She smiles back at him. "You're a natural." Then she turns to me. "Yeji-yah, you're next."

Wesley faces me. "Is that your Korean name? Yeji?" He says it with a vaguely American accent.

"Yeah. You can call me Eliza, though." I fold my dumpling peel over and try to pleat the edges, but accidentally let my fingernail tear through the skin. "Oops."

"That's okay. Just fold over the tear," my mom says.

I do what she says, and the dumpling comes out looking tolerable at best. When I place it next to the ones my mother and Wesley made, it looks less like a dumpling and more like an uneven lump. The pleats are irregular and I'm worried I didn't crimp them tightly enough. I picture dumpling filling scattered in the whorls of boiling water.

"Not bad," Wesley says.

I glower at him.

My mom teaches us another way of folding where you don't pleat the edges and instead keep it as a smooth half moon. Then you pull the two corners together so that it looks kind of like a circular pillow or a crown. "This one, you need to make sure you pinch these corners together very strong. Or it'll open up when you cook them."

Considering the stacks of wrappers and the amount of filling, it seems like we're here to make dozens of dumplings, if not a hundred or so. We fall into the routine pretty quickly and our folded dumplings look so beautiful lined up against one another. Well, two-thirds of them do.

My mom says, "When Yeji told me you were joining us, I knew we had to make mandu. For me, making mandu is like a social event. Sometimes, friends come together and make a bunch of them while they talk. Or in families, it's a dish that the parents and children can make together. When I was young, my mom would put out all the supplies and the whole family would sit on the floor and spend the morning making dumplings together. Then we would eat them for lunch." Her voice holds a note of nostalgia, and I know her head is halfway elsewhere right now.

"That sounds so lovely," Wesley says, and the wistfulness in his tone is unmistakable to me. Does my mother hear it, too? "I've always wanted to make dumplings, but the recipes usually make so many and . . ."

My mom nods. "It's always better with company. In my family, I was known for putting too much filling and then I couldn't close the wrapper." I'm surprised she's saying so much in front of Wesley. Maybe I was wrong, and it doesn't matter who is listening, as long as it's somebody. "My baby brother would only put a small dot of filling so that his dumplings were mostly just wrapper."

"Cooking is just a reflection of personality, I guess," I say. "You said you were always doing a lot as a kid."

My mom rewards me with a small smile.

I continue. "So what does it mean that my dumplings are ugly and Wesley's look fine?"

Wesley chuckles. "Let's not say out loud what we already know."

I push his shoulder, leaving a stain of egg-and-water wash and a dust of flour on his sleeve.

"Hey, no fighting while cooking," my mom says, but she catches my eye and gives me a wink. I immediately pull my hand back from Wesley and my cheeks are engulfed in flame. "Cooking is about coming together."

Now my mother is the one who sounds like a fortune cookie. But if she were a fortune cookie, I'd keep her message in my pocket for the rest of the day to reread when I got home.

Chapter 15

The girls and I don't talk about the incident in the parking lot for the whole week.

But on Friday, I'm the first one to arrive at Señora Molina's classroom for lunch. Once again, I'm staring at my blank personal statement document. If being out of ideas were an Olympic sport, I would take the gold. At least then, I'd have something to write about. People usually write about some sort of conflict they've experienced, and I feel like I've deliberately avoided that very thing for so long.

I'm about to text the girls (current group chat name: "domesticity is a curse," courtesy of Meredith after she sent a picture of her freshly laundered and neatly folded underwear—dozens of them) to see where they are when I hear a stream of giggles from the hallway. It doesn't sound like Kareena and Meredith, and there aren't many students nerdy enough to eat lunch in their teacher's classroom.

Then, Kareena and Jess arrive at the doorway.

I feel the beginnings of a headache pulse at my temples.

Kareena peers around, presumably looking for Meredith to give her better coverage. Seeing that it's just me, she puts on a wide smile and says, "Hey, do you mind if Jess eats lunch with us here?"

"I don't know," I say, trying to stay generous. "Señora Molina only trusts us to use her classroom for lunch because she knows us."

"Oh, actually, Señora Molina is friends with my mom!" Jess

chirps, happy to contribute to the conversation. "That's why I'm taking French, actually. Didn't want it to be awkward for Mrs. Molina to grade my things."

"Of course," I say.

Kareena frowns in disapproval. The bitterness in my tone must have been too evident. "Eliza."

"What?" The ice in my voice is a challenge.

"It's okay," Jess says brightly. "Maybe another time, right? I'll see you later, Kareena." She dashes out of the room and within a second, there's no evidence that she was ever here. Except for Kareena's attitude.

She drops her backpack with a resounding thud. "Eliza, that was rude."

I raise a brow. "I didn't even say anything."

"It's written all over your face. You were practically baring your teeth."

I shrug. "I don't think I should have to apologize for not liking her."

"Well, why don't you?"

I shake my head.

"No, seriously," Kareena demands.

"Okay, if you want to be serious, how is it that she mentioned wanting to apply to Penn all of a sudden and you weren't even fazed?"

Kareena crosses her arms. Her brown cheeks darken with frustration. "You know what I think? I think maybe you're still upset by the possibility that Jess is going to take your rank."

"That's not what this is about," I say, but I sound wounded even to myself.

"What's your problem with Jess, then?" Kareena demands. "You're not making any sense."

I watch her, her immaculately groomed eyebrows knitted in fury. How did it get to the point where my best friend is defending someone else against me? And it's not just anybody she's defending, it's the one person who I know would take advantage of Kareena if she could.

"How have you not noticed?" I say, exasperated. "She cheats off of you!" It seems so obvious, my head spins.

Her anger melts into shock and I watch her jaw slacken. She blinks at me in surprise, like this was the last thing she would have anticipated me saying. "What?"

"You didn't notice that sophomore year, after ranks came out, she conveniently started sitting in the row behind us in all our classes? Behind you, actually," I say. Jess followed Kareena's seat like a magnet, from class period to class period. Did Kareena really go around without detecting her academic shadow?

"That doesn't prove anything," Kareena dismisses.

"Sure, then how about this? Precalculus. We were taking an exam. She was staring at your desk the entire time. Of course, I'd noticed that she'd been doing it before, but gave her the benefit of the doubt and thought maybe she was daydreaming in class. But this time, *she saw me see her*. She looked mortified—Kareena, you should've seen her, she practically dripped with guilt. She glued her eyes to her paper for the rest of the class, like that would erase what I'd seen her do. But I'd seen her cheating off you and she knew it."

It easily comes back to me. How I stalked after Jess into the parking lot once eighth period ended, like a lion after its prey. How she only turned around when she realized I was intent on trailing her all the way to her car if I had to, that I would've climbed into the passenger seat if the situation called for it. Her delicate features were already twisted in fear, putting on a counterfeit show to make me feel like *I* was the one doing something wrong.

"Jess, I saw you," I told her when she finally surrendered the chase.

"It wasn't anything," she said. Her cardigan-draped shoulders caved in, another crafted display of disingenuous defense. Her act just made me feel more confident in what I'd seen.

"You were cheating." Of course, Jess, who probably didn't have to work for anything she had, was happy to lift answers from the smartest girl in our class. And, of course, she was making me feel bad for being the one to catch her.

"I wasn't, I promise," Jess pleaded. "Please, Eliza, I was just looking without thinking."

"I think it's a bad strategy to take an exam 'without thinking,' don't you?"

"You know what I mean."

I shook my head. "You do it all the time. Don't think you've been hiding it. I've seen it."

"I know you won't believe me, but I promise, it's not—I'm not—" Her ocean eyes looked even shinier with unshed tears. "Please don't tell anyone. I don't know how to convince you that I wasn't cheating, but I wasn't. I wasn't." A tear broke free to slide along her slim nose. I had to admit, if the academic thing didn't work out for Jess, a career in acting might go far.

The melodrama of it all fed my bitterness. It's not like our teachers would do anything too drastic to her if she were reported. She would only have to retake the exam. But other students were starting to stare at us as they walked to their cars, and I knew what it looked like. I was bullying someone in our year who embodied the quintessence of sweetness, berating her in public. Out of the corner of my eye, I saw Kareena and Meredith exit the building and make their way to the parking lot.

"Don't let me catch you again," I said, feeling defeated. There was no point in going up against Jess. Anyone could see her cry and the narrative would already be written. Jess Archibald did not do things wrong.

But she did. She does. I've known it, and the fact that Kareena refuses to see it makes me feel like I'm watching a fissure widen between us, threatening to swallow the ground from right beneath me. Even after telling her what happened, I can see in the grim set of her mouth, in the steel in her eyes, she's not convinced. All the strength of Kareena's determination, which I've always admired from beside her, is set opposite me now, and I feel much further from her than what the classroom allows.

Kareena grabs her backpack and slings it over her shoulders. "Eliza, I believe Jess. I think she was telling the truth." Her bottom lip wavers like she wants to say something else, but then her eyes constrict and she sets her jaw once more.

I want to shake her shoulders, puncture her delusion with questions like throwing spears. *She sits next to you in chemistry, doesn't she? She asks you to check answers all the time? And now she's considering the same college as you? What is she if she's not relying on your answers?*

But Kareena and I are not spear-throwing girls. We are shields, built for defense and stability. So I suck in my anger and say, "You can believe who you want. I won't fight with you about this." Of course, what I really mean is, *You can believe who you want, but how could you not believe your best friend?* Does Kareena hear what I leave unsaid?

Kareena straightens her shoulders. "Me neither. I'm going to the cafeteria."

The fissure cracks open into a canyon. Kareena leaves from her side.

I don't know how long I sit alone in Señora Molina's classroom before Meredith walks in. She sees me sitting alone and collapses next to me with a weary thud. "What the hell did I miss?" she asks. "God, I ask *one* question after class and this is what y'all do without me?"

Wesley picks up on my sour mood instantly. The second the bell rings for the weekend and the entire classroom rushes out, he turns to me and says, "Okay, tell me what's wrong."

I frown at him. "Nothing. What dish are we doing today?"

He shakes his head at me and I watch his dark hair tousle itself. "Not until you tell me what's wrong."

I open my mouth to say something snarky, but his chestnut eyes are warm with concern and it catches me off guard. Somehow, I end up feeling truthful. "Kareena—my best friend—and I had a fight."

His expression is oddly sympathetic. There's a groove in his chin when he frowns, like the shell of a walnut. I want to press my finger into it. "About Jess?"

I narrow at my eyes at him. "You are strangely insightful for a man."

He shoots me a smirk and corrects, "For anyone."

"That's all," I say.

"You don't want to talk about it?"

"I want to get to work."

"Nope," he says, shooting up from his seat. "You're upset and I'm hungry, so I'm going to cook for us."

"Well, we could cook together," I protest.

"No, this recipe is not on Mr. Treviño's list. Because it's too simple to learn from, or because it's not white—who's to say?" he says.

"So you're going to make me just sit here."

Wesley flashes me a grin that radiates so much arrogance, it might penetrate the ozone. "Do your homework. I know you love that." Then he starts to gather his ingredients, pulling from both the class fridge, pantry, and the corner cabinet that he saves for his own personal use. It's where he keeps ingredients he's brought from home, primarily Asian ingredients that the school doesn't already supply.

After lunch with Kareena, I don't have it in me to put up more of a fight. So I take his (obnoxious) advice and pull out homework. Unfortunately, despite how it makes me sound, there are fewer things more comforting to me than doing a problem set. There is something inimitably consoling about a subject where you know there is a right answer and you can trace your steps to check that it's correct. It's easy to lose myself in differentiation of inverse functions because you follow the same rules every time and arrive at the right result.

As Wesley cooks, the kitchen begins to fill with incredible yet familiar aromas. I feel like I'm back at home with my mother behind the stove. I get up and walk over to his cooking station. "I know what this is," I say.

"Yeah?" he says, stirring a brown gravy. Onions, carrots, potatoes, and cubed pieces of chicken poke out from the surface.

"I'm just shocked you're making it," I say.

"What do you mean?"

"Thai curry is so superior. I find it funny you would step into Japanese curry territory."

"I have room in my big heart for all sorts of curry. But it's good to know you like Thai curry. I'll store that in my equally big brain for future reference," he says. He's just added the curry blocks, so it's still in the process of thickening.

"My mom makes Japanese curry all the time. Except in Korean, we pronounce it like 'karae,' and I used to think it belonged to us. To Koreans, I mean. But actually, I think the Japanese brought it over when they invaded."

"That's cute," he says with a soft smile.

"Imperialism?"

He coughs. "Sorry, no. I mean, that you think of Korean people as 'us.' I don't know if I'd refer to Thai people as 'us.' I guess I don't feel that connected to Thailand, generally."

I look down at the countertop. Do I think of Korean people as *us*? I feel like I've been pointing to the opposite as an excuse for my lack of grief over my grandmother. I spent my childhood fighting my mom about going to Korean school on the weekends and I all but shat on trot in the car with Wesley. But maybe the reality is, I use the Korean parts of myself when they're convenient for me, shrugging them on and off like a jacket. The vague shape of hypocrisy takes form somewhere in my gut.

"Did your parents immigrate here?" I ask.

"My dad did in his twenties. My mom did, too, but when she was really young, sometime during the Vietnam War, I think. So she's more like me in that way. She feels very American." A grimace threatens his expression when he mentions his mother, but he doesn't elaborate. I get the familiar urge to crack him open, to see what's under his semifeigned arrogance, but I don't know how. "I think this is ready."

He opens the lid on another pot, which I see is full of cooked white rice.

"Before you say anything snarky about me cooking rice in a pot like a white person, I'd like to let you know that this kitchen does not have a rice cooker," he says defensively.

"I wasn't going to say anything," I say. Although I definitely was. I realize Wesley makes it fun, or at the very least interesting, to talk about being Asian, including all the various foods that come with the territory. It's different than the way it feels talking to my parents, and even from how I talk to Kareena. Being between cultures is like being a bead on a string, trying to balance between two ends. But no matter which end of the string I slide to, Wesley doesn't seem to care.

We sit down at our normal class seats with our plates of curry. When I have my first spoonful, I inhale deeply and smile. I hear the click of a camera shutter and see that Wesley has snapped a selfie of us with our food.

"Delete that! Curry is not even on the syllabus," I protest.

"This one's just for me." Wesley gazes down at the photo he's taken like he's about to say something else, but instead he locks his phone and tucks it away. "How is it?"

"Amazing. This was one of my favorite dishes as a kid," I say.

"Mine, too. Mainly because it was one of the easiest to make."

"You must've cooked a lot growing up," I say, trying to make the words sound thoughtful instead of curious.

He glances up and his expression tells me I haven't succeeded. "Are you asking if I had to take care of myself?"

I look down at my plate. "I'm not asking anything you don't want to answer." Then I take a deep breath and decide to be brave—or nosy. I haven't yet figured out where exactly the line is. "But maybe I'm a little curious as to what you mean when you say your parents weren't around to play music or teach you to cook. And maybe I'm a little curious as to why one would hypothetically walk home after saying they had parked their car in the school parking lot."

We eat in silence for so long, I have time to feel embarrassed for saying so much and then have the taste of the food wipe the embarrassment from memory. I do a little happy dance in my seat every time I get a chunk of potato in my spoonful. They're my favorite part of the curry, and Wesley has cooked them so that they're at just the right softness. Even with such an easy dish, you can tell he knows what he's doing.

I'm just getting settled into the silence when Wesley breaks it.

"What exactly are you asking?" Maybe he's trying to be brave, too.

I bite my lip as I consider how to phrase my thoughts with the appropriate tact. "I think there are a lot of things we take for granted at Highland Hills. The resources here, the academic prestige of the school, it's all like an idyllic bubble. And then I see this kid who, unlike everyone else, wants to stay here after school every single day and pretends that he doesn't walk home and doesn't do as well as he wants to in class and his parents aren't really around. . . . I don't know. I think it adds up to something. Do you?"

I force myself to look at Wesley directly. He seems at a loss for words. He opens his mouth to say something, then closes it.

I wait.

He stares.

I wait.

Then he starts laughing.

I look around me to see if there's something else going on. "What's funny?"

"You are."

"Yes, but usually, the funny part happens intentionally."

He laughs so hard, I start to get annoyed. I'm about to get up from my seat when he finally wheezes in a breath.

"Wait, stop," he says. "I'm sorry. I didn't mean to laugh."

I halt and turn to face him, still annoyed. "Then why did you?"

"Because you're cute."

I say, "What?" but it comes out like my throat was replaced by a malfunctioning incinerator.

"Like, your actions," he amends. "Your thought processes. All very cute."

"Right."

His eyes study my expression, and he quickly adds, "I mean, physically cute as well, but that's not—" He cuts himself off and pinches the bridge of his nose. "Just ignore me, please." I have never seen Wesley Ruengsomboon this flustered. Like last time, I see a blush creep up his neck, and I can't deny that it makes me almost giddy.

It's what gives me the confidence to say, "Okay, so I'm cute and funny. Obviously. But I'm funny *because* I'm cute? That's new." In my head, I congratulate myself on having my voice sound so steady when I can barely hear my own thoughts over the blood rushing in my ears.

He starts shaking his head. "It's not funny, but it is funny."

"Very logical, as always."

Wesley waves me off and continues on, disregarding my snark. "You thought I was poor, I guess is what you're skirting around. Having to walk home because I didn't have a choice. Using the school's kitchen because it's better than what I have back home." He laughs, but somehow, over the course of his words, it's turned bitter.

I take a breath to explain myself. "I didn't—"

"This is Highland Hills, Eliza. We're in a fully stocked kitchen that students have access to. Think about that! I doubt people can even be districted for this school unless they have money. And my family has a lot of it. My mom's an attorney for a gas company."

I rest my head on my hand for some stability. The sensation of being so wrong feels like vertigo. I hear Wesley's words from before echo in my head: *Maybe it should occur to you that some people just get these grades. Not because anything is happening in life, not due to some personal tragedy, and not because they slack off.* "Is that why she's a villain?"

"Partly." His sigh takes the length of multiple beats. "Obviously, yes, I would love it if her job aligned more with my values and less with oil lobbyists. But I think, more than that, I feel so . . ." Wesley runs his fingers through his hair trying to find the right word. "Unseen? You remind me a lot of her, actually."

Air escapes me like I've been physically punched. I didn't think I could feel worse today after lunch, but here we are.

Wesley must see the woundedness in my expression and he rushes to explain. "What I mean is that, she values what you value. Good grades, being involved, being the best. It's hard for me to remember that not everyone who is successful like her is as bad as she is. I think I can get caught up in my own worst assumptions."

His eyes meet mine and I think I see the trace of an apology there.

"Why do you think she's so bad?" I say.

Wesley spins his spoon in his bowl. "She thinks I don't appreciate her success and what she worked through to get where she is. To her credit, she's worked hard to gain her citizenship, to become the first immigrant woman hired by her company. She's always grinding toward her next promotion, closing deals that inarguably worsen Texas's environmental health but increase the number of designer bags in her closet and her status in the company. Sorry, you can tell I'm bitter." He shakes his head as if to clear it. "The point is—she has this one idea of success. She thinks I'm an absolute failure, essentially. Refuses to see the value in anything I actually like to do, like cooking. Every time she sees me, I can predict what's going to come out of her mouth. When am I going to get my grades up, should she send me to the military if I can't get into college, what is she working this hard for if her one son is this much of a disappointment?"

This is the most I've ever heard Wesley say at once. And every additional sentence adds more detail to someone I'm realizing I have misunderstood.

"That's awful," I whisper. "I'm sure she doesn't mean that."

"She does. She lets me know."

I shake my head. "That's not right."

"She would love if you were her daughter," Wesley says, and the bitterness is tinged with something much more vulnerable—hurt. *Carbon copy honor student. A regurgitation of others' expectations.* To him, I was a representation of all that he wasn't, but was expected to be.

"What about your dad?" I ask.

He rolls his eyes. It does not feel playful. "Consultant. Travels a lot. I rarely see him. I think my mom prefers it that way, too."

"So it feels like it's just you and your mom," I assume.

"I like to have any excuse not to be home if I don't have to be," he says. "As you've noted, I do like to spend my afternoons here until closing. As much of a loser as that makes me out to be."

"It doesn't. But the walking home?"

Wesley's laugh is mainly breath. "Small form of protest. My mom bought me a car and said, 'Look at what working hard can get you.' But of course, there's only one correct definition of hard work to her. It's silly, I know. And I can't even do it properly because Texas is a failure of urban planning, so I still have to drive just to get most of these ingredients I like to use, but . . . I like to think that every time she comes home, sees my car in the garage, and realizes I'm not actually there, maybe she's hearing me say something. Like, I can do things my own way."

He laughs again, but this time it's entirely self-conscious, and he dips his chin low like he's trying to make himself smaller. "God, this is really embarrassing. I am so sorry." He anxiously runs his hand through his hair again.

"Are you kidding?" I say. "Thank you for telling me. I've been so curious about you." And I immediately wish I could take the words back, because him being vulnerable is not an invitation for me to be embarrassing.

I see that he interprets my words just as candidly as I meant them because his chestnut eyes crinkle at the ends and his smile turns smirk-adjacent. "Oh yeah?"

In order to avoid responding, I scrape the last portions of my serving into my mouth and give him a puffy-cheeked smile. "Great curry."

He lets out a soft laugh and looks away. "Anyway, I know I'm being insufferable. I have every resource at my fingertips and yet I'm still bad at school and boo-hoo, my mommy is mean to me. I know how it sounds."

I swallow my food and frown. "No one said your problems have to be the worst in the world in order for them to exist."

He looks like he doesn't agree, so he says nothing.

"I think it's impressive that you taught yourself to cook," I say.

"I think it's impressive you have a good relationship with your mother," he replies.

"Sometimes," I say. "We haven't been close since my grandma passed away last summer."

"Oh, I'm so sorry," he says.

I twirl my spoon in my hand. "It's okay. I really didn't . . . You know how you said you don't feel connected to Thailand? I don't always feel connected to Korea either. Sometimes, it's like . . . events that happen there are just things that occur in a parallel universe."

He nods slowly. "You weren't that affected by it like your mom was."

I meet his eyes sharply. "Again, how are you this insightful for a guy? Or for anyone," I quickly add, because he's opened his mouth to correct me.

"You say more than you think, and the rest of it is written on your face."

I raise an eyebrow. "Oh, really? What's my face saying now?"

He studies me and I notice when his gaze drops to my mouth and back to my eyes. "I think," he says slowly, drawing the words out like syrup, "your face is saying something that you're not ready to put into words. So I'll wait." He stands up from his seat and takes our empty dishes to the sink.

The sound of the faucet running makes it so that I don't have to say anything. I'm glad for the distance because he's right. I'm at a complete loss for words.

Chapter 16

If I stop for a moment and let myself think about how much has changed since the first day of senior year, I don't know whether to laugh or cry. At the beginning, it felt like I had finally settled into a routine. It was like coasting, or letting the lazy current of a river guide me forward.

Now the waters jostle me. My best friend keeps choosing someone else over me. I'm opening up to a boy I swore was the most obnoxious person on earth. I'm probably the worst student in one of my classes. I thought I had the script memorized, but all the roles have been reversed.

On paper, everything is the same. The girls and I study at the boba shop. We go through the majority of our classes together. We still spend lunchtime in Señora Molina's classroom. But things don't quite flow the same way. The conversations are stilted rather than lightning quick. The laughter is half-hearted instead of rib aching. The group chat name hasn't changed in the past twelve days. We're closing off and I don't know how to fix it.

Then, one day during lunch, Meredith says, "Who was that boy you were walking with in the parking lot?"

"What?" I say, pretending like I don't remember.

Meredith cocks her head. "Unless you were recently diagnosed with amnesia, there's no way you don't remember because it was literally like a week or two ago. You were with this tall Asian guy."

Kareena nods. "He was cute."

"Yeah, I guess so," I say, as if the thought has just occurred to me.

"So who is he?" Kareena asks.

"Some guy in my Culinary Arts class."

"*The* guy?" Kareena gasps. "Your annoying, obnoxious, ridiculously talented rival who made you cry over onions? That guy?"

Meredith gives me a devilish grin. "That you just happened to give a ride home? The alternative is that you joined Uber, which I hope isn't true because I don't know if they're allowed to unionize."

Kareena waggles her eyebrows. She's gotten them rethreaded recently, I notice, although she didn't text about it in the group chat like she normally does. "Already bringing him home, are we?"

"Your place or mine?" Meredith coos.

"Can y'all stop?" I say with a sigh. "He's a friend, okay? Am I asking about who y'all are taking home?"

The room stills. I feel like I can hear my heart beating. Finally, because I figure no one else is going to say anything, I say, "Sorry."

Meredith shakes her head. "You're right. It's unfair of us to pry if you don't want to tell us. Isn't that right, Kareena?" She gives Kareena a pointed look, as if Meredith wasn't just as guilty of teasing me. Kareena looks at Meredith with narrowed eyes and pursed lips before nodding her head. She mumbles a soft agreement.

I turn to Meredith. "It's not that I don't want to tell you." This isn't entirely true. "It's just that there's nothing to tell." This is disappointingly true.

"Okay," she says, putting her hands up. "Change of subject. Let's talk about Halloween."

"What?" I say.

"It's only a couple of weeks away," Meredith says. "And we're not forgetting about it like we did last year."

Jess Archibald throws her annual party the Friday of Halloween weekend in her enormous house and invites every person in each of her classes, even if she doesn't talk to them, so that no one feels left out. You always know when it's the invitation day because she comes to school with the largest plastic pumpkin, the kind children take around the neighborhood for collecting candy. Stacked inside the pumpkin sit dozens of foiled stationery invitations, printed with a professionally designed, perfectly festive infographic with the party details. One year, the invitations were sealed with red wax that was placed to look like it was dripping blood from vampire fangs. Another year, the invitations were in handwritten calligraphy that someone said was a mimic of Edgar Allan Poe's handwriting.

"I totally forgot this was coming up," I say. "I can't believe it's already almost Halloween." This also means that my Culinary Arts reflection is due soon. Wesley and I still have one more dish to make. And even though it's inching toward November, not a single word of my personal statement has been written. Nor am I good enough yet to win the cook-off at the end of the semester. My head pounds. Or maybe it's my heart.

"Jess doesn't let us forget," Meredith says. "She and her parents started organizing at the beginning of October. Yesterday, Jess told us about how they couldn't find a giant cauldron that was big enough for the number of guests while also being functional to actually heat apple cider over their backyard firepit." She laughs and Kareena does, too.

This is the first time since my fight with Kareena that they've mentioned Jess openly. The intimacy with which Meredith mentions her stings, but what hurts worse is how casual that intimacy seems. This time last year, we weren't talking about Jess and her party at all. We would only remember it was happening the week of the event, when people in our classes would naturally chatter about what they had ordered and crafted for their costumes.

Kareena, Meredith, and I had a tradition of putting together sloppy, trio-based costumes. Our freshman year, we wore oversized pink, green, and blue shirts with a strip of black duct tape around our waists and went as the Powerpuff Girls. Our sophomore year, we dressed in all pink and went as the Plastics from *Mean Girls*, which was particularly hilarious because out of all the characters in that movie, we were probably most like Kevin Gnapoor. Last year was arguably our laziest attempt yet. We called ourselves Alvin and the Chipmunks and followed through by simply wearing a red, blue, or green sweatshirt with Kareena's red sweatshirt sporting an *A* made from masking tape. We always stayed together at the party, traveling together, eating together, sitting together. It didn't really matter what we were individually. People knew we were dressed as a group costume and that seemed to be effort enough, although the chipmunk year, someone did ask whether Kareena was referencing *The Scarlet Letter* or *Easy A*.

Group costumes clearly are not the plan for this year. Somehow, hanging with Jess and seeing firsthand exactly how much she puts into planning her party have converted Kareena and Meredith into people who want to take Halloween seriously.

Meredith shows us wig sites she's bookmarked on her phone. "I think this one is most like Daenerys's hair, but this other one is so much cheaper, and I'm probably only going to wear it once, you know? But I think it ships from Hong Kong, so it might not even get here in time."

Kareena nods. "I already ordered a shit ton of green body paint just to be safe."

"Why?" I ask. "Going as Shrek?"

"Don't be mean," Meredith chides. "She's going as Fiona."

Kareena rolls her eyes. "Elphaba. I figured I could buy a normal witch costume and paint myself green and—voilà. An effortful costume that will attract musical theater fans, too."

Meredith looks at me. "What about you, Eliza? Any ideas?"

I shrug. "You know me. I'll probably put something together last minute." I don't say: *Like we've always done. Like we should be doing this year.* It seems like *we* and *always* are being phased out of our vocabulary, especially when used in the same sentence. "Are we going in one car?"

I expect an immediate agreement, or reassurance that maybe all the deterioration is happening only in my head. But I don't get one. Instead, Kareena says, "Maybe. It's still kind of far away, so maybe we'll decide closer to the date."

"Cool," I say.

Even though things with the girls feel off-kilter, things with Wesley and my mother are more of a routine than they've ever been. It's the one reliable thing I have.

Each Tuesday, she walks into the kitchen after her piano lesson with a discernible lightness that only begins to shine through as the recipe comes together. She talks about Halmeoni, letting her mind go elsewhere, and comes back down to compliment Wesley on his skills. She teaches him the Korean words for common ingredients, like dubu for tofu, ganjang for soy sauce, maneul for garlic. He must practice during the week because during the next session, he'll use the Korean terms instead of the English ones. It's both endearing and annoying. Perhaps in the same way that Wesley sees me as someone his mother would appreciate, I get thorny seeing how effortlessly he wants to learn both the recipes and the language with an enthusiasm I've neglected before this semester.

The biggest difference doesn't need to be stated. My mother—and even Wesley, for that matter—cooks with love and with experience and with what I assume can only be innate talent. I'm getting better, and I think both my mother and Wesley recognize that. But I'm still behind. My cuts aren't as even, my timing isn't as precise. It would frustrate me more if I didn't love listening to her childhood stories so much. When she loses herself in a memory, both Wesley and I listen, rapt with attention. It doesn't matter to him that her English isn't perfect and it doesn't matter to me if she's sharing it with someone else, too.

Fridays are written off as Wesley time. If what I've started to teach him on Tuesdays before my mother's lessons is still confusing on Friday, we spend the first half of our afternoons working on schoolwork before transitioning to cooking. We're almost done with Mr. Treviño's syllabus. We only have one dish left, chocolate chip cookies, which Wesley suggested saving for Halloween as a sweet treat. We started off wanting to finish the list as quickly as possible, but now I think we're both drawing it out. The thought of completing the assignment makes me anxious, because I don't know what happens after.

The thing that really frustrates me is that besides our Tuesdays and Fridays, we don't really interact. It's a strange feeling, to have someone be in your own home, cook with your mother, but not text you on the weekend. I know his quiz scores—watch them slowly go up when he openly shows me on Friday afternoons—but I don't know what he does when he goes home. It's like there's a line drawn, a fence built around the parameters of our friendship. It doesn't seem to bother him, so I pretend it doesn't bother me either.

That's why it's so shocking when one Saturday, he texts me out of the blue to ask if I know a good place for studying on the weekend. His mom and dad are both home for once and he's itching to get out of the house. I say there's a place I know where there are plenty of outlets and natural lighting.

It feels weird to come to the boba shop with someone who's not Meredith or Kareena. The part of me desperate to hold on to a bare semblance of routine goes up to the register and orders my normal jasmine green milk tea. I don't think to ask Wesley if he's ready to order until I turn around and see that he's still studying the menu with comical intensity.

"Wesley?" I say, and he seems to be pulled out of thought. I almost laugh at him, and he scowls. He gives me a small wave to tell me to pay for my order without him.

As I wait for Wesley to battle his indecision, I consider texting Kareena and Meredith to see if they want to join us. At the very least, I consider texting Meredith. I'm sure she'd be excited to introduce herself to Wesley. But I don't. I can't tell if it's that I don't want them here, or if I'm scared to ask and have them say no.

Before I can debate this question too long, Wesley finally sits down with his ambiguous order. It looks vaguely pink.

"What did you end up getting?" I ask. "And why did it take

seventeen centuries? Empires have risen and collapsed. Dynasties have started and ended. My hair has grayed, fallen out, and regrown."

"There are *so* many flavors here," he says as explanation. "How does anyone make a decision ever?" He punches his straw through the sealed cap with no hesitation. "I asked the girl if she could be so kind as to mix the passion fruit with the Thai tea." He takes a long gulp and chews on his tapioca pearls.

"And how is it?" I ask, skeptically.

He offers his drink to me. Although we've shared countless meals at this point, it's never been such a communal experience. I take his drink and I have to look away when I drink from his straw. Wait a second. "What the hell?"

"Good, right?"

"It sounded so bad."

"But it's good, right?"

"So good." I hand his drink back. "Do you want to try mine? It's my go-to order. Jasmine green milk tea."

He takes my drink and I try my best not to think too hard about anything going on right this second, that our mouths are touching the same thing, but separated in time. When did I get so gross? When Wesley passes my drink back to me, I accidentally grab his hand, and the way he flinches makes me feel like I've killed a man.

"How is it?" I ask, keeping my voice bright.

"Great. I love that I can taste the flavor of the actual tea."

I nod. "This is the best boba shop in Austin. You're wasting your money if you go anywhere else."

"You're supposed to disclose sponsorships. I didn't know you worked here."

"You're lucky I don't. If you asked me for something custom, I would've sent you to the back of the line to think of a legitimate order while you wait. You're probably the reason that girl at the cash register is going to rant to her friends in a group text." I ignore the reminder of how my group text with the girls has been dry lately.

"Yeah, she did do this." He turns his cup around to show me a line of digits scribbled onto the cup below his order name.

I still. Look down, but not for too long. Look back up with a teasing smile. I hope it's convincing. "I stand corrected."

"She might start ranting when I throw the cup away."

I pretend to look behind his shoulder to study the girl taking orders. "She's cute," I say. "What's wrong with her? Remind you of your mother?"

"Ha. Love the way you turn my moment of vulnerability into a joke." But he does look genuinely amused.

I take a sip of my boba and take the time to chew my pearls, hoping that he'll revisit my question. He doesn't. Instead, he pulls out his homework, which feels like the cue to pull out mine. Again, I feel him drawing the line.

I do my part in respecting said line by opening my laptop and staring at my blank personal statement document. I let the cursor blink for a solid two minutes before I decide to work on my Culinary Arts reflection instead. This one is easier to write, at least. There's a very clear starting point—my pitiful cooking—and end point—my somewhat less pitiful cooking.

I'm shocked at how easily the words come out. It's easy to describe my multitude of shortcomings starting the class, the anxieties, the quiet embarrassment. Even easier is illustrating how capable Wesley was in the kitchen in comparison. With his instruction, every step became a learning opportunity, an understanding of how a decision made in preparation would help with the final result. I'm on such a roll that I only take a pause when I notice that Wesley is practically pulling his hair out working on something.

"Hey," I say. "Need help?"

He looks like he's about to shake his head, but then he looks down at his math notebook and drops his pencil in defeat.

I lean over to see what question he's on and jot down the relevant information onto a scratch sheet. I show my work, line by line, and then highlight my answer, the way we're taught to do for homework copies. "Here, come to my side. I'll show you what I'm doing."

He slides onto the bench next to me. I concentrate on showing Wesley the thought process behind each step, but I feel acutely aware of his leg lining up with mine and I suddenly wonder if my breathing is just a bit too audible. As I explain to him how to solve the function, I realize I've learned to tell when he understands what I'm trying to say and when he's simply pretending to. He asks me to check his thinking as he works through the next problem, and I do.

"You must think I'm embarrassing," he says.

"Why would I think that?"

"You probably took precalc, like, two years ago."

"What difference does that make?"

"All of it?" He raises the eraser end of his pencil to gesture all around him, exasperated. "According to anyone who has the power to decide what intelligence is—college, employers, adults in general." He looks away and I know he's thinking of his mother.

"I think you're smart," I say, and I do.

Wesley shakes his head. "It's easier for you. You're actually successful. Miss Salutatorian, Miss President of a Million Clubs. Who cares if you can't cook a meal without burning the building down? Colleges won't know, and they won't care. As long as your SAT score is astronomical and you have five awards under your belt, which I know you do."

I blink in surprise, unsure what to say. "Are you that worried about college admissions?"

"Who says I'm applying to college?" he replies.

For a second, I have to actively stop myself from saying something inconsiderate. I realize that talking with Wesley does not have the same parameters as talking to Kareena and Meredith. There aren't the same implicit understandings. "You're not?"

He shrugs. "I don't know who'd even accept me. You know my grades are shitty, even when I'm taking the easiest classes the school has to offer."

"Why are you so hard on yourself?" I scowl. "You're making yourself out to be some—I don't know. Someone so much lesser than who you really are."

Wesley grimaces like it's an instinctive reaction before smoothing his features out. He lets out a defeated sigh. "School is a specific kind of game, you know? And you play it so well—you, specifically. And it feels like sometimes, I barely even know the rules. I think I'm smart. I know a lot of things. I know how to entertain myself, how to feed myself, how to find new ways to do things. But it's like that kind of knowledge doesn't matter to them. There's no way to prove it."

"'Like only a certain sort of knowledge is valuable.'" It's my mom's voice coming from my own mouth. Wesley meets my eyes and his expression makes my heartbeat pause. Like he sees in me a mirror of himself.

"Right" is all he says. Then he laughs, but it's mainly breath. He sounds nervous. "I think I was so rude to you at the start because I felt like you would write me off, so I wanted to write you off first. My GPA sucks. And I know almost no one has a higher GPA than you. I think—maybe I thought that you'd . . . think I wasn't worth your time. Or something."

"What makes me worth yours?" I scoff. "I can't even write a personal statement and I've been trying all semester. My only skills are mooching off your great cooking and cockblocking you from cute girls who work at boba shops." I intentionally don't look at him because I don't want to see his reaction. "Besides, there are plenty of things that matter more than GPA."

There's a swallowed sound of amusement in his throat.

"What?" I say.

Wesley smiles in a way that signals apology. "Eliza. You have to know how ridiculous that sounds coming from you."

It's funny to be on this side of a familiar conversation. And he's right, ultimately. Although it's been nice getting to see these new layers to Wesley, and although I think my feelings might be moving in a direction I'm too afraid to follow, he is still my competition. I'm still hoping to beat him come the end of the semester, and I'm still aiming to keep my rank. I still want to give my speech, look out into the crowd, and smile at my parents and the dozens of Korean community members they've rallied to come.

I can't let myself forget the stakes. I can wax poetic to Wesley all I want about what matters more about a person than their grades, but for me, the story's already been written. I just need to finish it out.

Chapter 17

It's a rare occasion when both my parents are home for dinner. Between piano lessons and evening university lectures, the schedules get too difficult to coordinate, so I generally eat with whoever is available when I'm hungry.

But tonight, everyone's schedules happen to align and the three of us sit at the dining table with bowls of steaming white rice, kimchi jjigae, and an assortment of banchan. The kimchi jjigae is leftover from this week's lesson with my mom. I was particularly proud of this dish, because for the first time, it felt like an actually easy recipe. I didn't mess up the parts that were assigned to me, I could follow along with what my mom and Wesley were doing, and in the end, we had something so delicious that my mom insisted on sending Wesley home with a container full to share with his family. He said he would, and I knew he would not.

Another rare occurrence tonight is that my dad decides to initiate conversation with my mother. If I've been skirting around my mom since the summer, my dad has given her a mile-wide berth. For the first two weeks after my mom returned from Korea, she slept with the master bedroom door closed, the muffled sounds of hushed sobs serving as the only indicator as to whether she was behind the door. And while I thought I would want my spouse to try to comfort me during those nights, my dad insisted that what she really wanted was space. He slept in the guest room for days at a time, quietly dressed himself when he knew she was in a piano lesson, and left for work without disruption. I don't remember the last time I've seen them talk.

At dinner, my dad turns to her and says, "I'm glad you've been cooking more, yeobo." My parents really only ever refer to each other as the Korean term of endearment. It means honey or darling and suggests more intimacy than has existed between them for months.

She nods.

My dad continues, "It's nice to eat together, too."

She nods again.

A moment passes, and my dad turns to me. "Have you been working on your college applications?"

I lift one shoulder in a noncommittal shrug. "A little." The blank document comes to mind.

"College applications?" my mom repeats, like she's tuning in to the conversation.

"I'm not doing early decision," I say, trying to be proactive about assuaging her concern. "I have time."

"You're applying to college this year?" she asks. And that's when I realize that even though she's present in the moments that we're cooking together, she is still so lost in her own sea. She doesn't know when my school year starts or anything about the timeline of senior year.

"Yeobo," my dad says. "Yeji is a senior. Of course she's applying to college this year."

She meets my eyes from across the dining table, like she's seeing me for the first time. "She's growing up."

"Pay attention or you'll miss it."

"Appa," I scold. Even if it's what I'm thinking, I don't want him to say it out loud.

"Deciding what college you go to is going to be one of the most important decisions of your life," he says with firm authority. "It's important that, as your parents, we are here to support you."

A flicker of annoyance passes through me. It's the hypocrisy of my dad asking my mother to support me when he has hardly supported her through the last months. He tiptoes, whispers, never confronts the reality of her grief, and yet feels like he can demand more from her in the name of being a good parent to me. Who's a good partner to her? Who's a good daughter to her?

"Yeji's cooking has been getting better," my mom offers, like this is her contribution.

"Good," my dad says approvingly. "That'll help her with her grades."

"Grades?" my mom echoes.

I meet my dad's eyes and give the most minuscule shake of my head. My mother does not know about Culinary Arts, or that my desire to learn Halmeoni's recipes comes from anything other than being a good, curious daughter. It's not that I think she would mind so much, but the way she blossoms open during our lessons makes it feel so fragile. It seems too delicate to let some outside factor like the cook-off wedge itself into the conversation.

My dad continues, "My offer to teach you physics still stands. It would be really useful for you."

Of course, what remains unspoken is that Culinary Arts is not. And although I would have wholeheartedly agreed at the beginning of the semester, I'm not entirely sure I do now.

After dinner, I sit down to finally finish writing my reflection essay for Culinary Arts. It's not until I've already hit print that I notice I've nearly tripled the word count. There was too much to say.

The Friday of Jess's Halloween party comes sooner than I realize. At lunchtime, Jess asks to join us in Señora Molina's classroom and I say, "Yes, of course," even though I mean the opposite. I pointedly give Kareena a smile, like, *Look at this Herculean effort I'm exerting! I am such a trustworthy, peacemaking friend!* In return, her smile is the warmest I've received in a while.

Immediately, the three of them chatter about how excited they are for the party, which I realize belatedly is occurring tonight.

Jess turns to me. "Eliza, did you think of a costume?"

"Not yet," I say, trying to keep my response as simple as possible to minimize the chance of offense.

Meredith laughs. "Dude, it's tonight."

"Right. I'm bad about keeping track of things like this," I say, and shoot Jess what I hope is an apologetic smile. "But it sounds like fun," I add quickly. "I'm excited. What are you dressing up as, Jess?" Okay, good, redirecting conversation back to her. I imagine myself wiping sweat from my brow like a cartoon.

She glances over at Kareena before looking back at me. I wonder if she's surprised that I'm trying to make conversation, or if it's something else. Jess says, "I'm going as Galinda from *Wicked*."

Ah. Now it makes sense. Kareena has chosen a duo costume over our normal group costume. I look to Meredith to gauge her expression, but she doesn't seem affected at all. "I think you'll make a great Galinda," I say.

Jess smiles in gratitude. "Thanks. And also, I'm sorry if you think this isn't my place, but . . . if there's someone you want to bring to the party, like as a plus-one, I don't mind." She glances at Kareena again, like she's seeking affirmation. "If you want to bring someone, that is."

It takes me several seconds to understand what she means, to understand what Kareena and Meredith must be saying when I'm not around, to recognize how many conversations the three of them must have without me. It's a weird feeling to have a virtual stranger know more about your romantic life than even you seem to. "Thanks for the offer," I say. "Not really sure who I'd bring, but it's a nice thought." Meredith gives me a pointed look that says, *You're not kidding anyone.* Kareena keeps her eyes fixed on Jess.

"It'll be fun regardless, I promise," Jess says agreeably. "There will even be little mango cheesecakes that look like pumpkins. I know mango doesn't scream Halloween, but you'll have to try it. It's one of my favorites."

A chill runs down my spine. My jaw locks. I haven't forgotten our beginning-of-the-school-year picnic. "I'll be there," I say.

"Oh," Jess says, "I almost forgot." She pulls out two beautifully boxed cupcakes and slides one over to Kareena and one to Meredith. Each cupcake has their initial on top made from fondant. "This is congratulations for yesterday."

"What happened yesterday?" I ask.

"They submitted their early decision applications!" Jess exclaims.

"Oh my God, so did you," Meredith says. "This is too nice!"

"Seriously, Jess," Kareena agrees. "You deserve one, too."

"Well, sounds like you're offering half of yours," Jess says.

"Y'all submitted your applications?" I ask. Next to the three of them, I feel like a clock running two minutes behind.

Meredith nods. "We wanted to do it a couple of days before the actual deadline so we didn't run into any technical difficulties."

"But I didn't even get to read your personal statement," I say to Kareena. "I thought I would help revise it, like I did with Meredith's."

Kareena widens her eyes. "Oh, I didn't know. I'm sorry, Eliza. Although, honestly, I barely had anybody read it anyway because it felt so embarrassing, so . . ."

And even though she doesn't finish her sentence, I can tell that the people who have read it are sitting in this room. It's everyone but me.

After school, I set up our cooking station while Wesley moves toward Mr. Treviño's computer and projector. The start of another Pixar movie begins to play, and this one I recognize instantly.

"Feeling festive?" I ask.

"*Coco* might be the only one that can stand toe-to-toe with *Ratatouille*, in my opinion."

"I'm sure the whole *I want to pursue something my parents don't value* theme might play a part in that."

"I'm here to cook, not get psychoanalyzed," Wesley says.

"I read up on the chocolate chip cookie recipe last night," I say. "Sounds like the big learning objective is browning butter, which led me down this whole rabbit hole about milk solids and clarified butter, which is how they make ghee, and then I read, like, fifteen different recipe variations on biryani, which I totally think we should make next." I clear my throat. "I mean . . ."

Wesley catches my eye and the way he's looking at me makes my throat bob. He says his next words gently, a paper boat moving across the lake between us. "We can still keep cooking together, Eliza."

"But we're done with Mr. Treviño's recipes," I say. *We're done with the assignment. The group project is over.*

"Mr. Treviño's list was hardly all-encompassing. We can do some self-education."

I swallow. Is he saying that he still wants to spend time together? He wants this to continue?

Wesley shrugs and breaks eye contact. "Or not."

"No," I say quickly. I'm grabbing the paper boat. "Let's do it." To combat how warm my face feels, I add, "But let's finish the list first. Chocolate chip cookies."

We both watch as the butter slowly, slowly melts. I know from my research that the browning happens all of a sudden after a period of nothing, so we have to stay vigilant. We're standing shoulder to shoulder at the stove of his workstation.

Quietly, I ask, "Remember Jess Archibald?"

"Yeah," he answers, constantly stirring the butter so nothing burns.

"She throws a Halloween party every year."

He nods. "Right. We hear about it."

"We?" I ask.

He stops for a moment to look up at me. He expertly keeps his expression blank. "She only invites the kids in her classes. The AP kids. The rest of us just hear that it happens."

"Oh" is my only response.

Wesley resumes stirring. The butter is starting to bubble. If I look very closely, I can see the beginning of the milk solids turning visible. "I'm guessing you're telling me this because you're leaving the kitchen early to get ready? That's fine, Eliza. No worries."

"Actually," I say. "I was hoping you'd come with me."

I notice when his stirring hand stutters.

He laughs, a force of breath that almost buries his surprise. "I don't think I'm invited."

"You are now," I say. I figure it's best not to give the backstory and just hope he'll take my words at face value. "I want a friend there with me."

He raises an eyebrow. His chestnut eyes simmer. "A friend?"

I cough and look down. "Kareena and Meredith have been helping Jess with the planning and stuff, so I imagine they'll be too busy to really hang out with me. Will you come?" I try my best at making obnoxious puppy eyes.

Laughter breaks through his respectable poker face. "You look ridiculous."

"I can't believe butter can smell like this. Or look like this." The fragrance is heavenly. Toasty and nutty. I could bottle it up and drink it. The liquid is golden, shimmering above the dark brown milk solids. I'm proud of myself that I know this is close to being ready, even without Wesley telling me. "Also, I'm taking your lack of a no as a yes."

"I don't even have a costume."

"Me neither," I shrug. "I'm thinking of wearing a black turtleneck and going as Steve Jobs. Or The Rock."

He considers the idea. "I think I have a black turtleneck, too, actually."

I flash him a toothy grin. "Amazing. We can be twin Steve Jobses. Oh! Or you can be Steve, and I'll be The Rock. People will get it."

Wesley takes the pan off the heat and turns the burner off. "The first time I saw you, I distinctly remember thinking, 'My God, she looks so much like wrestler-turned-actor, Dwayne "The Rock" Johnson.' About time you finally cash in on the resemblance."

I give him a slight bow. "I've been waiting years for someone to make the connection. Seriously, Wesley. You'd be doing me a huge favor by going. But you don't have to if you'd rather not. I know spending an evening in a mansion full of people you don't know isn't the most enticing way to spend your Friday night."

"Eliza, don't you know the most enticing way to spend my Friday nights is to hang out with you?"

I look up to see if he's joking, but when I meet his eyes, I feel caught in something warm and serious. My face heats. My heartbeat amplifies in my ears. I want to say something, to respond with any semblance of coherence, but he looks at me with something so unfamiliar, I have to look away. I put my hand down on the countertop and lean on it for support, suddenly feeling shaky.

"Eliza!" he shouts.

"What?" I say—and he grabs my hand off the counter and jerks it away. My hand starts to burn and I finally understand that I unthinkingly rested it on the still-hot burner. "Oh fuck! Holy hell, that hurts!" My fingers are a rosy shade of pink and absolutely, painfully throbbing. Wesley turns on the sink to the coldest it can go and I gratefully put my hand under the running water.

"Jesus Christ, Eliza. Are you okay?"

"Yeah, totally fine. Just incompetent." My fingers still feel hot, even under the icy water. "It'll blister, but it's fine. Feels bad, though. Feels really bad." I wish I could keep myself from whining like a kid, but my hand is aflame. "I'm sorry," I say.

"Eliza, you're injured. Don't apologize."

"Can you believe we're more than halfway through the semester and I'm still injuring myself?"

"I'll finish the cookies," Wesley says. "Keep your hand in a bowl of ice water. Or get a towel, fill it with ice, and keep it pressed against your hand."

"You got it, Dr. Ruengsomboon," I say, giving him an exaggerated salute. After a few minutes of running my hand under the faucet, I fold ice cubes into a kitchen cloth and hold it against my palm. "Sorry I'm so inept," I say as I walk over to my normal chair, my hand a paradox of ice and fire.

"I can't tell you how many times I burned myself as a kid in the kitchen," he says.

"But I'm not a kid," I protest.

"But you have the same amount of cooking experience," he says. The signature smirk has made its return.

I have nothing to do but nurse my hand as I watch him finish making the cookies. This gives me an opportunity to sink into my thoughts. Even as I replay what he said in my head ad nauseam, I can't tell if his tone was sincere or joking. I want to revisit the conversation, but the moment has decidedly passed, and Wesley's expression is so different now that I wonder if I made up the way he was looking at me before.

As always, Wesley has left his backpack open. This time, I don't even pretend that I'm not looking. I reach in and grab the paper resting at the top.

It's an essay of some sort and I'm astounded to see a perfect hundred written at the top. "Holy shit, Wesley, how did you—" But I stop myself when I notice my name in the text of the piece.

Beyond an appreciation for Korean cuisine, Eliza has also taught me about authenticity to self. She is someone whose skills and successes are uniquely her own, who creates her own definitions and goals, and who inspires me to nurture ambition like it's a friend. She brings discipline to the kitchen, a thorough understanding of why something works, and an excitement to learn more than what's required of her. Her approach to cooking is evidence that cooking lies between science and art. If cooking with others is an exchange, what I have given Eliza is time and what she has given me is revelation. She reminds me that things are more than a sum of their parts, and it's only with Eliza's guidance that, for the first time, I've been able to see the sum of myself and others properly.

That's all I'm able to read before Wesley gently takes the essay from my hands.

I don't know what to say. I don't know how to react. I feel like I've done something wrong—illegal, even. My mind takes the path of least resistance and I ask, "How is it already graded? We turned them in today."

"Today was the latest we could turn it in," he corrects me. "I turned mine in early."

"I'm sorry," I say, and it comes out like a sigh. "That was incredibly intrusive of me."

He shakes his head. "It's okay. It's not anything I wouldn't tell you. Eventually."

I'm startled. "There's no way you meant it."

"Of course I did."

"But . . . it was so *thoughtful*."

"Your reaction is making me think that you wrote something awful about me in yours," he says with a nervous laugh.

"No, not at all," I protest immediately. "I couldn't stop writing."

"Too much to complain about."

"Shut up," I say. "I'd let you read mine, but Mr. Treviño has it now. Wesley, I . . ." For a long moment, both of us wait to see how I'm going to finish the sentence. There are a thousand ways I could. *I am so glad to have been paired with you. I think you are single-handedly changing how I think. I consider you one of my friends and still I want something else, too.*

I take too long, or I'm not brave enough to say any of those things, and the oven timer goes off, an incessant ping. "The cookies are ready."

I watch as he walks to the oven and pulls out the baking sheet. These chocolate chip cookies have to be the best I've ever seen. They're large and thin with giant gobs of melted semisweet chocolate poking through their perfectly brown crust. The entire kitchen smells like chocolate and butter and sweetness. Wesley was right about saving these for Halloween. They are the perfect treat.

When they've cooled sufficiently, Wesley plates them and pours each of us a glass of milk. He takes our picture and submits it immediately. "We are officially done."

He hands me a cookie and takes one for himself. We tap them together like a celebratory clink, but the cookies are so soft, the motion practically breaks them in half. We rush to catch them in our mouths before they can fall to the floor. Wesley's eyes dilate as he chews. "This is . . . kind of fire."

"Deeply insensitive considering my burn, but . . . you're so right."

"Are these the best cookies you've ever had?"

I nod vigorously. "Literally no competition. I hope you're satisfied with just the one, because I'm eating all the rest."

We watch the film while we let chocolate and butter melt in our mouths. Sitting side by side in the room, watching a movie together with a plate of warm cookies, I have to admit that it feels . . . romantic. I could easily lean over to have our shoulders brush. I could ask him if I have chocolate on my mouth. I could reach for his hand and see if he would let me keep it there. I want to ask him *something*, but I have no idea how to form the words or if he's even wondering the same things. So we sit in silence, letting the film reach its conclusion.

As the credits roll, I hear myself volunteer to clean the dishes. The cold water feels good against my tender hand and it's nice to do something so mindless when my brain feels so eager to dive into complications I'm not ready to think about. I try to let the film's soundtrack override the volume of my thoughts.

When I'm finished dishwashing, I turn around to dry my hands on a kitchen towel. I almost jump when I see Wesley standing there. He's so close, I bump into him just because there's nowhere else to go.

"Sorry, I didn't know you were there," I mumble.

I don't know that he's ever been this close to me before. Even though his face is in shadow, I can make out each eyelash and the small mole on the left side of his jaw. He gently picks up my burnt hand and inspects it.

"I wanted to ask . . . Does it still hurt?" he says quietly. The light from the film reflects off his black hair, giving him a halo.

My throat is too thick to speak, so I shake my head.

He looks at me, his eyes dark and glittering, and I have to swallow. I wonder if he can tell that I'm holding my breath. Then he presses his mouth onto my open palm, so softly, it feels like a whisper. It feels like he's asking permission.

"Wesley," I say, but there's no sound.

"Eliza," he murmurs against my hand. When he looks up at me, his expression is tortured. "Are we friends?"

"I think so," I say, the words on the cusp of trembling like autumn leaves. I guess we've never formally said it out loud, but something has changed. I don't see him and immediately have thoughts of needing to beat him by the end of the semester. I see him and I want to know him. I spend time with him and I like it. That's what friends should feel, right? "I hope you do, too."

He slowly lets my hand fall. "Okay."

I look at him, confused. Part of me is unsure if I'm actually here. My brain feels cloudy and my heart beats too fast. "Do you not want to be my friend?" The question feels silly, like we're back in kindergarten and sitting on playground swings.

He chuckles, but it sounds strained. "I don't . . ." For a moment, I'm terrified for him to finish. He doesn't want to be my friend. He wants to remind me of the competition. He doesn't think we should meet anymore now that our essays are turned in. He takes another breath and starts again. "I don't think about you the way I think about my friends."

"Wesley," I say again, and in the moment, it doesn't matter to me if I sound like I'm out of words, because I like the sound of his name coming from my mouth. I like to shape the letters like I'm gifting them away. Hesitantly, my burnt hand makes its way to his cheek. His eyes flutter shut when I touch him and he puts one hand over mine. I imagine our pulses chasing each other, one hand to the next and back again, as I lean forward slowly. I wonder if I'm even moving at all. There is a thick, heady feeling in the infinitesimal space between us and I want to swallow it whole.

I let my neck bring me forward so that our noses touch, his lips just a breath away from mine. "Wesley," I whisper, and I feel it for the first time—the friction of my lips brushing against his. His hand tightens over mine.

He takes a deep breath. It sounds desperate. "Eliza, please kiss me."

I let my lips fall onto his. His hand leaves mine to move to the back of my head and I feel it sculpt against the nape of my neck. Our mouths open, tasting of sugar and chocolate and warmth, and it feels like release. The cloak of pretense I've been wearing around him can fall away. *Here I am*, my mouth tells his. *Here is what I've been wanting to say for so long, what you saw written on my face before, what has finally caught up to my lips.* He pulls me against him and my heart thuds against his chest, like it refuses to stay trapped in. *Hear me, hear me, hear me.*

Suddenly, the door to the Culinary Arts kitchen opens and daylight floods into the space. I immediately untangle myself from Wesley and step back. In walks the janitor, Mr. Wilby, with a rolling trash can, and when he spots us, he lets out a loud whistle. "Sorry, kids," he says with a barely disguised guffaw. "Didn't mean to interrupt."

Wesley flushes as he smooths out his hair, scratches the back of his pink neck. "Hey, Mr. Wilby. Good to see you."

"Hi, Mr. Wilby," I say, although he doesn't know who I am.

"You know I love you, Wes, but I gotta kick you out. It's six p.m. and rules are rules."

"Of course," Wesley says. He runs over to Mr. Treviño's computer to shut down *Coco* while I awkwardly clean up the remainder of our mess. Wesley and I take our backpacks, and after he gives Mr. Wilby a final goodbye, we leave the kitchen together.

We walk in silence for a few moments, all the way through the courtyard and into the main building, before I can't handle it any longer. "That was embarrassing for you, too, wasn't it?" I say.

Wesley laughs and it echoes in the empty hallway. "More embarrassing for me, I think. Mr. Wilby and I are buddies. I see him every day at six."

"Right." I blow out a breath. "Maybe he didn't see anything."

Wesley shakes his head, amused. "Even if he didn't, I'm sure he can figure it out. I'm sure it was written all over my face."

"Yeah? What do you think was written there?" I know I'm pushing it, and I normally wouldn't be this brave, but I feel reckless and full of adrenaline in a way that feels so unfamiliar to me.

"Oh, I don't know. Probably something along the lines of, 'I just kissed possibly the smartest, cutest girl I know and am trying my hardest to act cool about it.'" He pretends to ponder for a moment and then adds, "Or maybe it said, 'Thank God this girl kisses better than she cooks.'"

I shove his shoulder as he laughs. We make it back to the parking lot and I move toward my car. Although I often drive him to my home or to other places to hang out, he never lets me drive him home. Instead, he insists on walking. When we get to the driver's door, I turn to him and say, "So you're coming to the party with me, right?"

He digs his hands into his pockets and nods. "As long as I can find my black turtleneck."

I frown. "Even if you don't."

"Fine. Even if I don't."

"Do you want me to give you a ride?" I ask. Jess's Halloween party is always very clean fun. There's no alcohol at the actual event, and although there will be a portion of my class that does, I don't plan on drinking anything beforehand.

He shakes his head. "That's okay."

"Are you sure? I don't mind," I insist. Mainly, I worry about walking into Jess's party alone, instead of with Kareena and Meredith as usual.

"There's no need."

"You're going to walk?"

"Yeah."

"Don't be ridiculous."

"We're neighbors."

I pause. "What?"

"Jess lives in my neighborhood. I'll walk. Don't worry." He looks uncomfortable as he says it. I guess I've known that Jess has a lot of money, and that Wesley does, too, so maybe it shouldn't be such a surprise that he lives near her. But the idea of Wesley alone in a big mansion feels like an unexpected addition to my image of him.

I slowly nod. "Okay. Well. I guess I'll text you when I get there?"

He gives me a small smile. "I'll see you soon. Do you prefer being addressed as Mr. Johnson or The Rock?"

"It's up to you, Steve."

He turns to start walking home and I watch his retreating figure for a second or two before I open my car door. I'm just about to get into my car when I hear footsteps running behind me.

When I turn around, Wesley is there. He wastes no time wrapping his arms around my waist and instantly, his face is so close to mine that we are sharing the same breath. He leans down, presses me gently against the car, and kisses me briefly before pulling away. "Sorry," he says with a devilish grin. "I couldn't stop thinking about it."

I reach up to move the hair—his damn shampoo-commercial hair—out of his eyes. The intimacy of it thrills me, but I try my best to seem nonchalant. "Don't miss me too much. The party starts at eight." Then I slide into my car seat and wave at him through the window. He stands there, shaking his head, laughing, and I laugh, too.

On the drive home, I realize he's right. I can't stop thinking about him either.

Chapter 18

At home, it feels more like a countdown until I get to see Wesley again. Now that I've let myself acknowledge the idea of liking him, it seems to be the only thing my mind wants to spend time on. The floodgates have been opened and the waters are misbehaving treacherously from their pent-up rebellion. I try to force myself to do homework because I don't need extra preparation time just to pull on a turtleneck, but my mind keeps wandering. I pull up my personal statement for college applications, but there is no chance of me being productive when I feel this way. I can't pin down an example of conflict or struggle or overcoming when my whole world feels like it's just now coming alive.

Giving up on the essay, I go downstairs and barely register the piano playing from the lesson room. My mom has been growing her student base this past month. She must have tapped into some kind of Asian-mom friend group, because half a dozen kids signed up within the span of two weeks. Even though she's been busy, she still keeps her Tuesday evening slot open for me and Wesley.

If it were April, I would have told my mom immediately. I'm sure I would've disintegrated into awkwardness saying the word *kiss* out loud, but prior to the summer, I couldn't have imagined not sharing something like this with my mom. The feeling in the pit of my stomach, in the center of my chest, in the tips of my fingers— it's all so overwhelming, it feels like an anatomical part of me. I would've had to tell her.

But it's not April. My mother doesn't even know anything about what my life has been like this semester. It would be too much to fill her in on, and she wouldn't remember it anyway.

My mother's last piano lesson for the day ends, just as I'm traipsing down the staircase in my low-effort costume. She sees me and raises her eyebrows.

"What?" I ask, suddenly self-conscious.

"You look very excited. Are you going somewhere?"

I try to resist looking sheepish. It's clear that this new feeling is written all over my face, even when I'm unaware of it. "I'm going to Jess's Halloween party," I answer.

She nods in understanding. "What is your costume?"

"Steve Jobs," I say. Technically, I'm The Rock and Wesley is Steve Jobs, but I don't think my mother knows who The Rock is, and I don't feel compelled to explain.

She tilts her head. "Are Kareena and Meredith going as Steve Jobs, too? What is the group theme?"

My mother has photos on her phone from every Halloween of recent memory. She always asks me to send a photo of Kareena, Meredith, and me in our group costumes so she can save it, so I know she's expecting a similar thing this year. But I'm annoyed by her questioning. She hasn't been aware of any part of my semester so far, and this is the time she's trying to trial her curiosity?

"We're not doing a group costume," I say sharply.

Surprise crosses her face. "Why not? It's tradition, I thought."

I roll my eyes. "Kareena and Meredith didn't really want to do it this year, I guess. They're busy." I don't know why I'm defending them. It feels too embarrassing to say that my best friends don't want to hang out with me as much anymore. And now really doesn't feel like the right time to tell her about kissing Wesley either.

My mom's eyes look surprisingly serious. "Yeji-yah, good friends are very important in your life, okay? You don't need to have a million of them, but the ones you do have, you need to keep."

"Eomma!" The indignation in my tone verges on hostility. "Stop pretending you know what's going on. You don't. You haven't in a long time."

She frowns at me, disappointment etched across her brow. She switches to English to say, "Don't yell at me, Yeji. I am giving you advice."

"I don't need your advice," I snap. "I'm going to Jess's Halloween party. I'll be home later." I grab my keys and head to the garage. I hate being angry with my mother, especially because I feel like we haven't had an actual fight since I was in middle school, but it feels so unfair. Once I'm in the driver's seat, I put my head on my steering wheel and I'm horrified by the threat of tears trying to leak out. My mom's questions are piercing right through the chinks of my mind's armor, taking me down paths I've tried to ignore the whole time.

When did Kareena and Meredith decide I wasn't worth their time anymore? Why did it take until now for me to name how I've been feeling—like I've been left behind?

And what gives my mom the nerve to think she knows best when she can barely even remember that I'm graduating this year? She thinks life paused in the summer and wants to come after me for having let things change? She's trying to make an argument without having done the reading.

I blow out a noisy breath and brush away any stray tears. Thank goodness The Rock is a minimal-makeup costume. I pull out of my garage and drive to Jess's house.

When I get there, cars line either side of the street for the entire block. It's only twenty minutes after eight o'clock, but it's already hard to find parking. This is why Kareena, Meredith, and I would always take one car. I see Kareena's blue Volkswagen parked closest to the door. She must've been here early to help set up. I park a street over and text Wesley, letting him know that I'm here.

By the time I make it to the walkway up to Jess's entrance, Wesley is there waiting for me. He's dressed in a black turtleneck, faded blue jeans, and even has on a pair of round-rimmed glasses.

"Oh my God. Did you really go out and buy glasses for this look?"

He shakes his head. "These are literally my glasses. I just wear contacts to school." He hands them over to me and when I peer through them, all I see is a heavy blur.

"Holy shit, Wesley."

"I know—very shocking that someone with corrective glasses would actually have poor vision. In other news, water is wet," he says, putting his glasses back on.

"They look really good on you, actually," I say.

"Don't flatter me, Mr. Johnson," he says, reaching for the heavy silver chain around my neck. The way he does it so casually is a reminder that it's everything but.

"All right, Steve. Shall we go in?"

"You sure I'm invited?"

"Of course." I'm about to begin walking when I turn to him, suddenly curious. "Which one is your house, by the way?"

"Agh. Promise you won't hate me?"

"Bold of you to assume I don't already," I say, putting up my burnt hand, which has started to form the gentle bubbles of blisters along two of the fingers.

He points to an expansive, gorgeous home three doors down from Jess's place. "That one. The Ruengsomboon residence. Pretty sure we're the only Asian family in the whole neighborhood."

"Well. I guess it's time you finally met one of your neighbors, then."

When we walk in, my first impression is that Jess has absolutely lost her mind. Her family is the type to go all out for any event they host, but the fact that this is our senior year and the last time she's holding this annual party must have motivated her to kick it up exponentially. Flashing lights are hung up everywhere in the form of neon spiders and cute ghosts. Immediately to the right are several tables with elaborate cupcake stands, each topped with intricate designs. One has skulls made from edible pearls. Another has glossy bats made from burnt sugar. I know that after our chocolate chip cookies today, Wesley is appreciating the dessert the way I am.

There's a caramel apple dipping station with an assortment of toppings. Hired staff work behind the bar, making a special menu of Halloween-inspired milkshakes. If it's like the previous years, the backyard has been turned into a temporary dance floor with a professional DJ curating the playlist and a line of photo booths around the edge of the pool.

"I'm assuming your house looks exactly like this," I say to Wesley.

"Down to the portraits of a white family hanging above the fireplace."

We navigate ourselves through the bustling party. I stop and say hi to people I know from class or from my student organizations. I find my Science Bowl teammates at a table playing one of the dozen available board games. One of them invites me to join their game, but I just wave and continue walking with Wesley.

"It's crazy that there are so many people from our school I don't know," he says as we finally move toward the back of the house.

I nod. "I mean, we didn't know each other until this semester. We wouldn't have ever met if my schedule worked out the way I wanted it to." I pause for a second and I can't believe I've never thought to ask this. I turn to him. "Who are your best friends?"

He looks caught off guard. "My best friends?"

"Yeah. I only ever see you when it's just the two of us, you know? Or the two of us and my mom. Who do you usually hang out with?" It seems strange to me that this isn't something I've asked before. Just because Kareena and Meredith have been relatively absent from my life this semester doesn't mean that's the norm for other people.

Wesley shrugs, and part of me regrets asking the question when I see how uncomfortable he looks. "There are guys I hang out with in my classes and at lunch. Sometimes, we'll play basketball together on the weekends. But I guess . . . I guess I never want people to get to know me too well."

I feel my eyebrows knit together. "What does that mean?"

He sighs and throws his hands up around him. "I don't want my friends to come over and see something like this, you know? I just want to be seen as . . . whoever I am when I'm separated from my family, if that makes sense." It does a little bit. The wealth and extravagance of the Archibalds—and likely, the other families on this street—is still an anomaly, even among my friends.

"That's not really fair," I say. "You're not even giving your friends the choice."

"And I don't want them to meet my mom. She would judge them, ask them about their career plans, and make them feel shitty no matter how they answer. I want to spare them from that." Then he changes his tone. "What about your friends? Why don't you let me meet them?" Under the accusatory words, almost undetectable, is the barest suggestion of hurt. I hear the hidden question: *Why don't you want them to meet me?*

"Let's go find them," I decide, and I grab his hand, leading him outside to the backyard. He holds mine in return.

The dance floor is covered in glow-in-the-dark Halloween stickers. String lights in the shape of pumpkins weave themselves through the air. I see Meredith dressed as a breathtaking Daenerys, dancing in a circle of her mock trial team. I lead Wesley over to her. When she sees me, she breaks from the group and gives me a wide grin. Whichever wig she ended up choosing, it looks incredible even up close.

"Meredith, you look stunning!" I say as we wrap each other in a hug.

"Thank you! It's an honor to meet you . . . The Rock?" she guesses.

"The pleasure's all mine, Khaleesi. I want you to meet someone," I say, turning to Wesley. "This is Wesley. Wesley, this is my friend Meredith."

Meredith reaches out her hand. "Good to meet you, Wesley."

"Same to you," Wesley says, giving her a charming smile. I wonder if he knows how great his smile is, or if he's aware of how his chestnut eyes crinkle at the corners.

"Are you Steve Jobs?" she asks.

"You're unbelievable for guessing us both accurately," he says.

"It's the glasses. Good touch. So, Wesley, why haven't I seen you around before?" Meredith asks.

Wesley gives a noncommittal shrug. "I'm not in any AP classes."

"Not in any?" Meredith asks. There's no judgment in her tone, just curiosity, but that in itself feels offensive. It takes me back to the first day of Culinary Arts, when Wesley turned to me with the same shock after I said I didn't have any cooking experience.

I give her a pointed look. She notices.

"Well, I'm glad Eliza brought you," Meredith says. "Jess's parties are always a lot of fun. I'm trying to convince her to throw one for our entire graduating class. It would be chaotic, but go big or go home, right?"

If anyone could throw a party for an entire graduating class, it would be the Archibalds.

"Do you know where Kareena is?" I ask.

Meredith's expression remains composed, but there's something practiced about the way she looks puzzled. "I'm not sure. I think she went to help Jess with some emergency?"

"It is a big event," I agree. "Maybe I'll find her eventually."

Meredith nods eagerly. "There's plenty to do! Y'all should find an activity station you like. I think Jess said there are at least a dozen this year. And in case you were wondering, they did find a big enough cauldron!" She points to a corner in the backyard where a giant cauldron sits hanging above a firepit. A worker in uniform is stationed there, ladling cider into ceramic pumpkin mugs.

Wesley and I walk around the rest of the backyard. The light in the pool changes colors so that the water flashes between orange and purple. I stare at it, thinking about how Meredith reacted to me asking about Kareena. Did Kareena tell her that she wanted to avoid me at the party? Is that why she drove herself and decided against the group costume? Maybe instead of ending our friendship to my face, she's slowly pulling away and hoping I get the hint. My thoughts are interrupted when Wesley intentionally jostles my shoulder with his.

"Okay, why do I feel like every interaction I witness you having with your friends seems weird?" he says. "Am I allowed to say that?"

"I think so, too." The words come out like a murmur.

"Hey," Wesley says, trying to get me to look at him. When I do, he flashes me a wide smile. "Come on, Dwayne. Let's see those pearls."

"I love it when men tell women to smile."

"Women? I'm sorry, Mr. Johnson, I thought this was a man-to-man conversation."

I reward his weak attempt at humor with a commensurate smile.

He laughs and swings his arm around my shoulders. He makes it seem so natural, but my blood warms instantly. "Why don't we check out one of the photo booths?"

The idea thaws my mood a little bit. There is something so earnest in his suggestion, like he genuinely wants a keepsake of the night. He leads me to one of the three photo booths that sit on the perimeter of the orange-then-purple pool. Wesley reaches for the curtain and pulls it open.

But two people sit inside it already. The photo booth light flashes as it captures a photo of two people kissing. One is dressed in a beautiful, shimmering sky-blue dress that poofs around her like a princess. I can only see the back of her head, but her blond hair is curled into perfect ringlets. The other girl is dressed in a witch's costume with a pointed black hat. I can vaguely see half of her face. Her skin is painted green.

It takes me that long to put the pieces together. It can't have been more than a second, but it feels like I've been staring at them for ages. It's like I've been studying a puzzle for so long, I've forgotten what the whole picture was supposed to be. Now I can suddenly remember.

"Oh my God," I say. At least, I think I must have said it, because Kareena and Jess pull apart and look up at me. Their faces hold twin expressions, reflecting shock, maybe a little bit of horror. I don't feel in control of my words or my expression. Whatever is written on my face must be plainly legible.

"We're so sorry!" Wesley exclaims immediately, quickly pulling the curtain closed again. I hear the two girls scramble inside the booth. "Come on, Eliza." He grabs my hand and pulls me into the next photo booth, which is thankfully open.

"Holy shit," I whisper.

"That was Jess, wasn't it?" he asks. "I didn't get a good look at her, but I think I could recognize her."

I nod. "Yeah. Galinda."

"What?" he asks.

"She's dressed as Galinda the Good Witch. From *Wicked*."

He nods, trying to understand. It's obvious he has no idea who the characters of *Wicked* are. "And her girlfriend?"

"Elphaba," I say. I sound numb to my own ears.

My mind reels so fast, there are only incomprehensible suggestions of thoughts. I can't believe Kareena would keep something like this from me. How long has she known, and how long ago did she decide not to tell me? I think about Meredith's behavior, her shifting expressions and the feeling like she knew more than she chose to say. The one day during lunchtime when Meredith asked me about Wesley comes racing back. Meredith looked at Kareena with sharp eyes and said, *It's unfair of us to pry if you don't want to tell us. Isn't that right, Kareena?*

Meredith has known this whole time about Kareena and Jess.

I'm the one they didn't want to tell.

In some way, I feel validated that my instincts were correct this whole time. My best friends didn't want me to know, and I consequently wasn't allowed in their space. But what eclipses that validation by tenfold is the undeniable feeling of hurt. What did I do to lose someone's trust like this? What about me gave the impression that I wouldn't love my friends fully for who they are? The hurt and anger meld together into venomous heat.

Wesley stares at me. "Eliza, are you okay?" His eyes are concerned, but noticeably confused. I'm unraveling in front of him and he has no idea why.

I give him a weak nod. My head feels too heavy on my neck. "Yeah. I just . . . I'm really—"

I'm cut off by the curtain of our photo booth opening. Wesley jumps in his seat and we both turn to see Kareena standing at the entrance of our booth. Her face looks distraught, her knuckles pale from grabbing the curtain so tightly.

"Eliza, we need to talk."

I say nothing, unable to streamline my deluge of warring feelings into anything verbal. Wesley anxiously looks at me to respond, but I can't.

Kareena pleads, "Eliza, come on. Please. Let's talk inside."

"I feel like we've had months to talk," I say. It seems like my mouth has finally decided for my head which emotion to prioritize, and the anger has teeth. "We have almost every class together. We eat lunch together every day. That's a lot of time. But there hasn't been that much talking." Even as I say the words, I hate myself for it. It's so unfair of me to be acting this way. Wesley's expression remains confused, but there's the introduction of something else— discomfort. He doesn't like the iciness in my tone any more than I do.

Kareena looks wounded. "Don't be like this."

I narrow my eyes. "I'm sorry for interrupting your photo booth. But it's a little mean to do the same to me in return." I pointedly look at her hand holding open the curtain. Then I notice Jess waiting a few steps behind Kareena, looking just as anxious as when I saw her in the parking lot sophomore year.

Wesley speaks up. "We can take photos at a different time. It seems like you two need to discuss something."

Kareena shakes her head, forcing her smeared green mouth into a thin smile. "No, it's fine. It's my fault for interrupting." She tries to meet my eyes, but I look straight ahead at the photo booth screen. Our shields are up. It's the only way we know how to be. She takes in a breath like she's about to say something, but instead she only says, "Enjoy," and shuts the curtain.

Wesley looks at me and holds my hand in his. "Eliza, what's going on?"

"Nothing important," I say.

"You're crying."

"I'm not." But I swipe my eyes and find them wet.

He pulls me into a warm hug, our black sleeves overlapping, and I feel so safe in his arms that the tears come out faster. "Eliza," he says into my ear, stroking my hair. "Whatever's going on, it's okay." He presses me tighter into him, lets me wet his sweater with my wretched tears. He says, "We probably don't want to take a photo, huh?"

I laugh and it sounds so wet, I would be embarrassed if he didn't laugh, too. "I'm sorry, Wesley. Really sorry. I forced you to come to this mess with me because I'm selfish."

He unwraps his arms from around me, brushes away a tear with the soft pad of his thumb, and gently presses his lips against my forehead. "How about we try those desserts? They looked immaculate and I've been thinking about them all night." He gathers me in his arms and guides me inside to the dessert table. We split one of each of the different cupcakes and after each bite, he says, "Not as good as what we made today," even though they're probably some of the best cupcakes in the entirety of Texas.

But when I think about how we made something incredible, the thought is instantly replaced by how I've just made such an awful mess.

Chapter 19

The weekend following Jess's Halloween party, my phone blows up with texts from Kareena. She spams my name over and over again, every so often adding a Please, let's talk. After a day, she seems to enlist the help of Meredith. Meredith calls me to meet at our boba shop, but I decline, saying that I'm feeling sick and shouldn't be spreading it to the public.

"Eliza, cut the crap," Meredith says sternly over the phone. "You know we all need to talk about this."

"About the importance of public health? I agree. The norm should not be that sick people can travel wherever, spreading disease, if they know they're sick," I say. I throw in a big cough for show. "Sorry, my mom's calling me downstairs to take some medicine. See you." And then I hang up.

Wesley texts me to have a picnic in the park and I want to go. It's the first time he's ever asked me to do something outside school, a deliberate crossing of lines we've previously set, and the last thing I want to do is discourage him. But I feel so awful and my head pounds. My mom does not notice that I have my door closed all day, or if she does, she doesn't come knock. I don't want to hear what she would say anyway. I force myself to take a nap just so I can get rid of this constant headache, but when I wake up, it's still there. I also realize I never responded to Wesley. I send him an apologetic text and he tells me not to worry, that he played basketball with his friends instead.

No matter how much I want to avoid talking to Kareena, I am too much of a rule follower to not go to school when Monday rolls back around. I purposefully slide into homeroom the second that the bell rings, so that I can directly take my seat and listen to announcements.

Kareena turns so that her entire body is facing me, but I sit straight and look ahead, like a model student.

Once the announcements are over, Kareena says, "Eliza, come on. You can't ignore me. We have almost the exact same schedule."

I look at her, purposefully boring straight into her eyes, taking effortful measures to keep my expression serene. "I'm not ignoring you. I just don't have anything to say. I'm sure you understand."

Kareena sighs and leans back against her seat. She looks drained.

Meredith turns to me with a pleading look. "Eliza, nobody meant to hurt you."

"Well, it's a good thing I'm not hurt, then," I say. I don't know what possesses me to say such pathetic things. I feel like I've been forced into role-playing the cool, unaffected girl. The dialogue has been written out for me, and I'm merely following the script.

"That's bullshit," Meredith says. "Why can't you be honest?"

I raise my eyebrows in disbelief. I almost curse myself for breaking my blank expression—surely this is not what the cool girl does. But it's too late now. Emotions I've tried to hold at bay creep back in. "You're talking to me about honesty."

Anger clouds Kareena's face. "Eliza, I know you're upset. But it's not fair to demand access to something that's private." Her voice trails off into a whisper at the end of the sentence as she realizes people in our homeroom are paying attention.

"When did I do that?" I say, my voice steely.

"Maybe not explicitly," Kareena argues. "But it's in your attitude, and in your body language. The way you're quick to bite back when you feel like you've been shut out."

I want to give her a withering glare, but instead, I force myself to give her a small smile. "Am I biting back or am I closed off? Which is it?"

Kareena's face contorts in swallowed anger. She clearly wants to say something, but the bell rings. It's our vicious cycle—not saying the things we want to say. Resenting each other for it. When did we forget how to actually talk to each other?

Although we have all our classes together until eighth period, it's still a relief to be able to simply sit and listen to a teacher's lecture without worrying about having to combat anything else.

For some reason, the feeling of guilt finds a home on top of my chest and settles there like a weight. I keep wondering if I'm the one pushing away my friends. Should I have said something earlier, about how I hated feeling like I was being left behind? Or should I have pushed harder for Kareena to doubt Jess's intentions? Was it really so wrong of me to want to protect Kareena from someone who was stealing answers from her?

The thought causes the image of Jess to flash in my mind. Precalculus. The desperation in her eyes, the fear and silent pleas written across her face. The mango cheesecake. The Halloween party. The understanding settles over me like a gust of wind. When I had caught Jess staring at Kareena all those times sophomore year, she insisted she hadn't been cheating. . . .

God, I need to talk to Kareena. I'm being so unreasonable. If

Kareena wants to talk, shouldn't I be grateful to listen? When I map things out logically, the answer spells itself. But when I picture myself talking to Kareena, I can only see the unmistakable horror on her face when Wesley pulled open their photo booth curtain. Like the idea of me knowing about something so personal was a nightmare of hers. I was her Halloween monster, someone demanding to see the most private parts of her, interrupting what should have been a cherished moment with my perverse sense of entitlement. Suddenly, it's getting more and more difficult to delineate who I'm actually upset with.

I'm reminded of the summertime when my grandmother passed away. My mother was still in South Korea then, but I had come back after the funeral. When I told Kareena I had made it back home, she picked me up from my house and drove me to hers. She emptied two pints of my favorite ice cream—Ben & Jerry's Chocolate Therapy—into a bowl and turned on *13 Going on 30*, a movie we had seen together for the first time when we were thirteen and had watched every year since.

"Kareena, you don't need to do this. I'm not grieving," I remember saying with a giant bowl of ice cream chilling the inside of my thighs.

"That's okay. You don't need a reason for ice cream and movies," she responded, turning up the volume on the film.

"No, you don't get it. I'm not numb. I'm not repressing anything. I just genuinely am not grieving."

"And like I said, that's okay."

Frustrated, I reached for the remote and put the film on pause. My body has the bad habit of producing tears in response to anger, as if anger alone isn't enough punishment. "Kareena. I'm serious. I feel like such a shitty person."

She turned her entire body toward me to tell me she was listening. "Why?"

"Because I don't feel anything! And not in the way where I know it's going to hit me later. I just . . . don't feel that affected by own grandmother's death. Doesn't that sound criminal? I sound like the world's greatest asshole!" Someone of my own blood, who gave birth to and raised possibly my favorite person in the world, was no longer alive, and when I found out, I hadn't mustered even a single tear.

Kareena began braiding her long hair, which she did often when she was concentrating. "You can't guilt yourself into feeling something."

"How do I not feel anything? She was literally my family," I said. The words came out strained. I felt so embarrassed saying them out loud.

"My parents moved here after they got their MDs," she said. "They go back to India twice a year. Sometimes I go with them. But it's different there, different expectations, different behaviors. Suddenly, there are servants moving around you. You eat your meals at different times. You don't say the things you want to say because you know it wouldn't be allowed. You don't let yourself be who you really are." Kareena had finished her braid. She unraveled it with her fingers before starting over again. "The world our parents came from is not home to us. You can't blame yourself for not missing something you never really knew."

"But I can," I said. "I do."

She shook her head. "This is part of the sacrifice our parents made when they came here. There's a reason that, historically, the ocean was enough to define old versus new worlds. It's not an easy thing to traverse. Sometimes, the people an ocean away are really only family by name. Your parents know this, and I know you do, too. So be gentle with yourself."

"You have family here" was how I replied.

Kareena furrowed her brow. "What?"

"You have uncles and aunts here in Texas. In Round Rock and in Houston and in Dallas. They're not all an ocean away."

Kareena's frown deepened. "Do you think I can't relate? Because I have relatives in the state?"

"I just think—I'm telling you something I feel so ashamed of and you're telling me something that's simply factual. They're not the same, Kareena. I have this disgusting guilt eating away at me and you have what?"

"I don't think empathy is about needing all the details to align. You're not the only person who has ever felt guilt or shame, Eliza. I say that to be comforting, not selfish. I'm sorry if it didn't come across that way." She looked like she wanted to continue, but chose to cut herself off.

I shook my head. "Forget it. I don't know what I'm saying."

We sat in silence for a long stretch of time, the guilt still pressing on my chest. Kareena let me sit there without saying anything. She didn't reach for the remote to continue the movie. She just stayed there, perched on the couch, braiding and rebraiding her hair. The ice cream melted in its bowl while we sat, both with so much to say but neither of us wanting to share anything else.

Thinking of this now makes me feel nauseous with guilt. Kareena had been trying to relate to make me feel less alone, had tried to keep the vulnerability open as a two-way street, and I had further isolated myself. Maybe I was the one who continuously put my walls up. Maybe I couldn't blame Kareena for giving up on waiting for them to fall.

During lunch, I don't go to Señora Molina's room. Instead, I head to the cafeteria, which I haven't actually seen during lunchtime in ages. I forgot people actually ate here. I slowly walk through the rows of long tables, painted blue and white like our school colors, and am about to sit with my Science Bowl teammates when I spot Wesley's tall head. He's sitting with a group of guys I've never seen before. Again, I'm struck by how strange it is that we don't know each other's friends despite having hung out for so long.

Wesley looks up when I walk toward him and his face breaks into a wide grin. My own smile reflects his like instinct. Maybe something about mirror neurons. I make a mental note to catch up with my Science Bowl studying.

He scoots over to make room for me on his bench. "Hi, Eliza. What brings you here?"

His friends all look at me with shy smiles, their eyes flickering back and forth between Wesley and me, like they're calculating the space—or lack thereof—between our shoulders.

One of them with curly red hair and freckles dusted all over his skin gives me a friendly smile. "Hey, I'm Joshua."

"Eliza," I say.

The rest of Wesley's friends introduce themselves, too. I don't manage to remember all their names, but I know the boy with the Afro is Michael and one of the white boys is Patrick.

"We didn't know Wes knew girls," Michael says. He shoots me a grin and his teeth are so straight, it's like I'm watching an orthodontics ad.

"Just the one," Wesley says good-naturedly.

"I didn't know Wesley had friends," I say.

Patrick snorts. "That tracks. He keeps turning us down. Now it all makes sense."

Lunch passes quickly as we eat and the boys take turns at trying to share embarrassing stories of Wesley to make me change my mind about him. Wesley takes it all in stride, laughing along with his friends, sometimes throwing in his own details. Michael recognizes my name from the Student Council emails and asks if it's too late to join. I tell him it's not and jot down his email in my phone to add him to the LISTSERV.

Spending lunch with Wesley's friends reminds me of what a normal friend group is like. Everyone is open. No one skirts about sensitive topics. It's nice.

When the lunch bell rings, Michael asks me if I'll be sitting with them again. He frames it as an offer, and this alone makes me feel a pang deep in my gut. I tell him that I would love to. I'm sad to say goodbye to Wesley and scared to go back to class with Kareena, so he walks me to my classroom, even though it's on the top floor and his is on the first. He leans forward to kiss my forehead before leaving to get to his next class. When he's no longer in front of me, I see Kareena and Meredith walking toward our classroom. Without saying anything, I enter the room and take the last available seat in the first row so that I don't have to sit next to them.

I know then that this is going to be a pattern. The girls are no longer the girls, the group chat name will stay stagnant, and I can't go back to how things were.

Chapter 20

It's amazing what a few weeks of intense studying can do.

Halfway through November, Wesley comes up to me in eighth period and shows me the results of his most recent precalculus exam. At the top of the page is an eighty-six circled in red pen with a smiley face drawn beside it.

"Holy shit, Wesley! That's amazing!" I exclaim.

"I credit this to two things," he says. "Number one, obviously there's this smart girl who's been helping me out a lot."

"Oh yeah? Can you introduce me?"

"Second is the passion fruit–Thai milk tea boba drink. When I'm taking an exam, I daydream about it and tell myself it'll be my reward if I can get through the rest of the problems. But now that I think about it, that's actually related to number one as well."

He wraps me in a hug that only ends because Mr. Treviño clears his throat and tells us to sit down so he can start class.

My Culinary Arts grade has also gotten substantially better since cooking with Wesley. Now that we're closer to the end of the semester, the majority of classwork has been kitchen lab work where we work at our stations and have to perform our hands-on technique. To my surprise, I am not obviously the worst student in the class. In fact, last week, when Mr. Treviño came around to taste everyone's tomato soup, he spent an extra minute at my station.

I watched surprise spread across his face after tasting, followed by a short laugh. "Wow! There's a little spice there, huh?"

I nodded, suddenly nervous. I'd added slices of chili pepper before removing them from the final product. "Is it too much?"

Mr. Treviño shook his head. "I think it's refreshing."

I almost slumped against my countertop in relief.

He continued, "You've really come a long way, Eliza. I still remember you pouring a can of diced tomatoes over your pasta. And now you've made your own tomato soup. That's progress if I've ever seen it." He gave me a warm smile and I returned it happily. I can't deny how good it feels to get someone's approval.

Kareena hasn't wanted to speak with me since I ignored her texts, and I will admit that I've been too much of a coward to break the silence. Any time I think of texting her, I remember her horrified expression and delete the draft. If she's decided to close herself off from me, I should let her. Maybe that's better than having a best friend you can't have a real conversation with. Meredith, on the other hand, has been trying her best to stay neutral.

I mostly spend lunch with Wesley and his friends. They're all really funny. I find myself wishing that they were in my AP classes, just so I could see them more often. I learn that Joshua plays saxophone in the school band and usually advances to the All-State Band, which in Texas is close to being prodigiously good. Michael loves video games and is always asking the boys if they can call in the evening to play. Patrick is on the school basketball team, and both his older brothers also played basketball at Highland Hills before graduating. I'm not particularly partial to high school boys on principle, but Wesley's friends seem genuinely sweet. They tease each other mercilessly, but no one ever gets hurt.

As much as I like hanging out with Wesley's friends, sometimes it's nice to be together when it's just the two of us. Every so often, we'll spend lunch in the Culinary Arts kitchen instead, catching up on schoolwork. There are times I look over at him working and get overwhelmed by how cute he looks when he's concentrating. His hair gets intricately twisted by his left hand, his eyebrows knit together and fall back apart when he's figured something out, and he keeps his lips parted just the slightest bit. The last part is really when I can't help but lean over.

My mother has definitely noticed the change in our energy during our Tuesday afternoon cooking sessions. After last week, she finally said something about it to me. I had dropped Wesley off at his house—a victory conceded to me after the Halloween party—and come back home, ready to try to fruitlessly tackle my personal statement again, when she stopped me and asked me to sit down at the dining table.

"What's wrong?" I asked.

"Wesley is your boyfriend?" she said. She phrased it like a question, but her tone said she took it as the truth.

"Yeah," I said. "Kind of."

"You didn't think about telling me?"

"I wanted to," I insisted. "I guess I forgot." I didn't say what I was really thinking, which is that she never asked. I also didn't want this conversation to direct itself back to Kareena and Meredith. Given how awkward class was now, they took up enough space in my head without my mother talking about them, too.

"He's a good boy," she said. "But you should remember your friends, too." There it was.

I rolled my eyes. "Eomma, my friends aren't really my friends anymore."

She looked concerned, her lips pulled down at the corners.

"What do you mean? Did something happen?"

The idea of talking about someone's sexuality to my mother was exhausting in itself, even without taking into account that I shouldn't know about it to begin with. So I simply shrugged and said, "They found a new friend."

"And you can't be friends with that new person, too?"

"It's not really like that."

She clicked her tongue in disapproval. "That's not good. This is your last year together. You girls should be appreciating that."

"Okay. Well, if that's all you wanted to say, I have work to do." I stood up from the dining table and went upstairs to my room.

My mom is still as kind and warm as she normally is when I bring Wesley around for our Tuesday lessons. But when it's just the two of us, I know she wishes I would reach out to Kareena and Meredith. I wish I could explain to her this nebulous concept of dignity I seem to have, where it would kill me to reach out when I'm the one who was left behind in the first place. I want to tell her that friendship is only meaningful when there's mutual trust, which I thought I had when I apparently didn't, and I don't know how we can get that trust back if we've been closing it off for this long. I want to admit that maybe I don't want to explore how I'm feeling about Kareena because I'm scared of finding the parts where I went wrong. It seems easier to pretend that only I have been hurt.

But I don't have the words to properly explain it, and even if I did, I'm not sure that my mom would fully understand. She can't pick and choose which parts of my life to care about.

Wesley feels like a reprieve from the mess of emotions I don't particularly want to dissect. He invites me to his house for the first time one weekend. His father is away for a business trip. His mother is spending the day golfing with clients or lobbyists—I forget how Wesley described it.

"Don't freak about my parents not being home," he had said. "I don't want to suggest anything. I'm just saving you the trouble of meeting them."

There is something ironic about him wanting to make sure I never meet his parents while he comes to my house every week to cook with my mother. But then I think about how he invites me to lunch with his friends whereas I never reciprocate. It seems like we're each choosing our own battles to fight.

I drive to his house on Saturday around lunchtime. I park in his gorgeous half-moon driveway and for a second, I stay in the car just to admire the architecture of his house, although the word *house* doesn't seem like it's doing the residence justice. The symmetry of the windows gives me the impression that this is an old home. I'm sure many wealthy white families lived in it before the Ruengsom-boons purchased it.

When Wesley opens the door for me, I take in the stunning interior design. The coordination between all the furniture and decor is immaculate. It's obvious that it's been professionally designed. But there's also an emptiness to it, like the home could belong to anyone. At least Jess's place has expensive family portraits hanging on the walls. I can't see a reflection of Wesley's personality anywhere here.

"You have this entire place to yourself?" I ask.

"Creepy, right?" he says. He leads me to the kitchen, which is so spacious and well supplied, it could be a set from the Food Network. "I'm cashing in on my most basic roots today for lunch."

"What's that? Pad thai?" I guess.

"Tell me you like pad thai."

"Love it desperately. But I would eat anything you cooked, Wesley. I feel like you should know that by now."

"I can't pretend I'm surprised that you're a noods girl."

Wesley walks me through the laborious cooking process. We start with the sauce, which already seems difficult because he chops up a block of palm sugar and melts it until it turns dark. He actually started the cooking process before I even came, he tells me, because the noodles have to soak for an hour. The countertop is littered with dozens of bowls and we slowly fill them as we prep the rest of our ingredients. As I follow his instructions, we eventually have a wok full of beautiful pad thai.

"This looks incredible," I say, "but this is so much work. This might be the most intensive recipe we've ever done together." It wasn't what I was expecting from one of America's most common take-out dishes. "And there were so many ingredients."

Wesley nods. "Honestly, a lot of Asian dishes are like that. I saw this video of a woman making homemade pho the other day. . . . Took the whole day, at least. It's ingredients, it's time, it's a lot of things, and it's like they never really get their flowers, you know?"

I don't know that I'm completely following, but I nod anyway.

Wesley plates the pad thai. He adds a handful of bean sprouts on one side, then expertly slices a lime into wedges and adds one to each plate. I walk over and help him sprinkle crushed peanuts and scallions as garnishes. "I've been talking to Mr. Treviño about it, actually," Wesley says abruptly, the words tumbling out.

I raise my eyebrows, confused by his nervousness. "About Asian food?"

He nods. "I was talking to him about how the Culinary Arts kitchen isn't supplied with Asian ingredients, or any *ethnic* ingredients at all. How that might put some students at a disadvantage during the final cook-off. I also talked to him about revising the syllabus for next year. I think we're ignoring a lot of very cool culinary things by sticking with the canon. I think there's so much to learn from Asian food, and it kills me that it's usually just relegated to . . . takeout."

"Why are you afraid to tell me this?" I say.

He reaches up to rest his hand on the back of his neck. "I don't know. I didn't want you to think that I'm trying to get an upper hand or something."

"Wesley, that's ridiculous."

"Well, that's not all."

I blink. "Okay."

"I don't know if I can make it to your mom's cooking lessons anymore."

I breathe in sharply and it almost whistles. "Why?"

Wesley grimaces at my reaction. "When I asked Mr. Treviño about expanding the ingredients, he said he'd ask the school. He also asked if I could teach him how to use them."

"You're teaching our Culinary Arts teacher how to cook?"

"He just wants to see how I would use them," he says quickly. "He's trying to write up a report to justify the costs to the school district or something. I don't think it should take too long. And of course, after I'm done, I'll try and run over to your house afterward. But Tuesdays work best for him, and I figure I'm not in a position to argue, you know?"

I nod slowly. "Yeah. Okay."

"I'm sorry, Eliza. It's such an honor to come and cook with you and your mom. But he was impressed by us submitting our shakshuka picture as our tomato sauce assignment. He asked me if I had other ways we can flip the syllabus, and if Mr. Treviño is asking . . . I mean, wouldn't you do the same?" he asks.

Of course I would. No matter what Wesley has become to me, I still want to give my speech.

Wesley takes a breath and continues. "I should thank you. My grades have been going up ever since you started helping me. I was almost failing two of my classes, and my mom had to be called in to half a dozen parent-teacher conferences about my grades." His eyes look distant, like he's remembering conversations I can't hear.

I shouldn't be surprised. I've been actively watching his grades climb over the past month. It's been impressive.

And in return, I feel like I'm relatively competent in the kitchen. Mr. Treviño will linger by my workstation to dispense a compliment. It won't be easy to win the cook-off, but it's not entirely out of the question anymore. Wesley and I are both different students than we were at the start of the semester.

Wesley continues, "I mean, I still can't go to, like, UT Austin, but at least I'm not failing."

"UT Austin's hard to get into if you don't make the cutoff rank," I say. There's a law in place that UT Austin has to automatically accept the top six or so percent from all the Texas public high schools. Without that automatic acceptance, it's pretty competitive to get in.

Wesley narrows his eyes in frustration. "Exactly. It's never even been an option. But now that my grades are better, and especially if I have a shot at winning the GPA boost, then maybe I could get in *somewhere*." He pauses. Then he says, "But I know this isn't relatable for you. You must think it's pathetic. How someone who has *this*"—he gestures around to his large, empty home—"still has to try so hard just to do okay in school."

"Wesley, don't say that," I say.

"UT Austin is probably your last choice," he says. "And I can't even get in."

I don't say anything. I don't know what would be worse: to confirm the truth or to pretend to deny it and have him see through me. Quietly, I say, "You invited me to your house."

Wesley looks up in surprise. "Yeah."

"You said you don't even let your friends come to your house."

His voice drops to a whisper. "Yeah."

"Thank you," I say. There's barely enough sound to make out the words, so I clear my throat before I continue. "It means a lot. To me."

"To me, too," he says. "I have nothing to hide from you."

His voice is so sincere, it makes my face feel warm. But I can't help the way his words bring my thoughts back to Kareena, and I feel hurt all over again.

"Eliza," Wesley says. "I like you so much."

I meet his eyes. The color of roasted chestnuts, yet they somehow feel even warmer than that. I want to tell him that being around him is like having a balloon inflate in my chest or like a hummingbird in my throat, but it comes out as, "I like you, too."

"I'm sorry about Tuesdays. I promise, I'm still going to try and make it. And I'll make something for your mom to apologize. Let me know what kind of food is her favorite."

Wesley's expression is so earnest, it nearly winds me. It's a foreign feeling, to have someone be so openly caring. To have someone let you know their secrets, but more than that, to have someone *want* you to know their secrets. It comes with an inexpressible feeling of gratitude.

The least I can do is admit to myself that I'll be working just as hard for the final prize.

Chapter 21

The following Tuesday, the first day that Wesley won't be coming home with me to learn a Korean recipe from my mother, I drive home alone after school. I've been skipping the Honor Society meetings on Tuesday afternoons so that I don't have to see more of Kareena than I have to. Part of me wishes I had a different student org meeting to go to, just so I could pretend to ignore the increasing feeling of loneliness. I'm on my block, just about to turn the corner to eventually get to my garage, when I see a car parked out front.

A blue Volkswagen.

I slowly park behind it. The license plate is one I've seen a million times before.

Sitting on my porch are Kareena and Meredith. It's been longer than I realized since I've actually spent time with them, and I can't remember the last time I saw them outside class. Across their laps is a pale gold blanket. Kareena's jeans are visible through the big hole in the upper left corner.

"Hey," I say. "Why aren't y'all at the meeting?" I try to keep my voice neutral. A bare canvas for them to paint a conversation on.

Meredith looks at Kareena, waiting.

Kareena looks up at me, her eyes already shining. "I canceled it. Eliza, I really want to talk."

I take a seat on one of the porch chairs. "Okay."

Kareena looks around her at the open space, then throws a helpless glance at Meredith.

Meredith turns to me with a pleading expression. "Maybe somewhere private? Like your room?" she asks.

I get up and the girls follow me upstairs to my room. I close the door behind me and the three of us, on instinct, pile onto my bed, like we've done a million times over the years. Our bodies are still working off muscle memory, even though the tension in the room is foreign and awkward.

Kareena closes her eyes and starts undoing her braided hair. When she opens them, I realize she looks so tired. The bags under her eyes are ashen. "Eliza, I didn't know how to tell you."

"That you're dating Jess?" I ask.

"Yes. And no. I'm dating Jess. But even before that. I didn't know how to tell you that I'm bi," Kareena says. She says this while looking mainly at the gold blanket that we've spread across us. I can hear her trying to file down the tremble in her voice.

"Kareena," I say. "Did you think I'd judge you? When did I give the impression that that's something you can't trust me with?" I hear my voice start to shake, too. At first, I think it's from anger— a reminder that my body thinks tears and frustration go hand in hand. But then I realize that it is simply hurt. I feel so hurt.

Kareena shakes her head, her braid halfway redone. "I just didn't know how to say it. And I only told Meredith because . . . obviously, she would understand."

Meredith gives me a soft smile. "She had a lot of questions. Understandably. And of course, I wanted to listen and help her escape the prison of heterosexuality." She clearly is trying to lighten the mood, but I'm too adrift to recognize the cues to laugh.

"I don't care that you're bi," I say. "Well, I mean, I *care* because it's part of who you are, but I'm trying to say that it doesn't change anything about how I see you. I'm just . . . I feel like I lost your trust. I mean, I had to invade your space—accidentally—in order to find out. And I don't know what I did, where I went wrong. Which is probably frustrating for you to hear, but that's really what's been haunting me."

Kareena bites her lip. "It's hard to explain, Eliza, but sometimes it's like . . . we're ships in the night about some things. I say something and you misunderstand, or it's the other way around. And pointing that out feels like opening a door to a fight, which neither of us ever wants, so then it seems easier to just . . . keep the door closed."

I wish I didn't understand what she means, but I do.

"I would picture telling you about Jess, and I—I couldn't imagine a scenario in which there wouldn't be some misunderstanding. Someone would get angry, but we wouldn't name it for what it was. We would just skirt around what we wanted to say and neither of us would be happy."

"I'm sorry," I say.

Kareena tugs her braid so tight, I almost reach out to stop her. "I think part of me hoped you would know. I hoped you would be able to tell. And when I was pulling away, I wanted to know that you cared enough to actually ask me what was going on. But you didn't even try, Eliza!" The words sound like they're being scraped from her throat. "How am I supposed to trust you with something when it seems like you don't care enough to know it?" Her eyes glisten with unshed tears, and she almost looks angry with herself for crying. I have no doubt I'm reflecting the same expression.

"I didn't want to pry. Or come off as insecure and demand to be included in something if I met any amount of resistance!" I say. "But I am insecure, Kareena. You know that. And so I decided to be patient. I thought you would tell me if there was something worth knowing. But you didn't. And you only wanted to talk about it after I saw you two."

Kareena sighs. The breath whistles through her clenched jaw. "I wanted support. I asked Meredith because she knew what I was going through, and even that was hard for me. And I kept thinking, should I even have to ask? Shouldn't a real friend be able to support me without me saying it out loud?" A tear leaks from the corner of her eye and skates down her face with frightening speed. I watch it miss the gold blanket and drop onto my duvet.

And finally, I escape the constraints of my own thoughts.

I see an image of Kareena struggling with this part of herself, unfamiliar and scary. I imagine her reaching out to Meredith, who came out as lesbian before we even entered high school. I imagine her seeing her parents every day, wondering if they would accept her for who she was understanding herself to be. And I imagine her wanting to reach out to a best friend who's doing nothing but moving further away. Consumed with something as frivolous as her class rank and cheating allegations that weren't even true. Who would react poorly if she told me the truth or if she continued to hide it. There was no winning.

I see my mother, in her bed in the months after Halmeoni's passing. I see her staying alone and my dad and me interpreting this as a message to give her space, when what she really wanted was someone to share this horrible feeling with her. I think of my dad not even staying in his own bedroom anymore, of me unable to remember her mother the way she desperately wanted to. I see my mother, lonely, grieving, isolated, with a spouse who avoids her and a daughter who fights her.

And most surprising of all, I hear Mrs. Porter. *I am all too familiar with the fact that some students have a very hard time reaching out for help when they're going through difficult times. Especially our high achievers.* At the time, I resented that Mrs. Porter thought her words applied to me. I didn't have the insight to know when to apply them outside myself.

God, I've been so selfish.

I see more tears drop down onto my duvet. Mine this time. "Kareena, I'm sorry."

She doesn't say anything.

I continue. "I'm sorry I wasn't there for you. I should have been. You shouldn't have to ask me to notice when my best friend needs someone." I look up at her. She's blurred from my tears, but I can make out that her hair is once again unbraided. "And I'm sorry about Jess. *To* Jess. I get the feeling she wasn't staring at your exam, huh?" I force a weak laugh, but the sound sticks in my throat, slick with tears.

"I'm sorry, too," Kareena says quietly. "It must have felt awful for you to see us all hanging out without looping you in. That wasn't fair. And with what's going on with your mom, too . . . I know it's been a hard semester and I'm sorry I haven't been here for you."

"Please don't apologize," I say. "I don't deserve it. I'm ready to act like a friend, and I mean it. Talking honestly, actually confronting our misunderstanding. Letting ourselves be open again."

"I know I hurt you by keeping it from you. I'm sorry." Her words are a tired whisper.

I don't know how to articulate that I understand, that I don't need to hear her apologies at all. The hot burning feeling of shame spreads in the deepest part of my stomach. I spent so much time making things about me—Jess's relationship to me, Kareena's trust with me—all in service of ignoring Kareena's pain.

Meredith says softly, "We miss you at lunch. You never eat with us anymore."

"Yeah, that's my fault," I say. "I thought you didn't want me there."

"It's not as fun when it's just me and Kareena. She doesn't laugh at my jokes," Meredith says, bumping her pale knee against Kareena's brown one.

I snort. "Yeah, but I don't think that's a Kareena problem."

"See?" Meredith says. "I missed this! God, I thought you two were never going to figure things out!"

Kareena rolls her eyes. "That's because you insisted on being Switzerland instead of actually doing anything."

"You say that like it wasn't my idea to drag you here! And for the record, the picnic blanket? My idea, too. I'm a fucking poet, you guys," Meredith says, flicking her faded blue hair. "Besides, if nearly four years of mock trial have taught me anything, it's that I have no interest in getting involved in fights that aren't my own."

"That's a bad take," I say.

"I agree," Kareena says.

"Okay, I'm clearly getting outnumbered," Meredith says. "This. This feels normal again."

Later that evening, my mother teaches me how to make budae jji-gae, which is a stew traditionally associated with the army, as *budae* means army base. It's the first time in a while that the lesson has just been the two of us. When I tell her that Wesley probably won't be joining us anymore, she looks stricken. "Did you two break up?" she asks.

"No," I say. "He just has something else to do on Tuesdays."

She gives me a cautious look, like she wants to make sure I'm not concealing a secret heartbreak from her. "I saw Kareena's car outside earlier today."

I nod. "Yeah. She came with Meredith. We all hung out."

She studies me carefully with that same watchful expression. "Friends are good after a breakup."

"Eomma!" I say with a laugh. "Wesley and I didn't break up!"

She seems to finally believe me because she gives me a nod. "Okay, good. Because that boy was a very good cook."

"That's what makes a good boyfriend?"

"It certainly helps."

"Appa never cooks," I point out.

"He used to. Actually, this recipe we're doing today is from him. Your halmeoni never made budae jjigae because you know how she would never want to eat processed food. But your dad ate it a lot when he went to gundae and he made it for me when he came back. That's when I thought I might fall in love with him."

"It was that good?" I ask in disbelief.

She chuckles to herself. "No, it wasn't very good at all. But he tried so hard when making it, wanting me to like it. He was putting on a whole show. I thought it was so sweet that he cooked, no matter how it tasted. Plus, not seeing him when he was gone for gundae made me figure out how I was feeling. I had never been in love before."

Gundae is the compulsory military service for South Korean men. Every Korean man is required to enlist in the military for two years before they turn thirty. As my mom and I make budae jjigae, she explains that after the Korean War, South Korea was in a state of desperate poverty. Kids at her school would be given American processed food so that they wouldn't go hungry. The military wasn't in any better shape. Using what was cheap and available, soldiers would make an easy stew with Spam and sausages and ramen noodles.

My mom must have tweaked my dad's recipe, because the one she teaches me to make is worth ordering at a restaurant. The stew is spicy and salty and probably so bad for me, but my mom and I eat it all anyway. Even burning my tongue with the soup does little to deter me.

"When your dad was in gundae," my mother continues, "I spent a lot of time with my friends. And even though they live in Korea and I live here, we're still best friends. That's special. Really, really special. Do you understand me, Yeji?"

I nod. "Yes, I do."

My phone lights up with a text at that moment. It's from Wesley. Sorry, he writes. Mr. Treviño is a huge talker. Tell your eomma I'm so sorry I missed the lesson. And I miss you even more.

I text him back, saying everything's fine. I add a smiley emoji so he knows I mean it.

"Are you texting Wesley?" my mom asks.

I immediately slide my phone into my back pocket. "Maybe."

"He seems like a good boy. What does he want to do?"

"What do you mean? Like, as a career?" I say.

She nods, slurping up a chopstick full of spicy noodles.

"I'm not sure, actually." I realize I've never asked. Wesley has never asked me either.

"What about his parents?"

"His mom's an attorney. His dad does something in finance. Consulting, I think."

"I don't know what that is."

"Me neither."

"What about you, Yeji-yah? Do you know what you want to do?"

"Computer science," I say automatically.

"Still?" she asks.

I nod. And then I stop. "Well, I don't know. Maybe I'd want to add something else, too. Something totally new, totally different. Like cooking was for me."

My mom puts down her chopsticks, balancing them across her bowl. "Yeji-yah, I had my entire life planned out when I was your age. It involved a bachelor's degree and a career that used that degree. It involved living in the country I was born in. Do you think that really mattered?"

"What are you saying?"

My mom shrugs and picks her chopsticks back up. "You can plan if you want. That will make you feel more comfortable. But unexpected and new things will always happen, too, and when they do, you have to believe that you will make things okay." Her expression gives me the impression that she is partially talking to herself. Halmeoni's death was sudden, unanticipated. Maybe my mom feels like it's up to her whether she makes it through the grief. Maybe when she's finding these words to say to me, she's also trying to convince herself.

I think of how every time I've messed up in the kitchen, my

mom or Wesley were always there to fix it. How making that mistake then meant that I tried harder not to repeat it next time. How some mistakes were small enough that when you tasted the end product, it was like it never happened. Maybe there was something to be said about letting go of the reins and knowing you would end up okay anyway.

I pull out my phone and reread the last text I've sent to Wesley. Everything's fine.

Maybe I can start believing that's true.

Chapter 22

Thanksgiving approaches faster than it has any right to. Every fall, Thanksgiving break signifies the beginning of the end, the sharp transition from practice to game time. As a student, you know that when you come back from Thanksgiving, it's a marathon to the end of midterm season. It's an important break because it's your last chance to breathe.

Highland Hills begins Thanksgiving break on Wednesday instead of Monday like the other schools in the city. It's some drawn-out logic to allow our winter break to be four weeks. They say that it's for some supposed administrative purposes, but Kareena, Meredith, and I have always thought it's because Highland Hills parents want to spend at least three full weeks skiing at their second homes in Lake Tahoe or Vail.

The Tuesday before Thanksgiving is our last day before our small break, so there's no Honor Society meeting. The girls come over to my house after school. We pile onto my bed, a mirror image of a week ago. Music plays softly over my Bluetooth speaker, and class folders are spread across the duvet in the false hope that we might be productive and do some homework.

"So how long have you and Jess been dating?" I ask.

"We've been, like, actually dating for a couple of months, I guess. Neither of us is out to our parents, so it's nothing, you know, public," Kareena says. "We had the same volunteer shifts at the hospital over the summer, so we spent a lot of time together. We got along really well, but I think it was watching how she was with patients. . . ." Kareena's cheeks redden noticeably. "You ever see someone so good at what they do, that it's like you're discovering beauty where you didn't see it before?"

"Oh my God," I say, bumping her knee with mine. "*Discovering beauty where you didn't see it before?* Rupi Kaur, are you in there?"

"Oh, so now all brown people look the same, huh?" Kareena laughs.

"Can we talk about the part where Jess just so happened to have a crush on Kareena for years already?" Meredith adds. "Like, this is meta-poetry."

Kareena's blush deepens. "She admitted to me that she had started liking me midway through freshman year. She said she spent the whole semester trying to figure out if she wanted to be me or be *with* me."

"Are you planning on coming out to your parents? Or are you going to escape to college?" I ask.

Kareena braids her hair. "I'm not sure yet. I don't think my parents would handle it really well."

Meredith doesn't say anything. Her parents have been vocal about their support. Since Meredith came out, they've marched together in Austin's Pride parade every year.

"Can we talk about you?" Kareena says. She takes her phone and it's a testament to how much time she's spent here that she easily connects to my Bluetooth speaker. The room fills with the sound of her favorite psychedelic rock band.

"What about me?" I ask.

Kareena rolls her eyes, throwing her braid over her shoulder. "Come on, Eliza. I'm not the only one who was in a photo booth with someone on Halloween."

Meredith hums in excitement. "Wow, Eliza. Sounds like someone's been keeping secrets."

I know my face is burning by the way they giggle. "I mean, yeah, we're dating. There's not really much to say." Just at that moment, I see my phone flash with a text from Wesley. I want to check it, but I don't want Kareena and Meredith to make a big deal about it, so I let it sit.

"I wish I knew who he was. Like had any sort of context for him. He kind of just appeared out of nowhere," Kareena says.

"Yeah, he's not in any of our classes. Has he ever been and we just never noticed?" Meredith asks.

I shake my head. I feel transported back to the flashing dance floor of Jess's Halloween party. Meredith in her Daenerys wig and her bell-toned voice asking, *Not in any?* Just a dash of cruelty in her casualness.

Kareena tilts her head. "Why not?"

I shrug, suddenly uncomfortable. I feel the blood slowly drain out of my face. "Uh, I don't know. Just isn't that good at school, I guess."

Kareena laughs. "I mean, I guess that's why we have classes like Culinary Arts."

Meredith shoves her. "Stop, she's literally in that class."

"But she had no choice," Kareena says. "It's different to *want* to take a blow-off class. I mean, Eliza wouldn't have taken that class if she wasn't forced to."

"I guess it's no AP Physics," I say. I leave out that I'd have to fight a lot less to do well in AP Physics. At least I wouldn't need someone to tutor me in physics the way Wesley helps me with my cooking.

"What's he like? Is he smart?" Meredith asks.

"Yeah," I say instantly. "Well, not like us, I guess. It's different."

"Does he know how to multiply?" Kareena teases.

I blanch. "What?"

Kareena gives me a small frown. "Remember? You said kids like him should go back to doing their times tables or whatever they do in their regular classes."

Had I said that? My chest thrums, absolutely horrified.

Meredith laughs. "Wait, what did you say about AP? The only AP he knows is all-purpose flour? That was honestly pretty clever."

"He's smart," I say, trying to change the subject. My previous words ring in my ears and I hate how I sound.

"Where's he trying to go to college?" Kareena asks.

Meredith gasps. "Would he go to MIT with you?"

"I don't think so," I say vaguely.

"Then where? UT Austin?" Meredith asks. It's the default choice for most Highland Hills students who aren't aiming for a top-tier university.

"Well, I'm not sure if he wants to go to college," I reply.

The silence screams. I can't look up, can only stare down at my duvet.

Kareena is the first to break it. "Like, taking a gap year?"

Meredith nods. "That could be cool."

"No," I say. "Like, maybe not at all?"

"Eliza . . ." Kareena doesn't finish her thought. She doesn't have to. I hear it in my own head.

Meredith tries a different approach. "I feel like this doesn't really make sense for someone like you."

"Someone like me?" I ask.

"At the top of her class," Kareena supplies diplomatically.

"Self-proclaimed nerd and try-hard," Meredith adds.

"Someone who really is trying to *get somewhere*," Kareena says.

I bristle. Meredith notices and tries to redirect.

"Okay, obviously Eliza thought Culinary Arts would be a waste of time at the beginning. We all did," Meredith says. "But clearly, she met someone she likes and that's worth something. It all balances out."

"Right," Kareena agrees, following Meredith's lead. "On one hand, it's a regular class you got stuck in. On the other, you get a boy and a guaranteed A."

"I wish I could end my day by mixing things in a bowl and getting credit for it," Meredith sighs dreamily. "You get an A for making yourself something to eat. I should've taken Culinary Arts."

"You're not really guaranteed an A," I say. But in my head, I think about the times I thought Mr. Treviño would give anybody full credit if he saw that they were trying. Even with my diced-tomato pasta sauce, I'm sure he would've graded me leniently. He has that type of spirit.

Kareena looks at me seriously. "Eliza. There's no way *you* can't get an A if those other kids can."

Again, my skin prickles. My heart flits rapidly in my chest. How often have I been guilty of talking like this without even knowing it?

"Right," I say, wanting to end the conversation. If I say what I really want to say, this fragile peace we just rediscovered will shatter. So I stand up and wipe my hands on my jeans like it'll wash away the icky feeling that's all over me. I grab Kareena's phone and raise the volume, trying to drown out my own thoughts. With the safety of Khruangbin thumping through the room, I do what I do best—redirect. "I think my mom's almost done teaching her lesson. Y'all can stay here if you want, but I'm heading down to the kitchen." I don't wait for their answer. I feel like I need to get away just to catch my breath again.

When I leave my bedroom and turn the corner to go down the staircase, Wesley is standing right there. I gasp, and my heart leaps into my throat.

"What are you doing here?" I ask.

I finally get a good look at his face and wish I didn't. His expression is cold and stoic, his eyes glinting like black ice with unmistakable anger. It kills me to see the hurt in them, too, because his face confirms exactly what I feared.

"I texted you," he says. The steel in his voice, so foreign to me, sends a shiver down my spine. "Mr. Treviño and I ended early, and I wanted to come to your mom's lesson."

"Oh," I say. My voice nearly trembles. "I didn't check your text. I'm sorry."

"Yeah, that's clear. I think I'll go home. Tell your eomma I'm sorry." He starts to head back down the stairs. I notice his key ring dangling from his fingers and I realize he was so desperate to get here on time that he drove his own car. I want to sob.

"Wesley, wait. Please." I run down and rest a hand on his back. I feel him tense underneath my palm. "You didn't hear—or I need to explain—"

He turns around and my hand falls away. He's only a few steps from the front door. "It's what people say when you're not around to hear—or I guess, when they *think* you're not around to hear—that shows who they are. So I've heard enough." His words fall onto me like a showering of needles.

"Wesley, please," I say again. I have no other defense, no other plan to keep him here. Just the compulsion to beg for him to stay.

"Do your friends know that you were paired to work with me because you were the worst student in the class? That the teacher took one look at you and said, this girl needs a goddamned miracle?" he sneers.

"Wesley," I gasp, and I hate the heat I feel when the tears leak from my eyes.

"That the only way you're getting through this class is because some regular kid who can't get into UT is pulling you through it?" I've never seen his eyes blaze this way before, like the chestnuts have been swallowed by burning coal. "Does it get nauseating, being so self-congratulatory all the time?"

Yes, I want to say. I could throw up right this instant. I hold my arms, hugging myself, to keep from reaching out for him. "They . . . we didn't mean—"

He narrows his eyes. "And what did you mean? When you agreed with what they were saying, you seemed to mean it."

"That's not—"

"Eliza, I was *so* jealous of you. When I first saw you, I would have given anything to be like you. To be successful in all the right ways. To have people you've never talked to know your name just because you were that smart." He takes in a deep breath.

I look at him, my vision blurred with tears. I wait for him to continue. I know he's not done.

He looks away and his face contorts into a pained grimace. "But you needed to use *me*, some regular kid in a regular class, in order for you to get through this course that your friends think is so beneath you. You're someone who would've sunk to the bottom if you didn't have me to keep you afloat. Some salutatorian."

"Funny coming from you," I say. For a second, I don't even register that the words are coming from my own mouth. I don't know where inside my brain these thoughts are coming from, or how they make it to my tongue. "You think I'm fake, don't you? But only one of us acts like he's above the ranking system when secretly, he's licking his wounds because he thinks he's not smart enough. And it's the same one of us who refuses to let his friends come over so they don't see how he lives. Not to mention there's only one of us who chose to hang out with Mr. Treviño on Tuesdays over a girl and her mom. But yes, Wesley, continue to villainize me. Someone did once tell me I remind you of your mother."

Wesley's eyebrows rise and something registers in him that makes his face turn slack. "I thought I was wrong not to give you the benefit of the doubt, when I first met you. Thought it was wrong to assume the worst. But I've never been more right about someone."

"Wesley, you don't even know me."

"I do, Eliza. You're a girl who clings to her grades because she's scared she doesn't have anything actually meaningful. You can't write a personal statement if you're nobody."

I shake my head. I stay silent. My mouth feels immobile, my head foggy. There's so much to say, but my mouth chooses this time to fail me. I can't explain to Wesley how wrong he is, how far off the axis this entire conversation has gone.

"I'm going home. I have to memorize my times tables," he says sardonically. Frozen in place, I watch as he leaves through the front door.

By the time my mom's lesson is over, Kareena and Meredith have gone home in a shower of quick hugs and goodbyes. And before I can tell my mom I don't feel well enough to cook today, she tells me she actually has a lesson at that time now, a new student that she just booked this past weekend, and she's sorry she forgot to tell me earlier. So I lock myself in my room and cry until I feel like I'll dehydrate myself if I release any more tears. And eventually, the house lights turn off and everyone goes to bed and there's no one who knocks on my door to check if I'm still in here.

Chapter 23

If there were a world record for the number of texts a girl can send in one day to a boy who is ignoring her, I'm sure I am breaking it. I send Wesley a million apologies, several crying GIFs, a dozen calls, and a few very embarrassing voicemails that barely disguise the snotty tears. But I might as well be trying to contact a disconnected landline. There's a deliberate effort he's putting into ignoring me. I don't know how I can make it better.

Among my many texts is an invitation to my family's Thanksgiving dinner. Every year, my mom does an incredible job of WASP cosplay and creates a beautiful turkey dinner, complete with mashed potatoes, creamed corn, green beans, and cranberry sauce. My dad's sole responsibility is to pick up the apple and pecan pies from our neighborhood bakery, but even for those, my mom puts the order in weeks in advance. It's a meal I look forward to every year, and I can't imagine that Wesley is doing something similar, given what I know about his family. And I want to see him. Even if he's angry with me, I know he wouldn't hold it against my mother. Not that my parents know I've invited Wesley.

The morning of Thanksgiving, I finally get a response, but it's only a direct reply to the dinner invitation. Two words: Can't. Sick. I sigh. I put too much faith in how much he cared for my mom. Or I overestimated his ability to forgive me. Either way feels like failure.

I come downstairs and something is unusual, but it takes me a moment to place it.

There isn't any commotion going on in the kitchen.

I check the time. It's ten a.m., which typically would mean that my mom is working on preparing the turkey. But I go into the kitchen and it's empty. There are no ingredients laid out, no pots on the stovetop, and no Eomma in her apron.

The door of the master bedroom is just slightly ajar. Through the slim opening, I find my mother in bed reading. My dad is still asleep next to her. She has one hand on her book, holding the page, and the other on my dad's hand. She doesn't notice me, so I quietly retreat back to the kitchen. Maybe this is my opportunity to do something nice for her. Maybe I can get started on most of the meal before she notices.

But when I get to the kitchen, I check the fridge. Then the freezer. Then the kimchi freezer.

No big bird. No pies. No evidence that there was ever going to be a Thanksgiving dinner to begin with.

My mom forgot about Thanksgiving.

I let myself get angry for a moment. Was she going to be surprised when her evening lessons just didn't show up today? Did she not notice that I was home from school on a weekday? Was it really such a big ask for her to be aware of a national holiday?

And then I let the anger go. This is a made-up holiday to my parents, something they only adopted for my sake when I was growing up. Koreans already have their own holidays, like the autumn festival of Chuseok, which my mom doesn't even celebrate here in the States anymore. When I was really little, maybe six years old, I watched my parents make songpyeon for Chuseok. I thought the colors of the rice cakes were so pretty—the white, the pale pink, the earthy green. I took a bite of one and made a face when the filling oozed into my mouth. My dad ate the rest so I wouldn't throw it away. I can't remember if my parents ever made songpyeon again after that.

Because of me, they've swapped out their Korean traditions for American ones. Maybe Halmeoni's death served as a reminder of what immigrating had taken from my mom, and now she's distancing herself from the country that never fully accepted her. This country invalidated her degree. Turned her daughter into someone who became estranged from her grandmother and a foreigner to her home traditions.

I slide out Halmeoni's stack of recipes and go through them, searching for something I haven't learned yet. We've covered great ground through our lessons, I realize, as I skim through and recognize most of them. Gimbap, japchae, doenjang jjigae, mandu . . . I've learned so much more than I thought. For each recipe, I can remember exactly what my mother said about it. Harabeoji eating Eomma's extra danmuji. Sick Halmeoni requesting dakjuk over doenjang jjigae next time. Samchon putting the smallest dollop of filling in his mandu wrapper. Wesley's perfect pleats. The recipes feel like so much more than instructions written on a page when they're associated with real stories and real people.

I finally land on one that we haven't gone over yet, but still looks manageable enough for me to follow. It's for dakdoritang, which is a spicy chicken-based stew. It's one of my favorite comfort dishes, but it's always been so intimidating to actually make. I force myself to read over the recipe, slowly sounding out the syllables of words I am not familiar with. At this point, the list of ingredients is pretty familiar, but the instructions take longer for me to understand. Ultimately, I think I've figured it out for the most part. I scour the fridge, and it's a Thanksgiving miracle that my mom happens to have all the ingredients needed. She might not have prepared for Thanksgiving, but she's always ready to make Halmeoni's recipes. My heart twinges at the thought.

The first thing I do is wash a couple of cups of rice and set it to cook in the rice cooker. Then I move on to the actual dakdoritang. The recipe isn't as hard as I expected and doesn't call for any crazy techniques or ingredients I haven't used before. Chopping up the whole chicken is the most difficult part, but Mr. Treviño just showed us how to do it a week or so ago in class. "Don't waste your money buying precuts," he told us. "With a good cleaver, you can always do it yourself." I wasn't convinced, but I appreciated the thought.

When it's time to add the spoonfuls of gochujang, I make sure the paste is heaping. I stir it in, and the stew becomes a gorgeous wine-red color that looks delightfully spicy. The potatoes and carrots are starting to get soft and glossy, and I can hear my stomach gently growl as I let the stew simmer. The rice cooker sings to let me know it's done and for a second, I let myself get swept up in the fact that I just cooked an entire meal on my own. And even more impressive, it actually turned out okay. I, Eliza Park, have just made a home-cooked Korean dish for my family without any assistance.

If it hasn't been proven to me yet, I now know that my halmeoni clearly knew what she was talking about when she wrote these recipes. I wonder if when she was writing them, she ever imagined that her English-speaking American granddaughter would be recreating her dishes across the ocean, even after she was gone. Or that a Thai American boy, a complete stranger to her, would be enjoying her recipes and using them as his introduction to cooking

Korean food. At least, he used to. I try to shake off the hurt of the past tense. I wonder if my halmeoni would have faith in me to do something to make my mom happy. I hope she sees me now and is proud of me for getting it right.

I'm ladling the dakdoritang into soup bowls when I'm startled by a voice. "Yeji?"

I've been alone in the kitchen for so long that the addition of a new person scares me. I jump in surprise. The dakdoritang in the ladle spills across the stovetop, across the countertop, and soaks right into the stack of Halmeoni's recipes I've left out. I look up and see my dad watching the flow of the red soup, blissfully unaware of the magnitude of what I've just done.

"I didn't know you were cooking," my dad says.

"Yeji's cooking?" I hear my mom's voice before I see her, and as I wait for her to enter the kitchen, all the pride I felt earlier has been replaced with nauseous panic. I can do nothing but watch as she walks in. A small smile starts to break when she notices what I've made, but then her eyes catch on the river of red that leads to the stained recipes. I see it like it's in slow motion—the recognition of the papers, the soft opening of her mouth in surprise, and worst of all, the shine of unshed tears starting to build.

She runs to the recipes and, so caught up in the distress of the moment, dabs them with her shirt. I hand her a kitchen towel silently and she takes it. The recipe on top, for the dakdoritang, is so damp, that when she lifts it from the countertop, the corner softly rips. "Yeji, what did you do?"

"I'm sorry, Eomma," I say, my voice small and anxious. "I was just trying to do something nice. For Thanksgiving."

A tear rolls down her face. She stares at the red-stained papers like she doesn't trust herself to look up at me. "They're ruined."

My dad tries his hand at piecing things together. "You remember the recipes, don't you, yeobo? You've made them for me so many times."

She shakes her head, and I know it's not that she doesn't know the recipes by heart, because of course she does. It's just so far from the point. "These . . . I've had them for so long." She takes in a breath so shaky, it comes out like a wheeze. "Yeji, how could you be so careless?" She turns to face me at last, and the devastation written in her eyes is accompanied only by anger.

"Yeobo," my dad says, a warning.

"You're always making a mess," my mom continues. I've never seen her upset like this. It's not that we don't fight, but it's never turned so ugly. "Never doing any part of a lesson right. I can't trust you with anything." *Always. Never.* I've been reduced to universal quantifiers. Because I wanted to make something of a holiday everyone else forgot.

"Yeobo," my dad says again, raising his voice.

It hits me all at once, that I am so tired. I am so, so tired. I'm tired of keeping my mouth shut just to say the wrong things when it matters. I'm tired of walking on eggshells around my mother, who waltzes in and out of my life when she wants to and turns on me now like she's the only victim in this house.

"The recipes don't even matter!" I say. The anger I clamped down earlier now flows from me like steam from a kettle. "You're the only person who cares about them. I'm only learning them in the first place for school, and for you to think that Halmeoni's cooking didn't die with her! Do you think I'm going to host my own kimjang? Do you think my kids are going to want gimbap in their lunch box?" My words are flowing faster, feeling dangerously free now that I've let them release. They're so fast, I can't strip away the venom before they come out. "I'm *American*. I'm never going to be the mom who forgets to make Thanksgiving dinner. I'm never going to forget my daughter's graduating, or have her cry alone in her room because I'm too ignorant to recognize that she got her heart broken, or think that a few sheets of faded paper are somehow more important than being there for my only child!" I let out a savage breath and say, "All I want is my mom, but she hasn't been here for the past five months."

My mom's eyes shine, and although the anger is still there, there's also the addition of something intensely vulnerable. It takes me a moment to recognize it, because I've never seen it on my mother's face before. Her bottom lip trembles and her chest heaves before she finally gets the words out. "All I want is my mom, too," my mom says in English, like she's using the language as a weapon. "And no one is here for me. Not even my own family." She takes the soaked recipes and flees the kitchen. I hear the slam of a door and the sound of a lock turning, and I know she's barricaded herself in the master bedroom.

My dad looks at me and for a second, we're both so stunned that neither of us says anything. Then he says, "You got your heart broken?"

"Don't talk to me," I snap. "Talk to your wife for once." And, like mother, like daughter, I storm up to my room, slam the door shut, and lock the door.

Chapter 24

The next morning, I wake up feeling absolutely awful. If there's such a thing as an emotional hangover, I think I'm having the strongest one of all time. I stare up at my bedroom ceiling and pray that my mattress will rip open and swallow me whole. I check my phone, see the wall of blue text in my conversation with Wesley, and throw it across the room.

Eventually, I crawl out of bed and trudge my way downstairs. The master bedroom is still closed. For the first time, I consider it as a challenge, or an invitation.

I find my mother in her bed. She has her reading lamp on and her book in her lap. Her eyes flicker up when I come into her bedroom, but they fall back down and she doesn't stop reading.

I gingerly climb into bed and sit next to her. "Are you mad at me?" I ask softly.

"Mm," my mom says. At least she isn't bothering to lie.

I look down at the quilt she uses each night. I remember picking it out with her in one of the countless, claustrophobic Dongdaemun shopping malls in Seoul. She haggled for it, which I said was embarrassing, but she said was the norm. My fingers anxiously pick at the green embroidery. "I'm so sorry, Eomma. I know that I was disrespectful and rude. I am so grateful that you're trying to teach me Halmeoni's recipes." Then, even though my grammar is shaky and my accent is noticeably American, I try to speak in Korean. "I'm proud to have you as my mother, and proud to cook food that you and Halmeoni love. I'm really sorry for hurting you." The odds that I'm speaking coherently are not favorable, but I'm hoping that the intention comes across intact.

My mom puts down her book and turns to face me. "I miss your halmeoni so much." Her voice wavers. "I'm sorry for yelling at you in the kitchen. I don't need the recipes, because they're in my head. But they were in Halmeoni's handwriting and . . . it's really lonely to be here in America."

At the sound of tears in her voice, my eyes start to prick as well. I barely know how to respond. Seeing my mother so openly vulnerable seems like uncharted territory. "I know. I'm sorry."

"Have you talked to your dad lately?"

"What do you mean?"

"He's . . . been trying to ask how I'm doing. It's different."

"I might have said something," I admit.

She closes her eyes for a long moment. "Sometimes, it feels like you and Appa are all I have. You two are the only ones here who knew her. And if you two don't want to talk about her, then who can I remember her with?" Tears leak from her closed eyes, and I watch them drip from her jaw onto the quilt. The green embroidery darkens to emerald.

It strikes me that my mother's loneliness runs so much deeper than I thought. The realization burns through me, chased by the hot feeling of unmistakable shame. I think of the months following my halmeoni's passing. The nights my mother would stay inside the walls of her closed bedroom, when even my father evacuated to the guest room. I would occasionally check in to see if she needed something from the grocery store. She always said, *No, thank you,* and I'd close the door, taking in a last glance of her tired frame leaning against the headboard. Every night, wanting someone to grieve with her, while the only people who could skirted further and further away.

The day my mother came back from that visit to South Korea was grim. My father and I had paid for the airport parking and stood there waiting at the arrival gate. I craned my neck every which way to see if my mother was the next person to come out.

When she did eventually walk through the final security gate, I didn't notice her at first. I couldn't recognize her. Who was that woman, hollowed and gray? Her eyes were sunken. Her hair was limp against her face. Everything about her just seemed to *lack*. There was not a single cell of my April mother in this person.

"Yeobo!" my father called out. "Yeongmi-yah! Nam Yeongmi!"

Finally, my mom glanced in our direction. Part of me hoped that her eyes would brighten at seeing us, that maybe the dullness could be swept away easily by the warmth of recognition. The recognition was there. It was clear by the way she walked directly toward us. But the warmth wasn't. It continued to be chased away by something I couldn't seem to fight.

That first night she was back, I heard soft wails from the closed door of my parents' room. The low thrum of my dad's tired voice, trying to soothe her. The thick cries from my mother. I left my bed and stood outside their door for what must have been half an hour. Twice, I lifted my hand to knock on the door, but couldn't force myself to go through with it. I was scared, I think. Nervous to see a kind of hurt that I couldn't fix. So I climbed back into my bed and fell asleep to my mother's muted sniffles.

"I love hearing about Halmeoni," I say, and I'm surprised to find that I actually mean it. Halmeoni is more to me now than she was in July. She was my mother's mother, there for her big moments and small ones, there to shape her into becoming the mother she is to me. I look at my mom now, compare her to the woman I saw come off the plane months ago. The warmth feels closer to the surface now than it did then, but I know that she is still processing her grief. It's an immeasurable process, one that has no manual. I take my mother's hand in mine and let my fingers slide between hers. "Sometimes I feel guilty that I don't miss Halmeoni like you do. I'd only see her every two years or so, whenever you'd take me with you to Hanguk. So when you tell me stories about her, it's like I can learn to miss her." I say this in English and I wonder if my mother really understands what I'm trying to say. I can barely even put it in the correct words myself. How do I say I'm sorry for not missing the person you care about so much? That when you moved from Korea, the distance thinned the familial ties I would have had to those you left there?

My mom reaches for my hand. "I'm sorry, too. I haven't been your eomma lately. Sometimes, I get so sad from Halmeoni that I become a bad parent, and then being a bad parent makes me feel even sadder. But, Yeji-yah, you don't have to learn her recipes because you feel bad for me. Or for school."

I feel myself blanch. "I want to know you and Halmeoni better. And I really do want to get better at cooking. The way you cook is like time travel, or magic. You go somewhere else, and food means something different, and you can fix any problem with the ingredients you already have." And then, even though it's nearing the end of November, and the Austin foliage is burgundy and russet, and the sun has been hiding behind the clouds for the whole week, I say, "You know what this weather makes me crave?"

* * *

I carry the bingsu tray to the table this time. A beautiful snowy mountain with golden injeolmi rice cakes and a mouthwatering scoop of pat.

Once we're digging in, I try to assume false courage and ask, "Why don't you talk to Samchon more?"

My mom nods. "Your samchon is really stressed. He's the only son and traditionally, a lot of responsibilities fall on him. Also, I live here, so it's harder for me to help. But he's the one trying to sell Halmeoni's house."

"Is that hard?" I feel like real estate in Austin is always going up. I don't know what it's like in other places.

"It's a really old house. Very run-down and the layout is not what modern people want anymore. Plus, it's very far from the newer, developed parts of the city, where young people want to live. He's having a very hard time getting people interested, and no one wants to rent it either." She puts her spoon down even though she's only had one rice cake so far. "And you know Samchon has three young boys to look after, so . . . He is busy enough."

I shake my head. "I'm sure he wants to talk to someone, too."

"He has plenty of people in Korea to talk to. Cousins, aunts, uncles. It's different being here."

She rubs her hands together like they're cold, which, considering the weather, they very much might be. "You should eat more."

"I remember your childhood friends were at the funeral," I say, sliding my spoon against the shaved milk. "Can you talk to them?"

"I have, and I do. But they didn't know Halmeoni like I did. There's only so much they can say." My mom sniffs and picks up her spoon again. "It's all right. Missing her is normal. I'll be okay."

I watch as she heaps a big spoonful into her mouth and I know she thinks she's said enough. Or maybe she thinks that's all I want to hear. "You can talk to me, Eomma. I want to miss her, too."

Before she looks away, I see her press her lips together, like she's trying not to cry in this bingsu shop. Of course, seeing my mom like this makes my eyes well, too. Finally, she looks back to me and gives me the most tentative of smiles. Our shiny brown eyes are twin reflections of each other. She says, "Thank you, Yeji-yah." She stares at me for a long moment before she sniffs and changes the subject. "You and Wesley aren't together anymore?"

I sigh. "We had a fight. He's not talking to me. I invited him over, but he made up an excuse and said he's sick."

"How do you know it was an excuse?" she asks.

I forget moms can be so naive. "He just doesn't want to talk to me."

She twirls her spoon in the melting puddle of bingsu at the bottom of the bowl. "A lot of my students have been getting sick recently. It's common now that the weather is cold."

"Eomma. Wesley doesn't want to see me."

She ignores me and pops the last tteok into her mouth. "You know what's a good meal to take to someone who's sick?"

I roll my eyes. "Dakjuk?"

"Dakjuk."

Chapter 25

For the first time, I try making a Korean dish from a recipe that isn't written in my halmeoni's handwriting. Instead, I found it online from a website run by a sweet-looking Korean lady living in New York. It's comically easier following a recipe written in English rather than Korean, and once again, I am impressed with myself for making a pot of dakjuk. Even my mom comes in at the end to taste test and she smiles in approval. It makes me want to run a lap around the neighborhood, yelling, *I'm a goddamn chef!* but I resist.

I pack the dakjuk in a Tupperware and slide it into a lunch box with some utensils. Before I can reason with myself and change my mind, I grab my car keys and neatly buckle the porridge into the passenger seat.

My heart sinks when I pull up to Wesley's house and the lights are off. I should've known he wouldn't be home. I can't remember the number of times he's told me he avoids being at his house if he can help it, but I find myself parking the car and getting out anyway.

I ring the doorbell and take three steps back, like I'm about to dash down the walkway and into my car at a moment's notice. I stand there for a minute. Maybe two. What's an acceptable length of time to be waiting? I know firsthand that the house is big and just getting from one end to another takes a while. But even so, I think I'm holding out hope for no reason.

So I turn back around. I'm about to reach for the handle of my car when the front door of Wesley's home creaks open and I see his face through the sliver. When we meet each other's eyes, he opens the door wider so I can see him fully.

"What is that?" he calls out. His voice sounds scratchy. Maybe he is sick? Or he just woke up?

"A car," I shout back. "I know you forget what it is sometimes." I don't know why I'm reckless enough to tease him, but it slips out like instinct.

"Ha," he says dryly. I'm too far away to see whether he's rolling his eyes, but it really sounds like it. It hits me that I've been able to imagine his expressions for a long time now. It's what I've been doing in my head every day since he stopped talking to me. "What's in your hand?"

"Oh," I say, too quietly for him to hear. I raise my voice. "A lunch box. It's for you."

There's a tense moment where neither of us moves or says anything. I wish I could study his expression just to get a hint at what he's thinking. I consider getting into my car and driving away, but I came all the way over here for a reason. Might as well wait to watch him close the door if that's what I came here for.

Then, he opens the door fully. He leaves it open as he turns around and walks back down the hallway, into the shadows of his grand home.

An invitation.

I retrace my steps down the walkway and close his front door behind me. The emptiness of the house seeps into me just like it did the first time. There are still no signs of personality or the family currently living here in any corner of the space. The furniture doesn't look like it's ever been sat on for more than ten minutes at a time and the only things on the walls are vaguely European-style paintings of fruit bowls and waterfalls.

I find Wesley lying down on the living room couch. He has a plush velour blanket covering most of his body, and his hair sticks up in the back like he's been lying down all day. I take a seat on the rug, channeling some evolutionary advice of keeping myself on the lower ground so I appear as sorry as I feel. It's unnerving to be so close to him, but still feel so far.

I try to study his appearance without transparently ogling, but I think I'm failing. He's sick. There's no doubt about that. His chestnut eyes are sunken, his lips are cracked, and his nose is bright red. I would make a joke about how bad he looks if the stakes didn't feel so high. I also am ashamed to say that even in his awful state, I still think he looks gorgeous.

Maybe if I wait long enough, he'll finally give in and I won't have to keep guessing what's going on in his mind. Or maybe we'll just sit in silence until one of his parents comes home, and that would still probably be an improvement compared to how things are when I'm not near him. When he won't look at me.

"Aren't you going to open the lunch box?" he says at last with a precise nonchalance. I can't tell if he genuinely doesn't care or if he's just perfected his ability to iron out the emotion in his voice. I pray it's only the second.

I unzip the lunch box and take out the Tupperware. "I made this. At the risk of sounding like a first grader, I'd like to say that I'm proud of myself and want to show it off."

"Does that mean you want me to eat it?" he says, coloring his voice with a hint of incredulity.

I bite my tongue to keep from saying something snarky. "Well . . . yes."

"I didn't realize you would try to poison me so blatantly. Don't most people try to keep it discreet?"

"Looks like you're already dying, so someone beat me to it."

He doesn't laugh, and there's a long pause. I debate whether this is a signal to pack the lunch box up again and make my exit.

"I have the flu," he says finally.

"I'm sorry."

"What is it?" he asks. He peers curiously at my dakjuk.

"Scared?" I say.

"Of something you made? Terrified."

The easy flow of the conversation makes my heart constrict. It feels so normal, when I know we're anything but.

"It's called dakjuk, or chicken porridge. It's a great food for people who are sick, because it's warm and nutritious and doesn't upset the stomach." I take a pause, wondering if I should say what I'm thinking. I think I want to, so I do. "I was hoping I could help take care of you. I was worried you'd be alone."

His lack of response makes me feel like I've said something out of line, and maybe I have. I just want to let him know that I care, but maybe that's what pushes him away further.

Wesley puts his hands on the sides of the containers. "It's still warm." He keeps his hands there for a long minute, and he is obviously thinking something, but won't share it with me.

"Of course," I said. "People don't get better by eating cold porridge." I unpack the spoon from the lunch box and take off the lid from the porridge. "Okay, open up."

"I'm not letting you spoon-feed me, Eliza."

I try not to show the panic that runs through me when he says my name. "What if I do the airplane thing? Or the train? What mode of transportation do you prefer?"

"My own hand," he says, taking the Tupperware and spoon from my hands. But the brush of skin is enough to know.

"Holy shit, Wesley, you're burning up." I lay my hand on his forehead and am reminded of the time I touched the burning stovetop.

"I thought I mentioned I have the flu."

"Have you taken any Tylenol? Or Motrin? Or something?"

"I'll be fine," he insists. He sits himself up and that's when I notice that there's the slightest sheen of sweat at the crown of his head.

"You're impossible." I get up and move to the kitchen. Even though it's technically rude to be digging around in someone else's home without their permission, I do it anyway until I find a bottle of extra-strength Tylenol. There's also an old, possibly expired bottle of some sort of grape-flavored decongestant, so I bring that as well.

"You're going to take these," I say, handing them over. "I will force each pill, one by one, down your throat until you're afebrile."

He opens his mouth to argue, but he must see how serious I am in my expression because he takes the Tylenol and downs it with a capful of the decongestant. The way his mouth twists lets me know that he thinks the cough syrup is absolutely foul. "You're just trying to make your food taste better in comparison," he grumbles. Then he takes a spoonful of the dakjuk and finally gives it a taste.

"Okay," he says after a painfully long moment.

"It's okay?" I say.

"No. I'm just saying 'okay.'"

"Oh."

"It's much better than okay."

I let myself full-on stare now. "What?"

"Eliza, this is great," he says. The sincerity of his words almost wounds me. Without my consent, I feel heat prick my eyes. I blink and look away, embarrassed by the volatility of my own emotion.

"You really think so?" I say.

"You think I'd lie?"

I think for a moment. "No. But I like to hear you say it."

For a split second, I see his face break into a small grin, but it's erased almost instantly and I wonder if I've only imagined it. He eats in silence and I try my best not to track his every motion. He moves slowly, like his joints are half-asleep, and he only eats half the juk before closing the lid. He falls back into the supine position and reconfigures the blanket over himself, like even eating has exhausted him irrevocably.

"I'm tired of being upset with you," he says, but it comes out more like a blurry sigh and I have to struggle to piece all the words together.

I fidget on the rug. "I'm tired of you being upset with me, too." Then I take a big sigh and decide to go for it. "I said this over text and over voicemail, but who knows how much of that you actually saw, because you never responded, which is fine because you have the right to be angry. But I'm so sorry, Wesley. I'm so sorry and I don't know how to make it up to you. I'm sorry my friends and I said some really awful things that weren't correct or okay. I was so wrong. I didn't know anything. I still don't know anything! But I do know that I like you and I miss you and I want us to be something real."

Wesley looks away and closes his eyes, like he's embarrassed for me. I feel my face get hot, but I don't know if it's because of the humiliation or the frustration. The silence that spreads between us feels like a burgeoning flood. How can I escape before it consumes me?

Then he chuckles, and the sound is so surprising, it takes effort not to react. He keeps his eyes closed, but the laughter continues to bubble out of him.

"What?" I say.

"Eliza, I swear I saw tears in your eyes."

I hastily brush at my damp lashes. "No."

"'Like I'd ever cry over you.' You said that to me once. Do you remember?" He is smiling to himself despite the fact that I can see the visible sweat collecting on his brow.

"I remember."

He sighs quietly. "You're cute," he murmurs.

"Oh, we're doing this again?"

He just continues smiling. Then he opens his eyes and turns his head to face me, but the motion of it makes his hair look even more chaotic against the couch cushion. "Holding grudges is a bad habit of mine. You know that." I know he's thinking about his mother.

"I'm sorry, Wesley," I say. "I hate it when you ignore me. You're . . ."

He tilts his head forward to listen better, and I worry for a moment he's going to tip off the couch. "I'm what?"

I sigh and lean forward to organize his hair. It's slick and warm. "I don't know. You're, like, my favorite part of the day. It sucks when you don't talk to me."

This time I see it plainly. His mouth breaks into a smile. His eyes crinkle.

"Don't tease me," I warn. "It took a lot for me to say that."

"I appreciate that," he says. His eyes are practically sparkling. I hope it's not the fever.

I nod. "Sure."

"You're my favorite part of the day, too." Wesley says it like it's a secret. There's an undercurrent of intimacy in his voice, and it covers me like chocolate.

"Really?"

"Mm," he mumbles. "I've thought about you every day. I couldn't forget you even if I tried."

I try not to smile. His tone makes me feel so warm, I wonder if I'm catching a fever, too. Flu is contagious, isn't it? I reply, "It really felt like you were doing a good job of it."

Wesley pats around to find his phone. He unlocks it and it's already open on a photo, but he doesn't try to hide it. It takes me a second to identify myself. I'm in the Culinary Arts kitchen, inhaling the curry Wesley made me. "There's a reason I always took the photos on my phone. I knew I would want to keep looking at you."

I might cry.

"Eliza, I'm sorry."

My brows knit together. "You don't have anything to be sorry for."

He shakes his head. "Not true. I said awful things to you, too.

You've tried to apologize to me countless times. I spend at least an hour every morning rereading all the texts you've sent me. I'm sorry for not wanting to listen."

"I don't have much to say that's worth listening to," I concede.

"You know that's not true. I was just—" He cuts himself off and there's a moment where I wonder if he won't finish his sentence, if he's about to fall asleep. Wesley's eyes are closed and his breathing is slow. Then he says, "I make a lot of bad assumptions. Have I said that before? I assume people think the worst of me, so I assume the worst of them. From the moment I met you, I always thought you'd think I'm some loser who's not going anywhere. And to hear it confirmed . . . Jesus, it was the cruelest form of humiliation." His nose is pinched in an effort to control his composure.

I want to reach for his hand. It takes everything in me not to. But I won't push him somewhere he doesn't feel comfortable going with me. "I'm so sorry, Wesley. That's not at all how I see you."

"You know what's wild?" he prompts. He says it with newfound energy, like he's recovering from his illness instantaneously.

"What?"

"I had this idea of who you were before I met you. Eliza Park. Perfect student. Projected salutatorian. Name on every organization's board. Perfect friend group doing perfect things, making Highland Hills proud. And I wanted to hate you so badly."

"Wesley, we've already been over this—"

"And then I met you," he continues as if I haven't said anything. "And what blew my mind was that you were actually everything you advertise yourself to be. There was some kind of energy about you, like you were somebody who genuinely had it all going right for you, that I couldn't resist. I bothered you so much that first week of Culinary Arts because I thought you were so *interesting*. And I wanted you to find me interesting, too."

I have to look away when I ask him, "Why are you talking in the past tense?"

"You're not letting me finish."

"You took a pause!"

"Because humans need to breathe! And I have a respiratory infection!"

"Fine. Then continue. I'm hoping for a happy ending."

A smirk spreads across his face. It's been a while since I've seen it and the sight makes my stomach twist. "As I was saying," Wesley says pointedly, "I wanted you to gravitate toward me like I did to you. How could I convince you to see me at all, if I was nothing that you wanted? And when I heard you and your friends in your room, it was like every negative view I had of myself was verified by some authority figure whose respect I'd always longed for. Things I've thought about myself—things that I wanted to think weren't true—were suddenly spoken out loud by somebody who wasn't me, and the truth of it all felt like something I couldn't deny anymore. And it hurt so fucking badly that I wanted to make someone hurt in return. So I pretended all the things I found out about you weren't true. It was a lot easier than having to realize I was only mad at myself."

"You were mad at me, too. You can admit that you were mad at me."

He shakes his head. "The truth is that all the things I thought about you before, everything I wrote about you for Mr. Treviño's paper, were correct. Are correct. I still believe them." For a moment, he lets himself laugh like he's being indulgent. "For Mr. Treviño's paper, I wrote, like, three different drafts. They kept coming out like love letters. I had to pretend I was writing a letter of recommendation instead." He smiles to himself and his eyes are halfway closed. I realize he is not in his right mind. Some combination of fever, sleepiness, and cough medicine is putting him on a different plane.

"Wesley, go to sleep," I say gently. But selfishly I think, *Keep talking. Tell me everything.*

"Eliza, I like you so much," he murmurs, and this time, I know he's falling asleep. He's barely conscious. "I'm done pretending I don't. And I like you so much more now that I know you can cook something on your own." He tries to smirk, but his face is already trying to sleep.

"I actually made a different dish by myself, too. It's called dakdoritang. I can show you," I say.

"Dory? Like *Finding Nemo*? Let's watch that one next."

I roll my eyes. "You're delirious."

And then, he's asleep. I'm watching Wesley Ruengsomboon, ill with the flu, sleep on his living room couch in his lonely mansion. Once I decide I've been creepy for long enough, I put the dakjuk leftovers in the fridge, tuck the blanket snugly around him, and—because I can't help it—give him a kiss on his too-warm forehead. "Get better soon," I whisper before I go. "I'll miss you."

Chapter 26

The weekend after Thanksgiving, I call Kareena and Meredith and ask them to hang out at our boba shop. When I arrive, they're already there, sitting at our normal table.

I order and take the jasmine green milk tea back to my table. Kareena and Meredith already have their work out in front of them and are diligently preparing for midterm season. I sit down and start to do my homework, too, but I feel something building up inside me until I can't hold off on addressing it anymore.

"Wesley heard us talking," I say. The words slip out without my permission, but once I've said them, I don't want to take them back.

Meredith looks up curiously. "What do you mean?"

"In my room. Tuesday before Thanksgiving. He heard us talking."

Kareena studies my distressed expression. "Okay. Did we say something wrong? I don't really remember."

"Yes!" I exclaim. "There was just this—this gross way we talked about regular classes and regular students."

"Like how?" Meredith asks. I recognize her mock trial attitude, her desire for evidence.

"We called non-AP students *those other kids*. We said they weren't trying to get anywhere. And then all those things *I* said at the picnic! The times tables, the AP flour . . . I was an absolute monster. And I don't think those things anymore, but I wasn't brave enough to say it out loud. Our whole thing was that we were going to be more honest, even if it meant confrontation, and the first time I was confronted, I folded *again*."

Meredith looks surprised. "You know we didn't mean anything by it. And you didn't either."

"But that's the problem, too," I argue. "We never mean anything by it."

Kareena puts down her pencil and looks at me. "Eliza, I don't know that I'm following."

Like ships in the night.

I look down at the table, trying to collect my thoughts, but they keep swirling around and bouncing off the walls, desperate to remain tangled. "We're oblivious to how much we've internalized this one idea of success," I say haltingly, feeling like I'm grasping each word individually and straining to connect them to one another. "This one idea of a good student. Get good grades, get into a good college, make your parents proud. And that's fine, because there's value in that, too. But that doesn't mean anyone who isn't that image . . . can't also be a good student."

I look up to see if Kareena and Meredith are listening. They both stare at me intently, foreheads crinkled in a demonstration of their effort. I continue, "You know, Wesley probably can't get into UT. His grades aren't good enough. But he's still one of the smartest people I know. He knows way more than me about cooking and culture and I don't know . . . It's in the way he talks, in the way he thinks. He thinks about things I've never even considered. I love listening to him. I learn from him."

"Do you want us to apologize to him?" Kareena asks. She offers it like a suggestion.

"That's not the point," I argue. "It's not like we did one bad thing and we just have to say sorry and we're all forgiven."

"That's bad news for the Catholics," Meredith says.

"Meredith, please," I say. "I'm saying that it's our mindset. It's prejudiced. It's elitist. All the things that make us believe we're better than others—none of that is actually real. Am I making any sense?"

Kareena stares at me with her wide, dark eyes. She's always been smarter than me. I want her to understand what I'm saying, to be able to connect my dots the way I've seen her do so many times in every class. "Yes. Yes, you're making sense."

Meredith tilts her head and says, "Okay, but just for fun, I'll play devil's advocate and say—"

"Meredith, please," Kareena interrupts, rolling her eyes.

"Kidding!" she says. "So . . . what does this mean for your Culinary Arts class?"

"What do you mean?" I say.

Meredith shrugs. "You basically admitted that Wesley is some culinary genius. Are you not going to try to win the cook-off?"

"Of course I'm going to try. But I'm not just trying because of rank. It's because I want to do well for myself, to be able to make something and be proud of it. This has been maybe the hardest semester of my life, but I want to prove that I've gotten through it." I turn to Kareena. "If Jess gives the speech at the end of the year, then so be it. At least I know I'm a smart girl and a pretty kick-ass cook."

Kareena waves her hand dismissively. "I promise, Jess is not trying to usurp your rank. She's been focusing more on this research project with the hospital than her actual classes."

"And speaking of Jess," I say, "it's weird that AP kids never talk to non-AP kids. Has it never bothered y'all? Like Jess's Halloween party: You can only get an invitation if you're in one of her classes. Everyone else just hears about it and then the Archibalds' land of luxury floods the Insta feed the next day." I shake my head. "There's this . . . gap, like we're not all at the same bougie school in the first place. And we leave the gap alone like it's completely normal."

"Jess talked about that, too, actually," Kareena says. "That's why she and Meredith were brainstorming ideas on how to do a class-wide graduation party."

"Where did Jess end up applying for early decision?" I ask, suddenly reminded.

"Vanderbilt," Kareena answers. "It's where both of her parents went. It's also only a two-hour plane ride away from Penn, granted that both of us get into our top choice, so that's nice. Are you still thinking MIT? Deadline's in a month, right?"

I swirl the remaining boba in my tea with the fat straw. "I don't know. I think I'll apply pretty broadly, actually."

"Still computer science, though?" Meredith asks.

I shrug. "I'm not sure about that either."

Kareena raises an eyebrow, but she's smiling. "Wow, I've never known Eliza Park to be indecisive."

"For real," Meredith agrees. "I don't remember this plot point in *High School Musical.*"

"I like theater and I like basketball," I say. "I think part of college is going to be figuring out what I want the balance to look like."

Meredith nods sagely. "So all this time, you weren't just Gabriella or Zeke. You were also Troy Bolton."

I shake my head in laughter. Then I nudge my chin in the direction of her open notebook. "Enough. Get your head in the game."

When Friday after break comes around, Wesley and I stay after class in the Culinary Arts kitchen like we used to before, even though there's no reflection essay due and no assigned pairings anymore. After I went to his house, it was like we pressed rewind, instantly falling back into our cooking routines and conversations like we never took a pause. As usual, Wesley runs over to Mr. Treviño's computer and puts a film on the projector before coming to our workstation.

"Did you bring what we need?" Wesley asks.

I nod. I pull out a lunch box full of ingredients the Culinary Arts kitchen doesn't stock—rice wine, sesame oil, gochugaru, gochujang.

"I've been looking forward to this all week," he says. "I can't wait to learn from you, Master Chef Park." He gives me a mock-ceremonial bow.

As expected, Wesley follows instructions easily. I brought my grandmother's recipe, which still bears the vague silhouette of instructions despite the giant stain and minor tear. Wesley is impressed by the way I can read the handwritten Korean, even when it takes me a while to actually do so. "I see you with your casual trilingual tongue," he says with a grin.

"Not even. I can barely speak English around you," I say, willing myself not to sound embarrassed. "My Spanish is elementary and my Korean is even worse."

He raises his eyebrows. "Look at who you're talking to before you say something so infuriatingly self-deprecating, okay?"

As the dakdoritang is cooking, Wesley pulls something from his personal corner cabinet and walks over with a small jar.

"Is that red curry paste?" I say warily.

"Indeed, it is."

"Wesley! The hypocrisy. You said you hated fusion food."

"Don't get it twisted. I hate when white people dilute Asian food to market it to other white people. But everyone loves a good Pan-Asian dish," he argues. "I realized that my purist attitude was a little unfounded." Then he looks up at me as if checking himself. "But obviously, I won't add any if you don't want me to. This is your grandmother's recipe. I don't want to give the impression that I don't respect that."

Hesitation gnaws at me. It feels too soon to be diverging from recipes, but then I remember Wesley's reflection essay. *Her approach to cooking is evidence that cooking lies between science and art.* And I want to be the type of person Wesley thinks I am. Part of the beauty of cooking is leaning into intuition. "Well, I guess this could be a fun experiment."

"You mean it, Chef Park?"

"Yes, Chef. Ten-four. Over."

Wesley rolls his eyes. He heaps a generous spoonful of red curry paste into a small bowl and begins thinning it out in some of the hot soup, before mixing it all together in the main pot. Then he puts the lid back on to finish cooking. "Now we wait."

"Should we actually pay attention to the movie now?" I ask. I finally look up at the screen and notice that it's not a movie at all, but an episode of *Chopped*. I turn to him and raise an eyebrow.

He shrugs. "Cook-off is around the corner. Thought we could get into the spirit of things."

I sigh. "I don't even know what I should make."

"We've made plenty of good things together."

I shake my head. "Mr. Treviño said the recipes should be original. I can't just claim my halmeoni's work as my own. I know you think I'm like a cutthroat scholar or whatever, but I'm not a plagiarist."

He chuckles. "We can brainstorm. Don't stress. Here, let me turn it off." He runs to the computer and closes the tab playing the show. The room is so much quieter once the audio cuts out. I think I can hear the small bubbles rising in the simmering pot.

"I thought we were over our sitting-in-silence era," I say, pulling myself up to sit on a countertop.

He walks over to me with his chin down, almost hiding his smile. He stops when his thighs touch my knees. The boost of the countertop makes it so that our eyelines match, an instant erasure of the head he normally has over me. "That's a shame, because what I wanted to do didn't really involve talking."

I avert my gaze, feeling my face heat. "If Mr. Wilby walks in on us again, I think I'll have to drop out. I can't have school staff knowing what my kissing side profile looks like. The shame would devastate me."

Wesley's lips quirk up at the corners. "I already checked the time," he says.

He raises his hand to cup my chin and gently pulls my face forward so that our mouths fall together. With the first contact of his lips on mine, I have to fight against letting out a sigh of relief. I missed him. I feel safe to admit it now that he is physically in front of me, physically touching me again. The thoughts I tried hard to block out for weeks are finally allowed to resurface and they are letting me know that they were gasping for air.

I let my hand slide against his cheek, taking note of his soft skin that transitions into the subtlest of stubble, his strong jaw that moves deftly to lock me in closer to him. His tongue joins mine and warmth bubbles in the depth of my stomach, like my insides are set to simmer. I marvel at how something can simultaneously feel so comforting and exhilarating. Kissing Wesley feels like flying through a free fall, knowing that he has me safely tucked in his arms. Is this the kind of special feeling that Kareena felt the need to protect from others, including me? This fragile bliss, newly brought into existence, but with the immediate recognition that something this alive could flicker out just as suddenly. In this moment, I understand her more than I have before. I would protect this flame with Wesley from anyone. It doesn't even register as an option not to.

Eventually, we pull away in a graceless effort to catch our breath. His eyes are dark, chestnuts swallowed by pupils, and the image of his mouth slightly hung open transforms me.

"I missed that," he says.

"Me too," I admit. The words come out breathlessly, but I don't have it in me to feel embarrassed. The warmth between us overrides everything.

"God, I love Culinary Arts."

"Because of me?" I say.

"Because of you."

The sound of a lid threatening to topple off turns our attention back to the stove. Wesley rushes over to release the steam building up. He grabs a spoon and uses it to stir the pot before bringing the dakdoritang up to his mouth to taste.

His eyes widen. "Holy shit." He immediately dips the spoon back in, brings it up to his mouth again. I don't even scold him about the double-dipping because I'm held hostage by his reaction. "Holy shit."

"What?" I say.

"Taste this."

I cautiously walk over to where he stands. "If it's gross, I trust your word. I really don't need to—"

He lifts a refilled spoon to my mouth, shaking his head. "Eliza, taste this."

I do as he says. I stay in silence, trying to figure out what exactly I'm tasting. My first impression is that it tastes like Thai red curry, but the longer I keep it my mouth, the more I get the gochujang. The character of spice transforms over time, but overall, it's . . . "Really good. I'm so confused by it, but I think I want more."

Wesley's face lights up. "Right? I'm sure some chef in New York or LA or something has already put this on a menu somewhere, but I think this is brilliant." He begins serving each of us a bowl of our red curry dakdoritang. I scoop us each a portion of rice and set them at our usual seats.

Every additional bite of the dish makes me like it more. "I think it's growing on me," I comment.

Wesley nods, his mouth full. "I think this is the best project we've made together."

"Really?"

He swallows. "Yeah, absolutely. It's like one level more interesting than the stuff I typically make."

I laugh. "I like it. I think I like the original more, if I'm being honest. Can I say that?" It feels sacrilegious to subvert in any way Wesley's talent, especially after the catalog of dishes I've witnessed.

He stops to look at me, and for a second, my breath hitches. Was

I insulting? I try to think of ways to backtrack, but Wesley says, "The original recipe is from *your grandmother*. Of course you can like that one more."

"I'm surprised you wanted to experiment," I say.

He shrugs. "I was cooking a lot at home when—when we weren't really talking. I was testing out new things and they just weren't turning out right. I was slapping things together carelessly. One time, my mom tried one of my experiments and told me that I better not be at risk of flunking Culinary Arts."

"Jeez. I'm sure it wasn't that bad."

"It kind of was. I was being unruly anyway, just the most undisciplined flavor combinations." Wesley shakes his head. "This is different though. Just a small change and it hits exactly right. I think I was going too big before, forcing flavors to behave when they weren't in compatible families, making random choices with the expectation of genius. Would you understand what I meant if I said I was being arrogant?"

There's something in the way he speaks when he's talking about cooking that I wish I could bottle up and open for Mr. Treviño, or his mother, even. His passion is revelatory. It's wild to me that Wesley ever saw himself as anything less than a good student. So many people around me are going through the motions of school without a fraction of the ambition or skill Wesley has, and in realizing this, I know I'm including myself. I say firmly, "Wesley, you should win the cook-off."

"What?"

"No one in this school cares about cooking like you do. I'm sure of it."

"I'm sure that's not—"

"I don't know anybody who would deserve the cook-off win more than you. You can't change my mind, I've already decided."

Wesley stares at me. He probably doesn't realize that I see it, but I do—the barest crinkle of his chestnut eyes at the corners, a sign that only I can decipher because no one has spent countless hours studying his face the way I have. It's the subtlest intimation that he's pleased, one sheer layer of restraint keeping him from cracking open like a sunbeam.

"Is it bad to say that compliments feel different when they come from you?" he asks, barely above a whisper. "Like they might actually be worth something."

"Don't let it go to your head," I warn. "I'm still going to try to beat you."

He grins at me, letting the sunshine seep through. "You wouldn't be the Eliza Park I know if you didn't."

Chapter 27

I spend the next week lost in trying to figure out my menu for the competition. It's tough because the dishes should be complex enough to show how much I've grown in the class, but measured enough that I can get them all done in the allocated amount of time. Mr. Treviño announced the other day the cook-off would be ninety minutes and would have three judges: Mr. Treviño; our principal, Dr. Richardson; and a special guest who he didn't reveal to us. The announcement, and the sudden feeling that the cook-off was actually happening so soon, got the entire class buzzing.

It's hard to balance everything going on: preparation for the cook-off, studying for midterms in the other classes, and trying to finally grind out the college application essay I've been avoiding. I'm jealous of Kareena and Meredith for having already submitted their early decision applications, because they have one less thing to stress over. "At least you don't have to study for the AP Chem midterm," Meredith says when I mention my envy. "Mrs. Pearson is absolutely killing us. Death by thermodynamics." Kareena pings a new group chat name: "Death! By Thermodynamics (Except Eliza, That Lucky Bitch)."

I yield the point to Meredith because I do remember Mrs. Pearson's exams being exceptionally brutal.

At home, I have the draft of my college application essay open. A few different first sentences, all watery variations on the definition of success. Reading it back over now, I don't know that I even agree with what I've written. It's silly that colleges ask for a personal statement as if our characters aren't constantly changing and evading summarization. Even if I'd written a full essay earlier this semester, I don't know that it would be an accurate reflection of me now.

I open a new document in case I get desperate later and want to revisit the success idea. The cursor of the new document blinks in rhythm as I rack my brain for a different topic to write about.

I hear a knock and turn around in my desk chair to see my dad leaning against my doorframe.

"Hey, Yeji-yah, are you busy?" he asks.

I gently close my laptop. "I guess not."

"Can I come in?" he asks.

I nod.

My dad crosses my room to sit on the edge of my bed. I turn in my swivel chair to face him. He asks, "What dates are you off for winter break?"

I furrow my brow. This is certainly not what I thought he would be asking about. I pull out my calendar and tell him the winter break dates. "Why?"

He nods to himself. "That's plenty of time. I was thinking . . . We should all go to Hanguk then."

My eyebrows shoot up. We usually only go to Korea every couple of years, and my mom just went this past summer. It's not time for another Korea trip yet. "Why?" I ask again.

He lets out a slow breath and leans back onto his hands. "I think it could be good for Eomma to be closer to her family for her birthday. And we can all visit Halmeoni's grave together. I think it would make Eomma happy."

I'm silent. Shocked speechless, actually, that my father is taking the initiative to do something to help my mother with her healing. At first, I think his suggestion feels deeply out of character, because this is the man who's been avoiding his wife since the summer. But then I think about how flattered my mother was when he tried to impress her with his budae jjigae all those years ago. Maybe it's more so that I haven't seen all his character to begin with.

"I think Hanguk is a really good idea," I say.

His face softens, and it's only in the melting of fear that I notice it was there in the first place. My dad, in all his knowledge of physics and academia and higher education, knows nothing about how to guide someone through grief. The notion that my own father is looking to me for any amount of direction is startling.

"You were right, Yeji-yah," he says. "About talking to Eomma. I was being a coward."

"I was, too," I say.

"I think I like being a professor so much because I get to have the answers. And with Eomma, after Halmeoni . . . I didn't have any." He nods his head, and keeps on nodding to himself, like he's wondering what to say next, or maybe recognizing the truth of what he just shared. Then he abruptly gets up from my bed. "I'll book the tickets soon."

He moves toward the door, and before I know it, I hear my own voice saying, "Wait. Appa?" Now that the silence of my room has been broken, part of me wants it to stay that way.

My dad turns around, surprised to be called. "Yes?"

"I, um . . . I need to think of some recipes to make for Culinary

Arts. Eomma told me that you made her budae jjigae a long time ago. Do you have any other ideas for me?"

He sits back down on my bed. "What did she say about the budae jjigae?"

"Well, she said she was charmed. But that it wasn't very good."

My dad laughs. "That sounds about right. Yeji-yah, I know I gave you a hard time about taking this class. But I'm proud of you for doing it. It's made Eomma really happy and I think it's made you ask questions you weren't thinking about before. As a professor and as a dad, that's the best thing I can ask for in my daughter."

"Thank you, Appa," I say, surprised by his earnestness.

My dad puts his hands together and blows out a breath. "Yeji-yah, let me be honest, okay? I have absolutely no advice for you on what to cook."

"Very helpful, thank you," I say.

"I think the best thing you can do is make a dish that will make someone feel happy. It doesn't matter if it's simple, or even if it tastes bad. If there's something there that lets them know you're trying, that'll be good enough. That was good enough for your eomma."

I smile. "That's very sweet . . . I don't think that applies to a Culinary Arts class, though. I think they're expecting something that's actually good."

He stands up then and brushes his hands on his pants. "Well, what do I know? I'm just an engineering professor." He's about to walk out the door when he turns around and snaps his fingers. "That dakdoritang you made on Thanksgiving? That was very good. Why don't you start there?"

* * *

The idea comes to me at lunch. Maybe it's unfair to say that it comes to me when it really is Kareena's suggestion.

I alternate between spending the lunch period in Señora Molina's room with Kareena and Meredith and the cafeteria with Wesley and his friends. Monday, Wednesday, and Friday are designated Kareena and Meredith days. Jess sometimes joins us, too, and although she makes a pointed effort to be kind, which I try to return with equal enthusiasm, it's a notably different dynamic. There's a need to explain myself when I make jokes or spew complaints because the common understanding of who I am is no longer a guarantee.

Nonetheless, it's a lunch without Jess when I let out a sigh so saturated with frustration that Kareena immediately narrows her eyes at me. Midterms are just around the corner and we've gradually been using more and more of lunch to study for our exams. Kareena looks like she's working through some chemistry. Meredith has a thoroughly highlighted AP study guide cracked open.

"I know you're not about to complain about the cook-off again," Kareena says.

"Honestly," Meredith agrees. "Isn't it, like, next week? You haven't figured it out by now?"

"Hey," I protest. "As my friends, aren't y'all supposed to be supportive and, I don't know, friendly?"

"My empathy is limited in proportion to how much of my brain is full of chemistry," Kareena says.

"Yeah, despite how it makes me sound, I would frankly kill someone to cook for a midterm instead of studying for another exam," Meredith chimes in, absentmindedly twirling her highlighter in her right hand. "If you cried me a river, I would happily drown myself in it."

"I just don't know what to do for the cook-off," I say, sounding like a broken record even to myself. "Isn't it kind of a ridiculous ask? That a high schooler could simply conjure up original recipes?"

Kareena puts her pencil down to stare at me with the full weight of her shrewd eyes. "Oh, come on, Eliza. Have you ever looked up a recipe online?"

"What?"

"Like, maybe you decided you wanted to make brownies. So you look up a brownie recipe online, and there are, like, two thousand white mommy blogs all claiming to have the best brownie recipe, and you have to scroll through a five-paragraph essay about their most recent Costco trip and the indignity of how they changed the price of paper towels just to get to the ingredients."

Even Meredith is staring now. "What the hell are you talking about?"

"I'm losing my point," Kareena allows. "What I'm saying is that if you look through all the different recipes, they really aren't that different. Maybe one adds more salt than another, or people have different preferences for which type of chocolate or cocoa powder they use, but at the end of the day, it's still a brownie."

"This seems like a very specific example," I say.

"Maybe Jess likes brownies, okay? The point: An original recipe can just be a tweaked version of something else. The odds that you find a recipe that is absolutely what you want aren't that high. So then you can workshop it until it's exactly how you like it, and voilà— original recipe. Don't reinvent the wheel. A brownie is a brownie."

"She's right," Meredith says, going back to her highlighter acrobatics.

"Of course I am," Kareena huffs.

"Cooking isn't, like, intellectual property. No one's patenting a brownie recipe. Unless Elon Musk has been up to something recently," Meredith says. "Eliza, I think you're worried about the wrong thing. Don't worry about it being a completely new dish. That sounds like an impossible task. Just worry about it tasting good."

"And not burning the school down," Kareena adds. "Unless it's the chemistry lab, which in that case, be my guest."

"Did you burn anything down trying to make brownies for your beloved Jess?" Meredith coos.

"What did the white mommy blogs say about mango cheese-cake?" I chime in.

Kareena doesn't deign to respond, instead turning her full attention back to studying.

The words of my mother come back to me, from when I first discovered Halmeoni's recipes. *These recipes are a great baseline, but even now, my taste has become Americanized. I'll find myself adding more salt or more sugar than what your halmeoni wrote down.* I think of Wesley mixing jarred red curry paste into our dakdoritang.

Could it be so simple?

The idea of mixing different ingredients jogs another suggestion I've been meaning to throw out to the girls. "Hey, would y'all want to sit with me and Wesley at lunch tomorrow?"

"Like, meet his friends?" Kareena clarifies.

I nod.

"Oh, hell yeah," Meredith says. "This is like in *High School*

Musical when the scholastic decathlon team hangs out with the basketball team! That means we're close to a happy ending."

I never realized how much of a jock Kareena can be until she's arguing with Patrick about whose sport requires more athleticism. I personally have never in my many years of friendship with Kareena held a conversation with her about sports, but the second Patrick teases her about the rigor of varsity tennis, the conversation turns feverish.

"Okay, but there is just so much more power when you get to hit the ball with another object," Kareena says. "Your arms can only do so much on their own."

"But don't you think it's more satisfying to know it's your own aim?" Patrick argues.

"No, because it's more impressive to know that you took into account the extension of your racket."

I look at Wesley and roll my eyes. "Imagine fighting over hand-eye coordination when I'm sitting right here. People are so insensitive."

He laughs. "I think Meredith is in awe hearing Joshua explain just how many competitions you have to win in order to get to state for band."

From her spot between Joshua and Michael, Meredith's ears perk up when she hears her name. "For mock trial, we just need to get through one! This guy goes through city, region, *and* area? And then state? You must be a fucking legend, man." She gives Joshua a playful shove on his shoulder and his cheeks match the red of his hair.

Seeing Kareena and Meredith interspersed among Wesley's

friends is simultaneously jarring and natural. I know that my best
friends can see what I've known for a while, which is that there are
reflections of each of them in Wesley's friends. The conversations
could go on for hours without anyone ever talking about what level
math class they're in or what schools they're applying to for college,
because those things ultimately don't matter as much to who they
are. Each of these boys has something we don't and it's a shame that
we waited until senior year to meet them.

The next week is a complete blur of recipe trialing. I end up sleep-
ing less and less, trying to fit my studying for my other classes
into the hours past midnight. When everyone else in my house is
asleep, I cram Spanish and history and calculus while lying in my
bed, because it makes much less noise than clanging around on the
stove. My mom notices me spending most of my evenings in the
kitchen, but she doesn't ever have more than a minute or two to
chat before she is swept back into the lesson room.

Wesley and I have put our Friday afternoons on pause as we
both attempt to put together our cook-off menus. He did suggest
working on our recipes together after school in the culinary kitchen,
but given that the cook-off is so soon, a lot of the other students
have been staying after school, too. I'm scared of being intimidated,
and I'm also scared of leeching their ideas when I'm not confident
in my own. I decide to stick to my own house.

I've printed out dozens of Korean recipes from a number of different blogs. I don't know what Kareena was talking about with
the white mommy blogs. The Korean mommy blogs introduce a
dish by talking about how they grew up eating certain foods with a
particular family member, or how they changed their methods over

time. It's not unlike what my Tuesday sessions with Eomma were like. Finding these websites feels comforting.

I repeat the recipes countlessly with a small tweak or two to distinguish each trial. I experiment with adding more green onion, no green onion, ginger and garlic, just garlic, two spoonfuls of gochujang, three spoonfuls. I cook the same dishes so many different ways, I almost get sick of the smell. There's still a little temptation to preen every time I get to the end product, though. I have to admit that they've been turning out great. I don't know if *great* can beat out Wesley's *masterful*, but I don't think I'm being delusional when I say I'm not too far off.

A couple of days before the cook-off, we all walk into the culinary kitchen for class and Mr. Treviño stands in front of the central table. The surface of it is barely visible through all the different ingredients placed on top. I freeze. Is this some sort of cooking pop quiz?

I see that Wesley is already sifting through. He holds a bottle of fish sauce and grins up at our teacher. "You got the brand I recommended!"

Mr. Treviño smiles. "You're a trusted source."

Once the bell rings and everyone is seated, there's still an audible murmur as the students chatter about the new ingredients. I'm shocked to see some things I recognize, like a large jar of kimchi and a tub of gochujang. Both brands are the exact ones my mom told Wesley and me were her favorites during our kimchi jjigae lesson. There are other bags of spices with labels in what might be Hindi alongside bundles of herbs I am only semiconfident in identifying. Is Mr. Treviño going to pull a *Chopped* and assign us ingredients to use?

"I'm sure everyone has been working diligently to craft their menus for this Friday's cook-off," Mr. Treviño says. "I'm very excited to see what everyone creates."

I scan the ingredient table for things I would be comfortable using. I steal a glance at Wesley and his face is brightened by a thinly suppressed smile. He must be so excited by the challenge. He lives for this kind of thing.

"I wanted to show you all some new supplies for the upcoming cook-off. One of your classmates, Wesley, and I have been spending the semester working on a budget proposal of sorts to submit to the school district, and I'm happy to announce that it got approved! Wesley let me know that the stock of our kitchen is not conducive to all kinds of cuisine, which, we then argued to the school board, was not a fair reflection of the student body here at Highland Hills. I don't want you all to limit yourselves because of what's available at the school. So if you don't see what you need here, I have a list here at my desk. Write down anything you might need for the competition. I'll secure everything Thursday evening."

I turn to Wesley, eyebrows raised. "That's what you've been helping with on Tuesdays?"

He nods. "At first, I was just concerned about the Asian ingredients, but Mr. Treviño wanted to expand it wider. It was a pretty good proposal, I thought. We would try out all different kinds of recipes, to prove how the ingredients we were requesting would be used in the class. Have you ever tried cooking with chamoy? I'm obsessed."

"You're really cool, you know that, Wesley?" I say. I am sincerely impressed by him. He took a complaint and turned it into something that the whole class could benefit from. I think of all my roles on campus, distributed across so many various disciplines—student government, volunteer service, science—and I don't know that I've ever come into any of them with the same ambition that Wesley has for cooking. It's humbling to realize over and over again the difference between passion and interest.

Wesley shrugs, like he's physically trying to let the compliment roll off him. "It's not really a big deal. We're just lucky we go to such a rich school."

I bump his shoulder with mine. "Let me compliment you."

Wesley takes my hand under the table. I try to resist the red warmth that creeps up my neck. We both look straight ahead at Mr. Treviño, intensely focused on pretending to look focused. His thumb taps a rhythm against the back of my hand, a nonsensical Morse code that serves as an outlet for the happiness he's trying to suppress, and the feeling wakes me up from the tiredness that's been accumulating over the week. I don't pay attention to anything said for the rest of the class period.

Chapter 28

All too soon, the day of the cook-off comes and I find myself in the culinary kitchen after school with all my Culinary Arts classmates. We stand at our individual stations with our ingredients and supplies stacked beside us. There's a palpable tension in the room, and for a second, I forget this is just a high school competition. It feels like something much bigger, and judging by the expressions on the other students' faces, we're all taking this very seriously.

I'm in awe of how much effort people have put into this class. I think of Kareena dismissing Culinary Arts as a blow-off class. I doubt anyone in this kitchen would agree. I can't put into words how much stress I've felt trying to create today's menu, and I'm so nervous I'm going to mess something up under pressure. I've made my dishes a handful of times each with the final recipes, but I still don't trust myself not to trip at the finish line.

The mood of the room electrifies when the Highland Hills principal, Dr. Richardson, enters the kitchen. Her black hair rests against her blazer in flawless waves and it makes sense to me that someone so front facing to some of the city's wealthiest parents would look her best at work. Walking alongside her is a brown-skinned man with perfectly gelled hair and an unusually tasteful mustache. He's dressed in a stylish button-down and perfectly ironed pants. He must be the special-guest judge, but I don't recognize him. My guess is that he's a member of the school board or some kind of administrative council.

Mr. Treviño greets Dr. Richardson with a warm hug. "Thank you for joining us, Dr. Richardson! We're very happy to have you as a judge tonight."

"Of course," she says. "You know I love the idea of the cook-off, Mr. Treviño. It brightens up the Highland Hills curriculum and lets us see firsthand the creativity and passion of our students. And I'm very humbled to introduce you to my friend, Chef Julian Salazar."

The mustached man holds out his hand and Mr. Treviño shakes it. I see admiration plainly written on Mr. Treviño's expression. "Chef Salazar, what an honor it is to have such a culinary talent visit my class. I think Grain and Garlic is one of Austin's most innovative establishments."

Instantly, a hushed murmur coats the classroom. Wesley and I exchange wide-eyed looks. This man is in charge of Grain and Garlic? This guy who was on a TV cooking competition against other amazing chefs and *won* is going to be tasting our dishes? I might pass out.

"It's really my pleasure," Chef Salazar says, and even from some distance, I can tell his tone is kind. My ears perk up to listen. "When Lucy asked me to help judge this event," he says, gesturing to Dr. Richardson, "I said I would be more than happy to. She and I have been friends since high school, you know."

Mr. Treviño nods. "What a joy to see where the two of you ended up! Now, if you don't mind taking seats at the judges' table, I'll get the event started."

Dr. Richardson and Chef Salazar take their seats at the front of the kitchen.

Mr. Treviño stands in front of us and claps his hands together.

His grin is so wide, I wonder how it doesn't split his jaw. His eyes glitter with excitement and his thrilled disposition is so sincere, I can't help but smile back at him. I look around the room and see my expression mirrored at every station. Something about Mr. Treviño has made each of us want to impress him. I can't help but think we would all be acting this way even without a prize.

"Welcome to the Culinary Arts Cook-Off!" Mr. Treviño announces with vigor. "Thank you all for being here. Today's rules are simple: You have ninety minutes to create an appetizer, an entrée, and a dessert for our panel of judges, which includes your principal, Dr. Richardson; renowned chef Julian Salazar of Grain and Garlic fame; and naturally, yours truly. No limits to ingredients or type of cuisine. I'll be walking around to observe your technique, and, of course, you'll be judged on taste. Don't forget that the winner of today's competition will take home a brand-new cookware set *and* a GPA boost. Any questions?" He takes the time to make eye contact with each of us, taking in our faces, our nerves, our antsy hands. His smile is reassuring, like he's already seen what we've made and it's blown away his expectations. Mr. Treviño's confidence in us makes me feel the slightest bit more relaxed, and I realize that's his intention.

"If there are no questions," he says, "then I'll start the timer now. You may begin!" He pulls up a ninety-minute timer on the projector that Wesley and I have screened so many movies on. I pretend that he's playing *Ratatouille* and that it's just another Friday afternoon with Wesley. *Anyone can cook*, I tell myself.

My hands move on autopilot, cutting my chicken parts the way I've done so many times at this point. Then I build the spicy paste that's the base of the dakdoritang. I add extra gochugaru because

I love the spice and nix the sugar from my halmeoni's recipe completely. Once the base of the soup is set to boil, I try to make my kalguksu dough, something I learned from a Korean lady's blog online. I've practiced making the handmade noodles enough times that I know exactly what consistency to shoot for.

While the dough rests, I peel and chop the potatoes before putting them into the boiling soup. Then I remember I haven't even touched the appetizer at all. I feel beads of sweat form at my hairline and I swipe them with my sleeve. I check the time. *I'm not behind*, I tell myself. *I just have to keep going.*

I open a jar of kimchi. Kimchi pajeon, or kimchi pancake, almost feels like a secret weapon to use in the competition. It tastes amazing, one of my favorite things to order from a Korean restaurant, while also being almost foolproof to make. It's essentially just kimchi and green onion mixed into batter that you then pan-fry. They're usually large, meant to be shared with the table, but for the competition, I've decided to make them individually sized, like dollar pancakes. I make the batter, adding a dash of rice-wine vinegar the way I've discovered I like it, and dollop the pancakes onto a sizzling pan before returning to my soup.

The dakdoritang is looking like it's finally starting to come together when I smell burning. Then I remember the kimchi pajeon.

Hurriedly, I flip the pancakes, but it's too late. They're completely scorched, the color of tar, and smell like the aftermath of arson. With a frustrated sigh, I throw them in the trash. When I hurriedly thrust my hand over the skillet to see how hot it is, I accidentally overshoot and burn myself. I curse under my breath, yanking my hand back. I know I'm scowling as I re-oil the pan that is clearly more than hot enough. I look up to see Wesley staring at me from his station with a questioning brow. He must have smelled my mistake.

You good? he mouths.

I nod and give him a half-hearted thumbs-up. Then I look away before I can take a guess at what he might be making. Despite Mr. Treviño's sweet smiles from earlier, I feel intimidated once again. I shouldn't have burned my kimchi pajeon. *Foolproof*, I repeat to myself bitterly.

With new batter frying up in the pan, I set a separate timer to remind me to flip them and return to my stew. That's when Mr. Treviño visits my station.

"Hello, Eliza. How's it going for you?" he asks.

"Um, I think it's been okay." I hope he doesn't see the beads of sweat that have already replaced their predecessors, or the rapidly reddening skin of my fingertips.

"You know, Eliza, I think you've demonstrated some of the most growth in the class. You've really become an excellent chef." I know he's trying to combat the tension I'm sure is apparent in my posture, so I try to give him a smile. He doesn't look very convinced. "Tell me about what you're making."

I explain to him my menu choices while I roll out the kalguksu dough. I have to keep sprinkling flour so that it stops sticking to the rolling pin. I hope it doesn't dry it out. Then I fold the dough and begin to slice my noodles using my chef's knife.

"This all looks very good," Mr. Treviño says. My timer goes off and I flip my kimchi pajeon. "Spicy, too."

I laugh. "Yeah, it's a good thing you can handle it."

"Let's hope Dr. Richardson is so lucky. I think you're doing wonderfully, Eliza," he says before departing for the next station.

I switch gears and begin the dessert. I racked my brain for a dessert that made sense with my appetizer and entrée, but my parents' idea of dessert is sliced persimmon and apples. Instead, I remember my mom's bingsu preference, and I work on my injeolmi rice cakes. The rice cakes don't take too long. It's a sprint of microwave work and then pounding in a mortar and pestle. I check the clock. I should have just enough time to get everything ready.

Slowly, things begin to come together. The kimchi pajeon looks crispy and, most importantly, not burnt. The dakdoritang bubbles, spicy red sauce washing over pale, freshly added noodles. The rice cake dough is getting close to the right amount of elasticity. When I glance at the timer, I note that there are somehow only ten minutes left. Didn't we just start? How did time go by so fast?

I pound the dough faster, hearing the bubbles pop beneath each stab of the pestle. When I think it's ready, I roll it in a small hill of injeolmi powder.

With less than five minutes left, I scramble to work on plating. I create three servings for each of the dishes, slicing the injeolmi rice cake into neat, bite-sized rectangles and coating them generously with golden injeolmi powder. I ladle the dakdoritang into three bowls and arrange the mini kimchi pajeons like fallen dominoes along a long, rectangular plate.

Mr. Treviño's ninety-minute timer blares through the room and everyone steps away from their station like we're on network television.

"Fantastic job, everyone!" he says with enthusiastic applause. "I am so incredibly proud of the work you've done this semester. I talked to each of you and saw some of the most impressive effort I've seen this year. I know the judges are very excited to taste your creations, so we'll begin visiting each of you, starting with the left corner."

Slowly, the judges taste everybody's three-course menu, offering their comments and compliments before scribbling something onto their notepads. Dr. Richardson recycles similarly pleasant comments to each of us, serving her role as diplomatically as possible while undoubtedly recording her genuine thoughts on her score sheet. Chef Salazar's notes sound like they're lifted directly from magazine reviews, complimenting one person on their bright acidity and another on their excellent rendering of fat. Based on what I can hear, it sounds like everyone's doing a remarkable job. My nerves build with unchecked pressure the closer the judges get to my station.

When they stand in front of me, Mr. Treviño asks me to explain my menu, just as he did before.

I take a deep breath and give a silent thanks to all the years of public speaking I'd signed up for when my voice doesn't shake. "My name is Eliza Park. For the appetizer course, I've made kimchi pajeon, which is a kimchi pancake. It's a popular appetizer at Korean restaurants and one of my favorites due to its simplicity and versatility.

"Next is the entrée. This is dakdoritang, a spicy braised chicken stew. I've also added handmade noodles called kalguksu to help absorb the sauce and provide a balance to the spice.

"And finally, for dessert, I've made injeolmi rice cakes, a traditional Korean dessert that is coated in soybean powder."

The success of getting through my descriptions makes me go a little numb. Somehow, I keep myself standing. I glance at Wesley for some amount of grounding to reality, and he gives me two thumbs-up. I do my best not to stare as the judges try my dishes, wondering if by not looking at them, they would be less likely to hear my heart pounding. I have to actively resist raising my arm to wipe off my nervous sweat.

Dr. Richardson coughs after trying the dakdoritang. "Wow, that's spicy, huh?"

Chef Salazar and Mr. Treviño chuckle.

"Really well done, Eliza," Mr. Treviño concludes. "I've never had this kind of bean powder before." He rubs the injeolmi between his thumb and forefinger. "It has such a unique, nutty flavor. Plus, the rice cake texture is perfect. I wish I could have ten more of these guys."

"Excellent work," Dr. Richardson nods. "I'll need to build up my spice tolerance the next time our salutatorian cooks for us."

"Ah, brainy and talented!" Chef Salazar says. "The vinegary bite in your kimchi pajeon is wonderful." I'm impressed by his pronunciation. I realize that unlike for Mr. Treviño or Dr. Richardson, this is probably not the first time Chef Salazar has tried these popular Korean dishes. I suddenly feel nervous that they don't compare to what he's had before. "I think the extra vinegar brings out the fermentation of the kimchi. And if I'm correct, kimchi pajeon is normally served with a dipping sauce of soy sauce and vinegar. I think it's smart to put it into the dish itself."

I'm speechless at his kind words. Luckily, he's not done.

"Dr. Richardson is right about the spice in your chicken stew. It's a very hot dish. It does a big favor to the hand-cut noodles, which absorb all that spice beautifully. You cut the noodles so evenly, too. That suggests great knife skill."

"Thank you," I say, bowing my head unintentionally, like this

Afro-Latino man is actually a Korean elder. The aura he gives, the dignity that emanates from where he stands, makes me want to show deference.

When they move on to the next student, I finally wipe my brow. I'll really have to throw this shirt into the laundry. I sit on my stool, feeling a swell of pride expand in my chest, competing against my thumping heartbeat.

I've done it. I've gotten through the cook-off with dishes that are worth complimenting. I can't believe I've gotten to a point where I can make food that other people, including someone who runs his own restaurant, would want to taste. Briefly, the thought of wanting to share this experience with my parents, especially my mom, pops into my head. I wonder how they would feel seeing what I've made, hearing how I talked about my dishes to people unfamiliar with my ingredients. It's no physics project, but I can nonetheless picture my dad's proud smile. And, of course, I wonder what my halmeoni would think. I wonder if she'd approve of me adding noodles to her dakdoritang, or whether she'd think my third scoop of gochugaru made it too spicy. I can't help but think that she would like it.

Wesley is the final student to be judged. I worry for a moment that he's put at a disadvantage, given that his dishes have had the most time to cool since being plated, but the second he starts speaking, I realize no amount of disadvantage would truly have made any difference.

"Hello, I'm Wesley Ruengsomboon and I'm very excited to have cooked for you tonight. For the starter, I have made a lobster bisque–inspired tom kha gai. Next is a Thai red curry carbonara. And finally, we end the meal with a mango cake that's part Filipino mango float, part chamoy mangonada. I hope you enjoy."

The simplicity of his explanations belies a quiet confidence, like if you asked him to elaborate on any of his decisions, he could easily cite exactly why he made each choice. It's written across his face, in the subtle traces of pride in his soft features, how much he loves what he's made. I have no doubt that the judges love it, too.

"Wow," Dr. Richardson says, almost like the word is pulled out of her involuntarily. "I would like to take this mango cake home. It's phenomenal." Her careful mask of diplomacy has slipped momentarily, revealing an extra serving of emotion and candor that has been intentionally absent all night. It's enough to confirm what I've known all along—Wesley is playing in a different league than the rest of us.

"The creaminess of the lobster bisque with the coconut of the tom kha gai, Wesley . . . It's really genius," Mr. Treviño says. "Also, I'll fight Dr. Richardson for the mango cake. I'm willing to put my job on the line."

"Oh, you don't want to fight me, Mr. Treviño," Dr. Richardson chides. "I'm wearing heels and I'm not afraid to use them."

It's not lost on me that while Mr. Treviño and Dr. Richardson banter, Chef Salazar has taken more bites out of Wesley's dishes than he has of anyone else's. It might be because Wesley is the last one to be judged and Chef Salazar no longer needs to save room in his stomach. But believing that would be kidding myself. There's a shift in the chef's disposition, like his kindness has dropped a degree or two in favor of becoming more studious. "Wesley, you said?" Chef Salazar says.

"Yes, sir," Wesley confirms. He's standing tall, but I can sense his nervousness.

"Really impressive job," Chef Salazar says. "The best type of food is one that takes you on a journey. Your menu does exactly that."

Wesley's deep blush can be seen from across the room. Chef Salazar gives Wesley a handshake, and I have to rack my brain to remember whether he did that for anyone else.

"Chef Salazar, thank you so much," Wesley says, his tone an endearing blend of admiration and astonishment. "And of course to you as well, Dr. Richardson and Mr. Treviño. This semester has truly been one of the best of my life." Coming from anyone else, the words would sound grating or obsequious, but from Wesley, it only sounds like the truth.

It doesn't surprise a single person in the room when Mr. Treviño announces that the winner of the Culinary Arts Cook-Off is Wesley Ruengsomboon.

Chapter 29

Wesley comes up to me with a stack of Tupperware dishes and sets them down at my station. I see his appetizer, entrée, and dessert neatly placed into their separate tubs. Even his leftover packing is precise. "Trade? Old times' sake?" he asks.

His food looks so tempting, and part of me is incredibly curious to know what the winning dishes taste like. What exactly did Chef Salazar identify in them that impressed him so plainly? But I take a look at what I've made—the crispy pancakes, the spicy soup, the chewy rice cakes—and I know that I want to keep it. "I think I'll take this home, actually."

He grins at me, like he suspected I would turn him down. "That's fine. You'll just have to make it all again for me to have later."

"I'll have to ask the same from you, champion." I look up at him, captivated by his easy smile and his burning eyes, like he's still riding the high of his victory. "Congratulations, Wesley. No one deserves it like you do."

"Thank you. You did an incredible job, too. Not one of your dishes looks like salsa."

I laugh. "Get over yourself." I finish cleaning my station and start packing my things. "I want to celebrate you, but I also want to get home, if that's okay."

Wesley nods. "Of course. We're still meeting tomorrow for boba, right?"

"Obviously. I can't let you go without me. Who knows how many phone numbers you'll leave with?"

He pulls me into a tight hug and gives me a kiss on my forehead. "All right. Go home, Eliza."

I set the reheated dishes up on the dining room table and wait for my mother's piano lesson to end. It seems to be winding down when my dad comes home from work, too. He notices the set table with raised eyebrows.

"Yeji-yah, what's this?"

"I made dinner for us."

"You made all of this?"

I nod. "For my Culinary Arts class. There was a cook-off today and I took home the leftovers."

"Did you win?"

"No, I didn't. My friend Wesley did."

He nods. "That's okay. I wasn't there to contribute my budae jjigae."

I roll my eyes. "I do great on my own, Appa."

"I know that's true, my salutorian. This looks really good." He approaches the dining table with genuine anticipation. "Also, who's Wesley?"

I try to imagine what I would be doing if I had dropped out of Culinary Arts after the first day, once I knew that everyone in the room was more experienced than I was. I would have missed the opportunity to learn from my mother about both her childhood and Korean cooking. I would not have grown so close to Wesley, would not have spent my Friday afternoons in the kitchen, would not know that there was an entire population of my school worth knowing that I was completely isolated from.

My thoughts are interrupted by the soft chatter of farewells, followed by the front door opening and closing. A few moments later, my mom walks into the dining room with a glass of water in her hand. She sees all the food on the table and says, "Yeji-yah, what's this?"

"I said that, too," my dad says.

"I made dinner. Now, everyone, sit and eat. It's getting cold." I let my voice sound uncharacteristically authoritative, and the shock value of it is enough to get my parents to sit.

I watch as they each slide a kimchi pajeon onto their plate. My dad ladles out some dakdoritang for my mom before serving himself. I move some food onto my dishes as well, but I only go through the motions of eating. I'm too nervous to actually put anything past my esophagus and too impatient to see what my parents think. I wonder if they'll find it silly that I'm attempting to make a big deal out of something they think is ultimately mediocre.

"You put kalguksu in the dakdoritang?" my mom asks.

I nod.

"That's not in Halmeoni's recipe," she says before slurping up some noodles.

I wince. "Are you mad?"

My mom frowns at me. "Mad? My American daughter is making wonderful Korean food all by herself. I'm so proud."

My dad nods. He vacuums a generous portion of noodles into his mouth and tosses chunks of chicken in. He eats like a cartoon character. "Very good, Yeji-yah. Halmeoni would think so, too."

"Really?"

"Yeah. I guess now you'll be in charge of making dinner."

I give him my best scowl. "I think you would be next in line before me."

My mom nods her head. "Yeah, if Yeji can learn, so can you." She points her metal chopsticks at my dad in accusation.

My dad changes the subject. "So if this didn't end up winning, I'm sure the actual winner must've been amazing. Or the judges were racist."

"Appa."

He shrugs. "Some people just don't know how to appreciate Korean food."

"No, I lost fair and square. I'm certain."

"Did Wesley win?" my mom asks.

"Who is Wesley?" my dad asks again, his voice suddenly an octave deeper. "You know him?" he says, turning to my mother.

"Wesley did win," I say.

My mom smiles. "He's a good student."

I think about how Wesley would feel hearing the words my mom uses to describe him. I'm sure he wouldn't believe me even if I told him verbatim.

"How do you know him?" my dad repeats.

My mom shakes her head in annoyance, the fringe of her cropped hair swaying. "Oh, be quiet. Let's eat what Yeji has cooked for us."

"Don't get used to it," I warn. But when I take a moment to think about it, I do want to get used to this. To feel this connected to my mother, to have her look up at me across the table and smile because I have made something I've learned from her and her mother. It's a kind of fulfillment that is both new and intoxicating. I want to believe that I'm finally starting to close the gap that my dad and I have let grow for so long. It's a reward so sweet, I can't imagine not chasing it again and again.

I'm waiting at the boba shop for about fifteen minutes past when Wesley and I agreed to meet. The cute girl isn't working the counter today. I vaguely wonder what she's up to in a poor effort to distract me from my college essay. The document is open and threateningly sparse in front of me.

The story of my family begins in the kitchen.

The cursor blinks with annoying persistence at the end of the first sentence. It's all I've written so far. In an attempt to work on everything but the essay, I have all the rest of my application filled out. I only need to enter my personal statement, and now that it's almost winter break, the deadline is approaching with nauseating speed. I told Wesley that he and I could work on our college essays together, serve as each other's sounding boards and editors. I should use the time waiting for him to actually draft something, but I feel so stuck.

By the time Wesley walks in the door, backpack haphazardly hanging from one shoulder, I've somehow written an awful first paragraph. Sometimes, you need to let out all the bad writing first, so that the good writing can find its way out. At least, that's what I'm telling myself so that I can get words on the page.

"Sorry I'm late," he says. The words all fall out in a rush. He sits in the seat across from me completely upright, like the back of the chair is ready to electrocute him if he were to slump an inch.

"It's no problem. What's going on?" I ask.

"Remember the special guest judge, Julian Salazar?" he says. His eyes are shining with a fervor I don't know that I've seen in him.

"Yeah. Grain and Garlic guy?" I smile at the alliteration. Maybe I can use poetry for my personal statement, a good old acrostic to beg colleges to let me in. I toss the idea out before it can even form. I'm desperate for inspiration, scraping the bottom of my metaphorical writing barrel.

Wesley nods. "Well, apparently, Mr. Treviño gave him my number. And he just called me."

I lean forward because he's leaning forward. "Oh, wow. Like to say congratulations?"

"He told me he's been wanting to start an internship program for recent high school graduates for a long time now. Like staging, but with a small stipend," he says. His speech is pressured with excitement. He reminds me of a blender that's a second away from blowing its top off. "And he was inspired by seeing our cook-off and thought, well, what is he waiting for? He's been wanting to start it, and why not finally get to it?"

"Staging?" I repeat, still hung up on the unfamiliar term. I carefully mimic his pronunciation. *Stah-jing*.

"It's like an apprenticeship you can do at restaurants where you learn from working in the kitchen. He said he was impressed with my cook-off dishes and that he would be interested in seeing an application from me! And I was thinking, I could do that for a year, and in the meantime, I could take some classes at ACC to boost my GPA while I figure out whether I actually want to go to college."

It takes me a minute to process everything he's saying. Part of it is how fast he's speaking. Another part of it is the stark departure from why we decided to meet in the first place. I glance down at my college essay open on my laptop in front of me. Then I look back up at him. "So I'm guessing you don't want to work on college essays today."

"I mean, I want you to."

"Have you told your mom about this?" I ask.

His brow furrows and his mouth turns down. "About the internship?"

"Yeah. And the not-going-to-college thing."

"No."

"Are you scared of how she'll react? I thought she was going to ship you off to the military or something. It would suck to have to write you letters all the time. I don't even know where to buy postage stamps."

"I'm not worried about what she'll say," he says. "I'll give her the benefit of the doubt and hope she'll be happy for me. Because I haven't felt this way, I don't know, maybe ever." He looks away, like he's embarrassed to admit it.

For a second, I can only marvel at the truth of what he's saying. In the semester that I've known him, I don't know that I've seen this Wesley before, with his gleaming eyes and barely contained movement. He's like lightning in a bottle. I wonder if he knows that about himself. "How do you feel?" I say softly.

"I don't know, Eliza," he says, turning to me at just the right angle so sunlight from the window cascades across the planes of his face. The lightning is leaking out. "It's like . . . like I'm making choices that are going to take me where I actually want to go."

I hear Kareena's voice. *Someone who really is trying to* get somewhere. Between me and Wesley, that person is Wesley. Of course, it's so easy to see now, with the acute clarity of hindsight, that it has never really been about whether we're trying to get somewhere. The real issue has always been over where the destination is set, and whether that destination is worth going to. Why does it matter if Kareena is aiming for the Ivy League and Wesley is aiming for Austin Community College, if each step is putting them respectively closer to where they want to be?

"I'm happy for you, Wesley," I say. My voice has a slight wobble and I realize I'm feeling too emotional.

Wesley looks at me with panic in his chestnut eyes. "Are you all right?"

I nod.

"Are you disappointed in me?" There's a scratchiness in his throat when he asks.

I shake my head.

"Is it because you don't want to tell your parents that your boyfriend isn't applying to college?"

"Wesley, stop. It's not about that. I'm really proud of you." I suck in a shaky breath. "I've been trying to write my college application and talk about who I am in a way that makes for a succinct-but-moving five-hundred-word essay, but I don't really know who that is. And then I look at you and I see someone who knows himself. It makes me happy for you. Maybe a little jealous, too."

Suddenly, he turns my laptop toward him and reads what I know is still open on the screen. It's barely anything, so I know he's done reading it within seconds, but he stares at it for a long moment. It's a rare instance where I can't read his expression. He begins to slowly nod his head. "Okay, this is good."

"It's, like, two words."

"Yeah, and I like it. Here's what I think—well, do you mind if I tell you what I think?"

"Wesley, you know I always want to hear your thoughts."

"Stop trying to make me blush. I think you should talk about how cooking has brought you closer to your family."

I raise my eyebrows.

"I think it's a really sweet story, the way you and your mom have gotten closer over your grandma's recipes. I envy that, you know? How close you and your mom are. And I think you should talk about Culinary Arts as a class, how you finally experienced, like, the one thing in the entire world you weren't naturally good at, but you put in the time to improve at it. I don't know too much about college admissions, but I feel like that's what they want to hear— something about overcoming, something about identity, blah blah blah, you know how it is."

I pause for a moment, letting Wesley's suggestions soak for a bit in my head.

Then I take the laptop from him and begin writing.

Chapter 30

When winter break officially comes, Wesley offers to drive my family to the airport. This is a big deal to me for two reasons. The first is that he obviously is not someone who typically offers to drive. The second is that this is the first time he'll be meeting my dad, who, for the most part, does not know about Wesley's existence or my relationship to him.

Wesley pulls up in a sleek, black Mercedes SUV. My parents have our luggage lined up next to the front door, ready for transport, and I watch from the window as he walks up the driveway. He's done this plenty of times before, but I see his nerves when he visibly crunches up his shoulders and forces them down again. I open the door before he can knock.

"Hey," I say. "Good to see you."

"You too," he says breathlessly.

"How are you feeling?" I ask.

"Like I forgot how to drive."

"Perfect." I turn around and shout into the house. "Eomma! Appa! Wesley's here to drive us."

Within minutes, my parents come to the front with their backpacks and shoes in hand. My mom lays her things on the ground so she can wrap Wesley in a hug. "Hi, Wesley, thank you for coming."

"Of course," Wesley says, returning the squeeze. When he pulls away, my dad is standing in front of him. Wesley is a couple of inches taller than my dad, but his anxiety makes him look smaller. "Hello, Dr. Park. It's good to meet you. My name is Wesley Ruengsomboon." He offers his hand out, and my dad shakes it tightly.

"Hello, Wesley. I appreciate you offering to drive us to the airport." My dad intentionally keeps his voice plain. Not a hint of emotion. I wonder if this is how he talks to his students.

"It's my pleasure," Wesley replies, and it sounds sincere. "I want to see Eliza one last time before the new year."

It hits me then that I won't see Wesley until a new calendar year. My parents and I are going to spend almost the entirety of my winter break, including my mom's birthday, in South Korea, and I'll return a few days before school starts back up in January. I try not to let myself get caught up in the sadness of our separation. "You'll forget about me in Korea," Wesley told me a few days ago with saccharine eyes. "There will be too much good food and too many pretty K-pop boys to even remember my name." I pushed his shoulder before pulling him back and letting my lips land on his cheek.

Wesley and my dad work together to load the luggage in the trunk. Then I let my dad take the front seat. I hope Wesley doesn't mind I'm prioritizing seniority over his comfort.

Wesley keeps NPR dialed at a low volume throughout the drive, while he asks my father about what he teaches. It's what I've trained him to do, knowing that as long as my dad gets to talk about physics, he won't have time to poke and prod Wesley's character.

I'm nestled in the back seat, taking note of how clean it is—probably because he never drives anyone anywhere—when I get an email notification. I swipe it open.

Hi Eliza,

Thank you for letting me read your college application essay. I absolutely loved it. The moments of remembering your grandmother with your mom were so powerful, and learning about how much you stumbled through the Culinary Arts course was tender and endearing. I'm glad something came out of your schedule mishap after all. I think your application is very strong and ready for submission. Please let me know if there's anything else I can help with, and have a wonderful winter break!

Best,
Mrs. Porter

"What are you smiling for?" my mom asks. "Not Wesley, because he's driving."

I lock my phone and tuck it away in my pocket. Then I reach for my mom's hand. She looks at me in surprise, but then willingly laces her fingers with mine. I give her hand a squeeze, letting myself feel content. My college application is complete. My parents are with me. My boyfriend is meeting my father. I'm heading to South Korea. In the moment, it seems like everything is moving in the right direction.

"I'm just excited for the trip," I tell her.

"Me too. I've missed Korea a lot," she murmurs, looking out the window.

I study my mom's profile. Her sparse eyebrows, her delicate nose, her chin and cheeks plump from her years in America. I see the silver of her hair and the shine of sunscreen on her face, applied religiously even though we'll be in an airport or a plane for approximately the next day. I see in her all the bits and cracks I've been avoiding looking at for the past half year, the lines in her face or the slight frown in her lip I've willingly ignored since June. They are less noticeable now, I think, as if the closer we get to the airport, the more she gets to let go of.

"I think I've missed it, too," I say, before turning forward and waiting for the airport to come into view.

The story of my family begins in the kitchen. It served as the backdrop for when my father attempted to make a grand cooking gesture to impress my mother before they were married. It was the setting for the only comforting meals my mother had in the first few months after immigrating to the United States from South Korea. And it was the place where I learned to miss someone I would have claimed not to know.

When my grandmother died the summer before my senior year, the worst part for me was the lack of grief. The separation of not only generation, but country and culture, made me feel like there was little to actually miss. Our visits were infrequent, our communication was stilted, and our time together was always so short. The concept of loss loses its sting when it feels like you didn't really have someone to begin with.

An accidental enrollment in a Culinary Arts course changed everything for me, in a number of ways. For the first time in recent memory, I was in a class I was absolutely awful at, surrounded by students much brighter and better than I had ever seen. There was so much for me to learn, starting with humility. Of course, I had to learn how to cook, too. I discovered that my grandmother had given my mother handwritten Korean recipes before my parents immigrated. I asked my mother to teach them to me, and she agreed.

Our cooking lessons were sprinkled with stories of my mom as a child. In addition to teaching me how to make her favorite childhood Korean dishes, my mother also taught me that memories could find new life in someone else. These stories of my grandmother came with accompanying imaginings, and with each recipe learned, I felt like I was meeting the person I lost. I began to recognize a country through the smells of the kitchen. I found the beauty of language in ingredients and dish titles. I felt the connection of family while preparing these dishes, passed from mother to daughter, mother to daughter. I learned to taste home.

I've always been a fan of school and learning. My father is a professor, my mother is a tutor, and school has always been one of the things I was best at. But even with all the education surrounding me, I was missing the most crucial lessons. Focusing too much on the classroom kept me from understanding that some of the most important knowledge is revealed elsewhere. Burning my hand on the stove, spilling soup all over the countertop, forgetting to salt my eggs—the list of my cooking disasters could fill a book. Finally, after making mistake after mistake, I realized that creating a mess in the kitchen and finding ways to clean it up were the real moments of growth. I discovered by doing, and the rewards could not have been sweeter. It was only in the kitchen, where I felt the most lost, that I began to find out the parts of myself I didn't yet know.

The story of my family begins in the kitchen, so I should have known that the story of me would start there, too.

Acknowledgments

It probably goes without saying that Eliza's obsession with school is somewhat autobiographical. I've spent so many years being a student, and throughout that time, I've been blessed to have encountered so many incredible teachers. In an effort to make what could be a novel-length paragraph into something slightly succinct, let me start chronologically. I would like to thank Mrs. de la Garza for creating the association between school and love so early on. Mrs. Krell for being the pivotal lighthouse that made me fall in love with writing to begin with. Mr. Krell for pulling me aside one day to tell me that my work ethic could get me anywhere I wanted to go. Mrs. Yost for comparing my sixth-grade "novel" to *Flipped* by Wendelin Van Draanen and consequently giving me the highest praise I have received to this date. Señora Acosta, who still serves as a second mother to every student she taught. Professor Waters, whose immense support and care indelibly shaped my entire Vanderbilt experience. It has been my dream for so, so long to be able to write your exact names into a book I wrote and send you a copy. I hope you know that your impact on us as students is nothing less than life-changing. Each of you has done exactly that and I thank you so much for it.

This book would literally not exist without Penny Moore, the most extraordinary literary agent of all time. Thank you for taking such good care of this story and seeing something in its roughest of drafts. Thank you so, so much for choosing me. I truly couldn't have gotten luckier. Thank you to Penny for guiding me to Jen Ung. Thank you, Jen, for your endless passion and creativity, and for always approaching this story with excitement and understanding. If any part of this story sings, it's all credited to you. Thank you to the rest of the team at Quill Tree and HarperCollins for giving this story a home, and particular thanks to Jessie Gang and Sihyeon Park for creating a beautiful cover that I still can't get enough of.

My parents got the dedication, so hopefully they're okay with waiting until the third paragraph. My parents are actually my everything, and I owe every blessing in life to them. Thank you for giving me the space to find what I love and for being just as excited about this book as you were about medical school. Thank you to my sister, Vivian, for your support and generosity, as well as for having the cutest dog in the world. If you read this book, you probably thought it sucked, but I've never trusted your book taste anyway!

It's funny that I wrote this book before I started medical school, back in 2020, and it's coming out now that I'm finishing my intern year of OB-GYN residency. It's been a long journey, but I've had the most wonderful people alongside me. Thank you, Agatha, for being my platonic soulmate and the owner of our one shared brain cell. Shaz Noo for being the most loyal, trustworthy friend anyone could have. Alice for giving me my Camp NaNoWriMo prompt and actually being the reason this story even exists. (For anyone curious, the prompt she gave me was "a character that consistently puts herself up for humiliation.") Elizabeth, Annie, and Kristine—who are collectively the sole reason I survived medical school—thank you for turning something so difficult into something so joyous. Thank you to internet friends, too—to everyone who spent even a moment interacting with me on my old book blog or on YouTube, when I wanted to be surrounded by readers who understood me. If you or a loved one spent a minute watching my BookTube videos, you may be eligible for financial compensation.

And finally, thank you to Connor. I wrote Wesley before I ever met you, but you have all his best qualities and even more. It's almost like I wrote you into existence, but not even my imagination could be so good. Thank you for being my favorite person and always saying that I'm yours.